FROM THE MIDST OF WICKEDNESS

FROM THE MIDST OF WICKEDNESS

A Novel

NELSON COVER

Epigraph Books
Rhinebeck, New York

From the Midst of Wickedness: A Novel © 2017 by Nelson Cover

ISBN: 978-1-944037-64-2
Library of Congress Control Number: 2017941114

Book design by Colin Rolfe

Epigraph Books
22 East Market St., Suite 304
Rhinebeck, NY 12572
(845) 876-4861
www.epigraphps.com

For Gretchen

I
A New Friend

FTER THE FIRST DAY OF CLASSES BEGINNING THE AU-
TUMN SEMESTER, Zoltan and I resumed our practice of
having a drink at the faculty club.

We sat at opposite ends of a small table in the bar, my beer
and his vodka between us amongst small glass bowls of potato
chips, pretzels and party mix.

Zoltan rummaged in the pretzel bowl, his colossal fingers
almost unable to extract the loops.

We had just finished talking about our first impressions of this
year's undergraduates, who seemed ever younger and less prepared than the prior year's, inspiring in us head-shaking disbelief.

There was an awkward pause, as often occurs when two colleagues resume meeting again after a long hiatus. Zoltan had
spent much of the summer in his lab. I had spent mine shuttling
our kids to various day camps and teaching a summer course.
We were that close and had barely spoken to one another.

"So, what happened this summer on the home front?" I asked,
wincing immediately at the inappropriate stupidity of the question.

Zoltan looked at me as if I had lost my mind. He spat out, "I
have no home."

I watched members and guests at other tables look our way,
eying him.

The fact is Zoltan frightens people.

More than his massive size and his hulking demeanor, it's the
disturbed, crazy Hungarian seriousness of him that causes peo-

ple to shift uncomfortably when he walks into a room, to glance about furtively for the closest exit. The unshaven mass of his scowling, mustached countenance, penetrating black eyes, the coils of black-grey hair springing from his head, he looks as if he has emerged from some basement torture chamber for a breath of fresh air still absorbed in the work at hand. Zoltan moves through life unaware of the seas of humanity parting before him.

Putting all his idiosyncrasies aside, Zoltan is my good and loyal friend, the first person I would call in an emergency. I know many of his secrets; he knows way too many of mine.

For instance, we will have our drinks and Zoltan will pay me in cash for his portion as we exit the club. Despite being a tenured professor and senior cancer researcher, Zoltan is not a member of the club. He will pay me, an associate professor of communications, from the stash he keeps in his bottom bureau drawer, his life savings.

Kicked out of his house by his wife years ago, living in a third floor room he rents near the university, my friend is a man of the here and now. He and his wife have fought over money for all their years of marriage and separation. He is on the one hand reluctant to get a divorce because of what it might cost him and on the other hand understandably paranoid about her knowing how much money he might actually have, so he has no bank account, no credit cards, no memberships. He pays his rent in person; he pays what few bills he might have by money order. I wonder at myself at times because I have been immersed in Zoltan's life for so long that all this seems normal to me.

"I'm sorry. I meant how are things with your family?"

"Frida is the same, a nagging, ungrateful shrew. Anna is back at Swarthmore, her junior year." Then his whole countenance changes as he asks with real interest and concern, "How is Janet and Sarah and Tommie?"

These inquiries are not only totally caring and sincere but of an unusual depth and as such they routinely make me struggle to respond in some meaningful way. Unfortunately, no matter how I might try to embellish any description, our lives as two professionals raising two children in a metropolitan community are ones of frantic and mind-numbing routine.

I hear myself let out a small, exasperated sigh. "Janet? Good." I shrug. "Her practice is going well but along with Tommie it's wearing her out. The usual."

"And Tommie and Sarah?"

I shake my head. "Tommie?" How does one describe a caring and affectionate child who is unfortunately obsessive and inappropriate in all his behavior? "Well, daily issues but nothing major this summer. Sarah? Too bright and perfect for her own good. Sailing through school. If she wasn't such a cutie, it would be disgusting. She's a good sport about Tommie. But he grates on her like he does all of us, and the fact that he absorbs most of our attention doesn't help."

"Hmmm, yes. I can see that."

Occasionally in emergencies we have had to call on Zoltan as a sitter for our kids. Uncle Zoltan. He invents experiments or games, totally ignores their bedtime, let's them eat junk food and sweets. By the time we return they are in the midst of a liquid color-changing chemistry experiment, our kitchen turned into a rank-smelling laboratory. Or he endeavors to teach them about his first love, opera, and we return home to opera blasting from the speakers and Zoltan acting out different parts with the kids, including female, for which he has borrowed some of Janet's clothes, which, as you might imagine, ticks her off pretty significantly. I mean, it's not like he can actually fit in any of her garments, so he pins them to himself. Needless to say, Tommie and Sarah find him endlessly amusing.

In my peripheral vision I became aware of a fellow patron approaching our table. His ruddy face reflected years of alcohol and stress, his complexion irregular and his forehead marked with small, sharp crevices, damage undoubtedly from a collision with a car windshield some years before. He wore a funereal store-bought suit, nondescript gray print tie, white shirt, black loafers. There was a reassuring presence about him, of a man inured to the foibles of life, even appreciating and seeing the humor in them, a fellow traveler in need of some company.

"Buy you fellas a drink on a Thursday night?" he asked in a pleasant tone.

At some point the previous year, when I was having lunch at the faculty table, he had been pointed out to me as one of the president's "henchmen," which in summary was all I knew about him. I always found this kind of name-calling interesting, as faculty, while professing an ardor to protect all entities from discrimination, invariably criticized the administration and its members with stereotypical bias while holding themselves aloof from any real interaction. It was as if they could not help themselves in their need to feel superior.

"We're just..." I began.

"Yes," said Zoltan. "That good. Thank you. Sit down."

Our new acquaintance pulled a chair from another table and sat down. Our waiter came. "Martini on the rocks," he ordered, "four olives, four onions. And another round for these gentlemen. Thanks."

"Frank Lusby." He extended a hand, and leaning over the table shook ours.

"Zoltan Vastag."

"Good to meet you."

"Thomas Simpson."

"Likewise. I saw you fellas here all the time last year, figured I should make your acquaintance. You guys seem like real compadres. It's not everyone who pauses on a daily basis for reflection and a bit of socialization. Makes life worth living, I think. How do you guys know one another?"

"We met at faculty orientation a dozen years ago," I told him. "Something clicked. We were both recently married for one thing, both starting our careers, both new to the area. Epic adventures followed. None of which can be discussed."

Lusby chuckled. "Yes, that I do understand. It's good to have real friends."

"What you do besides sit here and buy people drinks?" Zoltan asked.

"Ah, good question, Zoltan," Lusby said. "Thank you. I'm a consultant to the university, working out of the president's office on the capital campaign."

"The big one?" I inquired.

"That would be the one—$4.5 billion."

"That a hell of a goal," Zoltan remarked.

"Yeah, pretty overwhelming until you break it down into the various potentials for different schools, divisions, programs and projects and match them up with donors. Then it begins to look doable. Of course, the board will play a major role."

"All them billionaires."

"We are fortunate enough to have several."

Our drinks came.

"You still not told what you do," Zoltan said.

Lusby shrugged. "Hard to define really. To some degree whatever the hell they tell me to do. I'm a strategist and an organizer for the campaign both from a prospect, staffing and choreography point of view. But you know in that kind of role it's not too long before you're caught up in the whole ball of wax."

"So, you're something of an administrative tar baby?" I joked.

Lusby laughed hard, reddening. "Yeah, that would be me. I think I'll tell Bryan, rather, our president, that one. He'll get a kick out of it."

"You're on the road permanently?"

"It doesn't quite work that way. I'm home the majority of weekends. A lot of times I can stretch it to three days. Then we have a summer vacation of a month."

"You have kids?"

Lusby looked at us glumly, a world of troubles surfacing in his expression. "Yeah, my lovely wife, Mary-Beth, holds down the homestead while my daughter, Elizabeth, screws up her life."

"What do you mean?"

"She's a Goth."

"Oh.... Jesus."

"He has nothing to do with it, I can assure you."

"Yeah."

"Frankly, there are times I wonder whether I have any role in our household at all, other than bringing home a paycheck and being taken for granted."

Neither Zoltan nor I knew how to respond to this strangely intimate confidence, so we were silent.

Lusby continued in his soft, smoky voice, a voice tailored to not carry, "We have a cocker spaniel, you know? Very sweet dog. When I come home after a long week of killing myself here, I walk in the front door and the damn dog barks at me. How do you like that?"

"Frank, you need more home time," I counseled.

"Yeah," he agreed. "Or a lot less!"

We laughed with him.

"So, do you guys mind if I ask you a couple questions? I just like to hear the unvarnished truth once in a while from folks who have no vested interest in the politics of this place."

"Sure," I said, "but we have to go in a couple minutes."

"Okay. So, for now, just one question. If you had one word of advice for the president, what would it be?"

It did not take me long to reply. "The president's going about selling himself to his constituents in all the wrong ways. Your communications from him are predominantly in print, which is static and out-of-date by the time constituents read it. He needs to be on the web. The more you can get him as a participant or host on podcasts and other media broadcasts the better. This will humanize him. You might consider a regular virtual town meeting in which the president discusses university programs and plans and takes questions from the audience. Broadcast it online and allow it to be interactive.

"As for your publications, get rid of as many of the grip-and-grins as you can. Feature small articles and thought pieces from him that articulate his vision or a genuine emotion or idea so people feel like he has a soul, that he cares about higher education and this university and that he has interesting, informed opinions and ideas to share. You'd also do well to assemble an email from him to constituents several times a year reporting and discussing what's happening at the university, recognizing and giving as much credit to everyone who's doing good work as possible—the more conversational the tone the better. It would likely have high readership."

Lusby nodded thoughtfully as he took a sip of his martini. "That's very sound and sensible advice, Thomas. I wonder why our public relations and marketing folks haven't ever made any of these recommendations?"

"Beats me. We never see them; never hear from them. I know they're busy, but that's all I know. Like many things around here, we live in two separate worlds."

"Hmmmm," Lusby mused.

Zoltan said, "At medical center we have head of the hospital and we have dean of the medical school. I have dual appointment and report to both dean and department head. Department head report to head of oncology center. We have no clue about the president. He not a player in our game. He need to have a meeting of the entire faculty and research people and tell them what he doing to help us, what he think, who he is."

"Well, he very definitely is a player in your game, but I'll let that go," Lusby said. "The fact that you don't think he is I find very interesting, and I like your suggestion.... Thanks, guys. I appreciate your thoughts. Get on with your real lives now while I think about what you just said."

He pulled a small leather card holder from his suit jacket pocket and handed us each a card. "By the way, there's a welcoming reception at Stewart House for deans and department heads next Friday at four. Could I count on you fellas to attend? Be good to have a few at large folks from the university and medical campuses there. Be happy to introduce you around—to the president and other members of the administration."

"We let you know," Zoltan replied, standing. He turned to me. "You give me ride?"

"Sure."

Zoltan paid me as we left the club and we walked across the quadrangle to my car amidst the general undergraduate celebration of cooler days, turning leaves, fraternity rush and an upcoming football game, people passing in the other direction giving Zoltan a wide berth.

I looked at Frank Lusby's card. On one side it was printed with the university seal and had him as chief consultant to the president for the Campaign for Progress. On the other was a corporate logo fashioned out of dollar signs and his title as senior vice president for Blakum, Inc. in Pittsburgh.

"What you think of that Lusby?" Zoltan asked me.

"Kind of a creepy guy but also very likable. I find myself wondering why he bought us a drink. Why did you even agree to have a drink with him?"

"He know everything. You take Zoltan's word. He like some kind of spook for administration. Nothing happen without him. His fingerprints nowhere to be found. There are reasons he want to buy us a drink. Not to say I know what reasons are, but one thing you can be sure of, he know exactly who we are and exactly why he want to know us."

"Very Machiavellian," I observed.

"Yes. That why I let him buy us drink. I am a curious fellow."

"You going to this reception?"

Zoltan shrugged. "Sure. Why not? Be interesting to meet our boy wonder president and all the ass kissers and others, like his assistant. Very attractive, capable, scary woman. You come too. We fuck with them."

II
Genius

No matter what one thought of Bryan Q. Fitz-Hugh as president, and I had met him in passing on one or two prior occasions, he was a very likable and appealing fellow. He had the charm that often accompanies Irish descent. He was engaging and fun with a witheringly quick wit. He had an ability to size up people and situations instantly and project as quickly and creatively how they might best be positioned to support him and his future plans.

He had been appointed President of Sessions a little over two years before after serving at a previously nondescript college where he garnered a national reputation for its transformation, and he had brought much of that energy, experience and acumen to Sessions. Fitz-Hugh, as a president, was essentially a man on fire.

His first initiative has been to form an energy task force with the university's faculty, administration, maintenance staff, students and outside vendors and advisors. The aim: to make the campus energy self-sufficient over a five year period through the implementation of solar and wind turbine systems and through a rigorous conservation program that identified and rectified the university's many energy-wasting buildings as well as policies, procedures and practices.

The team effort and resulting *esprit de corps* from all levels of the university working cooperatively had brought the president very favorable reviews. A major celebration of the university's going off-the-grid was already being planned two years in advance for Earth Day.

As this success unfolded, Fitz-Hugh took steps to integrate public service into the university's core curriculum. He held a joint retreat in which local community agency CEOs and their boards rubbed elbows with the college's faculty, board members and student leaders. From this, an internship program had evolved where students in various disciplines worked in social service and other public, private and non-profit community service agencies and faculty joined their boards.

A signature program had also been developed in which 'at risk' youth from the area were trained via the university's groundskeeping and maintenance crews in landscaping, maintenance and construction, and then through state and federal grants were employed by area agencies working on revitalization projects within their own neighborhoods. Their successful completion of work on these projects either led to securing full time employment or, if they chose, to taking GED courses in the university's College of Continuing Education—in several cases on a university scholarship.

Lately, Fitz-Hugh had turned his attention to the Campaign for Progress, a comprehensive effort which sought funds not so much for endowed chairs as for moving forward present day initiatives under the theme of creating, in Fitz-Hugh's vision, 'The Global University,' one dedicated to greater access for all, not only through admissions of international students to Sessions but through international alliances with other key universities worldwide, including plans for a Sessions campus in Beijing.

"So," I asked Zoltan the following Friday as we walked across campus to the reception at Stewart House, "refresh my memory. Why are we doing this?"

He shrugged. "I have curiosity about all of this administration and politics. You have to admit it is interesting. When president's consultant invite you to attend a reception, even if it only for deans and department heads, and you are not supposed to be there, you should go. Never know what you learn."

"Yeah. Maybe. Look, I can't stay long, gotta get things straightened away at home."

We climbed the marble stair, wrought iron rail entry. Stewart House, formerly the president's residence, was now vacant except for special events and the occasional overnight dignitary or professorial candidate, because Fitz-Hugh, and his wife Celeste, an attorney in private practice, having two young daughters, did not wish to live in what Celeste described as "a fish bowl." Accordingly, off-campus housing had been negotiated as part of Fitz-Hugh's compensation.

Zoltan opened the massive mahogany door and we were assaulted immediately with overheated air from too many bodies in the large black and white marble tiled, high ceiling foyer, a cacophony of conversations resounding in the room.

It took me a moment to acclimate, plus I had to work my way around Zoltan's bulk to get a good look at the crowd.

The president and his retinue were over towards the doorway to the living room. He was impeccably dressed as always, in a light-weight cream colored suit as befitted the Indian summer weather, pale yellow silk tie and sky blue shirt that set off his tan. Other department heads and faculty were scattered around in small clusters talking among themselves, including the provost, Samuel Kravitz, and my department chair, Howard Calhoun.

Kravitz was a linguist. As erudite a scholar as we had at Sessions University, he spoke French, Spanish, Portuguese, German and Russian and had a working knowledge of many more languages. All this knowledge was carried proudly in his distinguished, over-large, handsome head with its broad forehead, swept back dark hair graying at the temples, bushy black eyebrows atop a remarkably small yet fit body (Kravitz had been a champion gymnast in college). This physiology created the impression of a political cartoon caricature somehow come to life.

He was best known for his ability to get his back up about issues involving academic principles and integrity and for his idiosyncrasy of using a foreign phrase while conversing to illustrate a point. While some of our more multi-lingual colleagues found this edifying and gamely went along, those of us less fluent found this form of one-upmanship genuinely annoying.

My boss, Calhoun, was an avuncular pie-in-the-sky theorist, a lovely older gentleman with white, unruly hair, skin troubled by eczema, gravelly voice and glasses with over-thick lenses distorting his eyes to the degree that they resembled two small, brown minnows darting in sequence behind a prism. While in his pleasant and genial way Howard welcomed all considered discourse on any intellectual subject, and could hold his own in any such conversation, outside of this he was a remarkably disorganized and forgetful person, and so also, as head of our department, he was always troubled by the sense of not having done something that should have been done, which was usually the case.

His office in our communications department in Hart Hall, on the upper quadrangle, was a dumpster of twenty-five plus years of work at the university. It was so full of dust and mold that because of my allergies I could barely make it through more than fifteen minutes of any meeting with him. As I blew my nose and looked around at yellow—and even brown—stacks of papers and research that had accumulated over the decades of his tenure, I honked monosyllabic responses designed to get me the hell out of there.

There was a bit of an air of homecoming amongst the crowd, as many of us had not seen one another since the spring. I was struck by the aging of some, the transformation of style or hair, weight gain and weight loss in others.

I moved toward Kravitz and Calhoun instinctively while Zoltan went to talk with his colleagues from the medical center.

Howard paused mid-conversation when he saw me, pleasantly surprised.

"Ah, Thomas, good to see you." A puzzled expression came to his face. "What are you doing here?"

"Zoltan and I were asked to show up by Frank Lusby."

"Ah, yes, 'the henchman,' as my colleagues say."

"That man," Kravitz sniffed, "overtly slippery. Had the presidency fallen to me, we would not have those kinds of people making a mockery of our university administration."

Howard nodded sagely, "I don't doubt it for one moment. As I was saying, Samuel, how was your summer? How is the family?"

"Ah, thank you Howard. All are very well. Joan has been working on a Mozart violin piece for the coming chamber orchestra concert. Natalie and husband are at the University of Chicago. She's continuing her career as a concert pianist and he's teaching mathematics. Young Samuel is finishing up his PhD in modern languages at Yale. All very satisfying for the old man."

"Wonderful! You know, over the summer, Samuel, I've been giving some thought to creating a new course for our department. I look at the pronouncements being made by our national leaders and the leaders of our allies and those who are opposed to us and I wonder whether the time has not come for a joint department course titled, perhaps, 'Communications and Linguistics in Politics—the Art and Science of Manipulation.' You realize, of course, as I do, that not only do our students not bother reading about international affairs on a daily basis, but they also do not understand remotely the grotesque distortions that are being reported as honest truth. This might help alleviate that problem, as well as give them some capacity for independent analysis. We could perhaps link arms with our colleagues in political science."

Kravitz frowned. "Howard, you may not realize it, but that idea could be as abidingly dangerous as it is propitious. First, I commend and agree with your intent. However, as you may have noticed, there are pockets of zealotry on this campus and around the city. What happens when we begin revealing the ugly truth behind linguistic and communications manipulation being applied by some leader whom zealots revere. *Gefährliche!*"

Howard was crestfallen. "*Wahr,*" he replied, shaking his head. "Unfortunately, you have a valid point there, Samuel."

"Let me consider this idea," Kravitz said, "and vet it with others. I'm not saying it's impossible, but we must consider what safeguards to apply."

"Of course, Samuel."

There was a pause, both men cogitating the departmental communications and manipulations required to pull off this newly proposed course, at the same time weighing the political risks of possible disruption.

"Well," Kravitz said to Calhoun, ignoring my presence, "I must corral a department head or two, catch up with their summer."

"Yes, of course."

Kravitz was a step away but stopped suddenly and turned back to us with an afterthought. "Say, Howard, do you know anyone who has younger children who might serve as a babysitter for Natalie's two children when she and her husband visit us? We haven't a clue whom to call."

"Oh," Howard said, bemused, "we would be in the same boat…" I could see an idea come to him. "But Thomas here… Would this be of interest to your daughter, Sarah? She's about the right age for that, isn't she?"

"Yeah," I said, a bit taken aback that I was suddenly relevant because of my fifteen-year-old daughter, "she's never done it before. I'll ask her though."

"Good man!" Kravitz said, reaching out and shaking my hand. "Much appreciated."

As Kravitz turned and walked away, Howard looked at me abstractly, clearly still a bit puzzled by my presence.

"How was your summer?" I asked. Howard had a place in Maine.

It took a moment but this brought him back into focus. We became colleagues again. "Ah, paradise. The sailing was marvelous, the lobsters in plentiful supply. We had weeks on and weeks off with the grandchildren. I conducted a thorough review of Schramm and then Berlo. How was your summer? How are the classes?"

"Good summer; the summer course I taught went well, kids are fine, Janet's practice is thriving and of course driving her crazy. New classes seem to have begun well. Students evermore challenged."

"Yes, they are less and less prepared, less able to think with any analytical depth. The world to them is a monochromatic simplicity, flat and grey. As for Janet, I'm not sure how anyone like Janet deals with troubled people all the time."

"Just look around."

"Yes, Thomas, but we have the luxury of avoidance. She does not." Calhoun smiled.

"True."

"Thomas, the proposed course we were discussing—you have any interest in teaching that?"

"Sure."

"Good. I'll let you know how things develop. Doubtful anything will come of it, but you never know."

As I turned, Zoltan walked by and said, "Bar this way," and we headed off into the opposite dining room where a table had been set up and two of the university club's waiters were pouring drinks.

The crowd around the bar was several deep except on the right side.

One person stood there patiently waiting to place an order. He turned to us—dark eyes enlarged by optics peering at us through round black spectacles with center hinges, black hair cut close to his head, a bedraggled orange mustache connected in an 1800s manner to copious orange sideburns. He was skinny and was wearing a frayed herringbone sports coat, an ancient button-down collared blue shirt, corduroy jeans, a rope belt and boat shoes without socks.

"You guys go farhst," he said to us in a Boston accent, motioning toward the bar. "You look thirstier than me. Plus," he held up an empty glass of ice cubes and remnant scotch, "I'm ahead of yah."

"We catch up," Zoltan said, giving him a rare smile that somehow possessed a touch of maniacal and rictus grins and elbowed his way to the bar, expanding the space our bar mate had left.

"Good, don't need to hold back with this crowd. After all, they all are exspurts. I'm just a poor Jewish kid off the streets ah Boston. The only thing you can do to even the keel is drink along with them."

Zoltan ordered our drinks and another for our new friend and turned back toward him. "What you do beside grow sideburns?"

Our compatriot laughed. "I like that! Mark Berger," he said, reaching out and shaking our hands. "For some damn reason awhile back they put me on the board of trustees. Guess they want some of my money. I've given 'em a little bit. I love the job Bryan is doing—world-class leader. How are you fellows involved with the university?"

"We crash receptions for free drinks."

"We're both professors here, Zoltan in cancer research and I'm in communications. The president's consultant asked us to attend for some reason."

"You mean Frank. Yeah, that figures. I like Frank. There's always an angle."

"You look like you just step off boat."

"Well, actually, I just did. I have a boat in the harbah."

"That's interesting," I commented. "You live on it?"

"Nah. Just reserve it for when I'm down here for board meetings, other than winter, and when it's not being chartahed. You know, for many years I hated the idea of owning a boat—just another possession that owns you—but finally my accountants convinced me that this chartah/lease business helped with my taxes, and I have to admit having it down here at my disposal is kinda convenient."

"On occasion Zoltan and I talk about getting a boat."

"You sailahs or stinkpottahs?"

"I like to sail. Zoltan just likes being out on the water."

"I like to fish," Zoltan added. "Rockfish very special catch."

"You'll have to come see my boat sometime."

"Sure, we'd like that."

There was a bit of a commotion behind us. We turned and saw the president making his way toward the bar, the crowd parting politely as his retinue moved in our direction.

There was his assistant, Ursula Mueller, steering him toward us. Young, perfectly groomed, with strong flawless features, she had a sleek, purebred look. From what I could tell, Ursula was all business, took herself, her job and her loyalty to the president far too seriously. Worked 24/7/365. Had no life beyond the office that anyone knew about. Given that she was handling a personality whose tendency was gregariousness beyond all bounds, it made sense that these two were paired professionally. Before now she had never given me more than a stern and dismissive look. As she approached, she smiled at me as if we had long been the best of friends.

The dean of the College of Continuing Studies, Jack Wentz, was also following along, joking openly with the president. Wentz was a laughing porcine figure, with small, squinty, fast-moving black eyes, slick hair, wearing an acetate suit, cheap shirt and tie. Why he and the president seemed glued to the hip was beyond many of us. Frank Lusby of course was part of the group, as well as a few deans and department heads, thirsty now that the president was headed toward the bar. I recalled that Celeste Fitz-Hugh, occupied as she was with matters of litigation and billable hours, rarely made an appearance at these functions.

"Mark," the president called out to Berger genially, repeating, I thought, what Wentz had just whispered in his ear, "I see you've found your usual pre-occupation."

"Hey," Berger held his freshly filled glass up in a toast, "for some reason this time of day I get very thirsty."

The president turned to those around him. "Without Mark's sober financial and investment acumen, the university's endowment would not be nearly as robust as it is today."

"Nah," Berger demurred. "You had something to do with that, Bryan. I just help direct traffic here and there."

"Thomas, how nice to see you," Ursula said. "I hope your summer was a good one."

"Yes, thanks. And yours?"

She rolled her eyes. "Too busy." She glanced at Fitz-Hugh, who smiled at us. "He never stops."

Lusby moved imperceptibly forward and said to Fitz-Hugh,

"These are the faculty members I was telling you about."

I noticed that Lusby was not drinking.

"Ah," Fitz-Hugh smiled.

"Frank told me your ideas," he said to me. "Spot on, my friend. Thanks so much. It really helps to have your expertise as a resource. Frank met with our public relations department yesterday and I believe you will find your suggestions incorporated into upcoming communications. As well, the idea of online presidential forums is just right; exactly the kind of platform I was looking for. They can become a conversation with our worldwide alumni and friends, donors and affiliates. Perfect. Thank you so much. I also particularly liked the idea of the president's email—low key, reporting on the state of the university, a great way to engender interest and engagement among all our constituents. And this is one time," he laughed, "because all the news is about them, they won't shoot the messenger!"

He turned to Zoltan. "I also thought your commentary about perceptions at the medical campus were very interesting. I've talked with the dean and the hospital director and we're going to have a presentation to the entire medical faculty, researchers and clinical staff about two months from now filling them in on our planning for the future, our roles and how we can all work toward common goals. Very helpful. Let me also commend you on your research. Your recent paper on the genetic potentiality for altering immature cancer cells is most interesting."

"Thank you," Zoltan said with the expression of an axe murderer. Zoltan hated it when people talked about his research.

Fitz-Hugh turned back to me.

"So, you're from Baltimore?"

"Originally, yes," I said, surprised that he had checked me out this thoroughly.

"I spent a couple of very good years there as a dean of students. Fascinating city. Such an innate provincialism. The suspicion they have that the rest of the world regards their city and therefore its citizenry as second rate drives them even further toward insular behavior. I found it most interesting when I first moved there that if I was at a gathering and came upon a group in conversation they would continue their conversation as if I was not there, did not even exist. On one hand, it was because they had no idea of what to say to an outsider; on the other, they had not grown up with you, so in some very real way in their world you actually did not in fact exist. After a time, I became accepted as part of the scene, but until then, it was rather strange."

I laughed. "That's a hell of a summation. It might even have some truth to it."

"Lovely folks once you get to know them."

"Some of them. Maybe not so much the family members."

Fitz-Hugh laughed. "That's true of any hometown, isn't it? Even in my lovely hometown of Palo Alto."

I laughed in return. "You're right.

Few things in life are certain. One of them is that while I might know my field of study and area of expertise backwards and forwards, upside down and inside out, I am by no means a genius. Our president, on the other hand, was. Geniuses remember and know everything. So, our president could at any time converse knowledgeably about anything from the mysteries of sea turtle mating to the rates of crime in the largest inner city neighborhoods. For all I knew, he not only had read Zoltan's most recent paper, but actually had some idea what it was about.

While on the surface, in this politically correct world I expressed enthusiasm for these remarkable individuals, the fact was that if I looked more deeply into my real feelings about them, I found myself resentful. Part of it was rank jealousy, a larger part was an uneasy distrust. Distrust of the confidence and self-affection such capability brought to their possessor and what it could do if it ever got off track

So, I listened to the president as he continued to lead the conversation around him, all of it casting a glowing gold light on himself, his youthful vitality and charisma, his sparkling blue eyes, his brown hair with highlight wisps of blond, his whitened teeth, while feigning amused and admiring interest.

He turned to Zoltan. The conversation had veered to football and the coming Sunday's game.

"I don't suppose our star researcher ever played American football. It would be soccer, wouldn't it?"

"Yes," Zoltan replied. "That what our family liked. And you can imagine in school where they put me on team."

"Let me guess. Goalie."

"Yes, of course."

"Were you any good?"

Zoltan shrugged. "Not really. Teammates say though that other teams too scared to score. Afraid of what I might do to them after match. Teammates spread rumor that our family worship Satin and practice cannibalism."

"Yes, a competitive advantage. I can see that."

Zoltan took a long drink of his vodka and deadpanned, "I pussycat."

Everyone laughed.

"We must go now," he said, draining his glass.

As we walked back through the foyer, beginning to empty now as the reception wore on, a "Wait a minute guys," from Berger coming up behind took us by surprise.

"Hey," he said, "I wasn't joking about your seeing my boat. Let's exchange cards. Why don't you guys come out sometime? Bring your wives, girlfriends, kids, whatevah. Hey, bring a girl-friend for me! Seriously, love to see you guys. Enjoyed meeting you."

"Okay," I said, somewhat taken by the intensity and sincerity of his interest. "We'd love to do that. We'll be in touch. See you then."

As we walked across campus, I told Zoltan, "Why don't I give you a ride over to your place?"

"Good, I need to do something like listen to opera to recover from that mess."

"Yeah, was that everything you wanted it to be?"

"Well, yes, interesting but very…what is word…?"

"Bogus?"

"Yes."

"Before we get going let me Google this Berger guy."

"Yes, he funny guy. But…what…he lonely?"

I nodded. "Yeah, that's my read."

"Yes, but he good man."

I worked my phone as I sat in the front seat of my car.

"Je-sus," I heard myself say.

"What?"

"This guy, Berger. I thought his name sounded familiar. He's world famous, a currency and commodities trader. Owns hedge funds and God knows what else. A multi-billionaire." I read on. "Je-sus, and he's got a Ph.D. in political science from BU and a law degree from Harvard. Just a poor Jewish guy off the streets of Boston, huh?"

Zoltan shrugged. "We forgive him this. I like him anyway."

"Yeah, so do I. Be interesting to see his boat."

"Yes."

"So," I turned toward Zoltan, "what the hell do they want with us? We're just peons in the scheme of things."

"That a good question. I bet we find out soon enough."

I shook my head. "Yeah, maybe. It's all a bit strange, don't you think?

"Yes."

III
Home

AFTER DROPPING ZOLTAN OFF AT HIS PLACE, I drove out the expressway to our neighborhood, the neighborhood Janet and I thought would be so great and which we aren't wild about. It's pretty enough, with relatively big, showy but cheaply-built houses on small lots.

What really attracted us was that it was near a school with a highly-reputed program for Tommie, had a great number of activities for the kids, a community pool, tennis courts and a nearby park and river. We had not, however, expected its residents to be so very cliquey. The stay-at-home mommies hang out with their ilk, as do the working mothers. Families who send their children to certain private schools hang out together. Families who go to the same church hang out together. On their own, the dads, immersed in their money-making pursuits, hang out with no one. Janet and I, whose life philosophies embrace independence, have discovered that we have little interest in hanging out with any of them. Often we feel like modern day seekers, looking for honest, genuine people whose priorities are not skewed by false and ephemeral pursuits. It's a long and fruitless search.

At least Tommie's school has worked out well. He's comfortable there and not anxious and unhappy as he was in the "can't win" environment of a regular school where he was told he was stupid and was bullied. He seems okay at first, a good looking kid who wants to please but who presents us with a daily challenge of trying to channel and guide him toward a normalcy we know he will never reach. Janet's a professional psychologist and even she's a bit confounded by him. The more you get into it, the more you realize all these labels that shrinks and psyches throw around are just that, and that each child or adult is his or her own unique creation and being. Labels may describe them in part or describe tendencies but they do not in any way sum up the whole.

I parked the car in our garage and headed into the house through the laundry, which opens into a large family room with a double doorway to the kitchen.

Sarah was sitting in front of the TV on one of the leather couches watching a program where hip kids interact in colorful and completely bogus ways around contrived circumstances.

She actually had the grace and presence to mute the TV and chirp, "Hey, daddy!"

I bent over and gave her a hug as I glanced into the kitchen to see Janet stir frying chicken and vegetables, the smell of it drifting through the house, a bottle of white wine and glasses on the counter.

"How was school?" I asked as I stood up again.

Sarah shrugged, twirled one of her braids with an idle hand.

"The SAME!"

"Thrill a minute, huh?"

"So bor-ring!"

"Yeah? Get used to it."

"That's what you always say."

"Yeah. You have homework, right?"

"Done, daddy. I do that in school."

"Okay. I should have known. Where's Tommie?"

Sarah looked at me as if I might be the most stupid person on earth, which was how I felt for asking the question.

"Okay. I should have known."

She was in the gifted and talented track in her freshman year of high school and yet was still jogging in place unchallenged. Her saving grace was being good-natured and perceptive enough to maneuver her way out of any situations that might not work out well—relatively easy when one is smart and popular.

I walked into the kitchen to my honey brown haired, brown eyed, no nonsense, practical to a fault, smart as a whip spouse, who has more common sense than any crowd of people combined. She looked only mildly harassed.

"How was your day?"

"Some interesting cases today. Some progress. Then there's Dr. Compton."

"He'll make it another week?"

She shrugged. "One can't be sure. He's very determined and willful to be forever unhappy, so it's a struggle to keep him upright."

I poured a glass of wine for each of us. "I guess I should go check on Tommie."

"Probably a good idea."

"Okay," I said, picking up my glass of wine.

We gave one another a parting kiss on the cheek.

Tommie was in Tommie Town or, to the uninitiated, the basement.

His fascination with fire engines had begun at age four, the first time in the car one had passed us on the way to a fire, sirens blasting, lights flashing. His eyes had widened and he had shouted, "What THAT!!!! What THAT!!!! What THAT!!!!" and we had explained and the questions had continued unrelentingly: Where did the engines live? How did fires start? Who were firemen? Where did they live? What did they eat? How did fire hydrants work? Where does the water come from?

Over the years his fascination continued and extended to everything in connection with fire engines, fire houses, firemen, famous infernos, the history of the fire engine, different fire companies, our local fire department—where all the crew knew him by name because if I didn't take him over there on a regular basis he would become just impossible.

Eventually his obsession had taken over the basement: first, with a collection of model fire engines, then he invented a village in which his fire engines resided and then, when that wasn't enough, he hectored me into helping him build a much more extensive model village.

I had worked with Tommie to help him build Tommie Town, setting up sawhorses and building a platform of plywood, partly because it was a good father-son project but also because he was relatively uncoordinated and might learn from doing some of the very basic work himself. He had at least pantomimed helping mix plaster, building mountains and ridges of chicken wire, setting down model railroad track, painting the landscape, installing shrubbery, then badgered us into buying not one but two very nice model fire stations from which he ran his collection of model fire trucks and could tend to a village of stores, a hotel and residential housing.

So, here was the problem. What do fire engines put out? We had concocted a system of a flashlight with a tinted orange lens, which was used to simulate a fire for Tommie's extensive collection of fire engines to help extinguish. So, I or Janet or Sarah would stand by with the flashlight, shining on a building of his choice while Tommie made all the attendant imaginary noises of bells and sirens and with his model firemen dispatched an engine, or several, to put out the incendiary threat to the town.

Frankly, his daily three alarm needs wore us all out, but the option of leaving him alone for any extensive period of time was not palatable. Needless to say, our house had been cleansed of any matches and lighters. Our fireplace had fake cloth flames activated by a blower and lit from behind. Smoke detectors and fire extinguishers were carefully placed in unobtrusive places throughout.

I opened the door to the basement to discover that the lights were out.

"Tommie?" I turned on the lights and went down the stairs.

Tommie came running up to me, his brown hair tousled, the perpetual anxious and overly enthused look on his face, blinking in his awkward, almost manic way. He had the most beautiful, long-lashed, china-blue eyes that made his blinking seem all the more unfortunate. He hugged my leg and hip, looked up.

"Dad! I invented a time machine!"

"Well, that's interesting."

"It will take me back in time and then I can put out fires with my antique fire engines because it will be back then when they were new!"

"Okay."

"Let me show you how it works. You have to turn out the lights."

He had converted one of the remnant plastic kiddie cars that probably should have already gone to Goodwill, surrounding it with cardboard with cutout windows of orange, red and blue colored clear plastic panes he had crafted from three ring binder dividers and taped in place.

I hit the light switch on the wall and Tommie turned on an old portable CD player that probably also should have gone to Goodwill long ago. Music blasted through the basement, some mysterious and galactic space theme. He was sitting inside his time machine and turned on the flasher switch to a LED flashlight so that it lit up the time machine, which he rocked as if it were traveling through the time space continuum. I must admit his time machine looked kind of odd and spooky rocking and vibrating in the dark.

He rocked it for a time way beyond my attention span. I started assembling lesson plans as I stood by the light switch, occasionally taking a sip of wine. Eventually, he stopped and said, "Dad, you can turn on the light now."

He came out from the time machine with a fireman hat on and handed me what was known as the "fire light," and I shined it on the grocery store while he ran an antique model fire engine from a fire house to the store and went through his ritual of dousing the flames with invisible water and appropriate sound effects and saving the shopkeepers and customers with some dialogue thrown in. "Oh, thank you, sir." "You're most welcome, madam."

When he had finished, I asked, "Don't you have some homework?"

"I don't know…maybe," he blinked his awkward rapid blink, almost a tick, as his mind came back to reality, his eyes large and blue and not yet quite focused. "When's dinner?"

"Almost ready, I believe. Let's go upstairs."

As we climbed the stairs, Tommie asked, "Dad, can we get a Dalmatian?"

IV
Clubbing

LIFE AT SESSIONS RESUMED ITS AUTUMNAL PACE, September running seamlessly into October.

In the club bar one afternoon after classes, Zoltan and I sat across from one another, the discussion, a familiar one, about our dim prospects for advancement.

"They keep on giving me more lab supervision work, then as far as they concerned I am gone, yet I stuck with all the work and no raise in pay, and I have to do research on my own. Like all the research I do for my last paper was on my own time this summer. I go to department head about this and he say I in line to make great discovery and when that happen I be famous and money pour in. I tell him he full of shit. They load me up with crap and that mean anything I do is slow and always interrupted."

"What of your findings or discoveries do you own, or have a right to, if you are doing the research in their labs?"

"I do not know."

"You'd better find an answer. Go back and look, find the employment contract you signed and have an attorney review it."

"Yes, this make sense. Mother university want everything all the time, yes?"

"Damn straight. But you're too cheap to hire an attorney, aren't you? Plus the word 'attorney' scares the shit out of you."

"Do not bet on this, Thomas."

"Then do it. Use some of that damn money in your big God-damned bottom drawer. Invest in yourself."

"Maybe you right."

"My problem is I'm stuck teaching the same courses every year. Okay, so I can update them in terms of bringing in the newest developments, survey methods, social media techniques etc., but where's the time for getting out in front of any of this with a seminal work of significance? Without that I'm just going to be stuck in the same rut, and sooner or later get deep-sixed because of the lack of recent publications."

"Yes, but we should be thankful. Many would kill to be where we are. It just mean we must solve our problems."

"How?"

"Maybe our new friends can help?"

"Oh, right. Why would they help us? They're too damn busy helping themselves."

Zoltan shrugged. "I don't know. We see... You ever hear from this Berger?"

"Actually, yes. He called me in his inimitable way, like he was at a trading desk completing an order. He wants us to come down and see his boat next Saturday."

"That good."

I heard someone call my name. We looked up and saw John Fein hurrying down the Karastan carpet toward us. Fein was the director of public relations, and by all observations present-ly a desperate man.

"Thomas!" he called out to me in an animated voice as he ap-proached, raising his arm and forefinger. "I need a word."

Fein was known as Fine-Fine Fein because "Fine" was his basic answer to any inquiry. Balding and overweight, high-col-ored, he routinely conveyed an unwholesome anxiety and ner-vousness that assured an abiding lack of respect from anyone with whom he was dealing.

When he reached us, he said, "Hi Zoltan," distractedly. He pulled up a chair, sat down across from me and said, "What the hell did I ever do to you?"

"What?"

"The president's office is all over me for these new programs. We're completely overrun as it is. We don't have the staff for this shit. What I am supposed to do? Tell them we can't get the magazine out? I am fucked! Especially this interactive online forum idea; we don't have any of the expertise required for that. How are we supposed to do that?"

I thought for a moment. "Hell, John, a couple of my grad students could take on the online set-up for that and work with the president's office on the program."

"They could? Oh my God, you'd do that?"

"How's your intern budget looking?"

"Oh, it's toast, man. Covering all these new community initiatives is eating us alive."

"Let me see what I can do. No promises."

"Awesome. That would be so fine, Thomas. Thanks. You've made my day. Hell, you've made my year! You're the best, Thomas."

"So, how you doing otherwise?"

"Oh, fine, fine. Gotta go. Deadline. Thanks again."

We watched as he scurried back down the hall.

Zoltan observed, "He like out of *Alice In Wonderland*, yes?"

"Yeah," I laughed, and was somehow comforted by the thought that Zoltan knew about *Alice In Wonderland* not only from the opera but from reading the book to Tommie and Sarah when they were younger.

As we walked through the bar on our way out, Wentz, Ursula Mueller and Lusby were having drinks toward the front with Bernie Reve, the vice president for university advancement. Reve was dressed in an even darker suit than Lusby's, but one of considerably higher quality, white shirt, elegant silk tie of green and gray, glistening black shoes. Reve was known as a weak administrator who left the running of his operation to his associate VP. However, he was reputed to be the consummate pro when it came to major gifts fundraising, a charming and delightful persona masking the personality of one who was never happy with himself. This self-contempt led to binge-eating and it was said he gained and lost on average over forty pounds a year, which affected his mood. When he was not dieting he was an ebullient soul, full of good cheer, fun and mischief, a sweetheart, thoughtful, caring, creative but also all-consuming of any food or alcohol in his vicinity. Dieting, he became a conniving paranoid monster. Given this, it was important to pick up clues on the state of his consumption, or lack thereof, to know how to deal with him. Judging from the martini and onion rings in front of him, I figured that all was good with Bernie's world. Everyone else was also drinking martinis, except Ursula who was sipping cranberry juice.

"We're having a little celebration," Lusby said as a way of greeting. "Care to join us?"

"Sure, thanks," I said. "I need a word with you anyway."

"Hey, Zoltan," Wentz greeted, "you cure cancer yet?"

"No, it very difficult, like obesity."

"Whoaaa," Reve chortled, rubbing his hands together gleefully. "Nice rejoinder, Zoltan."

Lusby waved at the waiter and ordered drinks for Zoltan and me.

Ursula said directly to me, "You sit down," not unpleasantly, but more of an order than a request, and indicated I was to find and pull up a chair next to her. She was wearing a dark blue pinstriped pantsuit and a white blouse with a bright blue scarf that picked up the color of her eyes. As always, her short, light brown hair was combed back, accentuating her well-formed forehead, high cheekbones and the fine lines of her jaw and chin.

"How such a beautiful woman get involved with these scumbugs?" Zoltan asked her as we sat down on chairs we had pulled from other tables.

"There's no accounting for bad taste," Lusby observed. "What can I help you with, Thomas?"

"I just had a chat with the always desperate Mr. Fein. I offered to help him pull off these new communications initiatives by providing him with some of our department's grad students, but his intern budget is shot. We actually have a couple of kids in our department who know more about webcasting than any of the professors. I can talk with our department head, Howard Calhoun, about their helping Fein and the president's office pull the program together."

Lusby shook his head in mock disapproval. "You would ask me to make yet another wholly inappropriate and inexplicable expenditure of funds from the capital campaign budget, possibly incurring yet even more wrath from our esteemed provost?" he asked, smiling ruefully.

"Ummm..."

He shrugged matter-of-factly and smiled. "I've got you covered. Send me a budget and I'll inform that imbecile Fein of his good luck and back you up with your Calhoun... So, what did you guys think of our little reception at Stewart House?"

"Usual cluster fuck," Zoltan commented dismissively.

Everyone laughed.

"The president was in fine form," I added.

"He loves those gatherings. If he wasn't a president, he would be in politics, which may account for why he does so well on Capitol Hill. By the way, he loved you guys, is very appreciative of your input, as you could tell."

"We like this Berger," Zoltan told them.

Reve perked up, his voice was high and tight, yet smooth and conspiratorial, like he was letting us in on a great adventure. "Anything you can do to cultivate *him*..." he said, moving both hands outward to indicate the amount of largesse involved. "Well, it would be *very* much appreciated. He's one of our campaign's top prospects and a bit of a wild hare. Hard for us to pin down what his interests are and what he might want to do; keeps his cards close to the vest, but his capability is, well... pretty much infinite."

"What you mean 'infinite?'" Zoltan asked.

"He could be a billion dollar donor!" Wentz snorted, coughed and slapped Reve on the back.

"Okay," Zoltan said, "we think about that. So, what you celebrate?"

Lusby said, "The founding of our university's Beijing Center, thanks to Bryan and dean Wentz's persistence, plus Bernie's very significant score. Confidential at this point, so we won't use any names, but in the near future there will be an announcement at the School of Foreign Service of a $150 million gift to name this new center." He paused, thought for a moment and smiled. "Bernie, why don't you tell these gentleman the story behind this generosity? It's..." He paused and a bit of slur crept into the next word, "iconic."

Wentz interjected, "I've got to get out of here in a couple minutes to meet with the president, so let me tell you about the center first. Something I've been working with Bryan on for some time." He took a slug of his martini and filched one of Reve's onion rings with stubby, fat fingers, an onyx and diamond ring flashing on his pinky.

"I have to go to the same meeting," Ursula said.

Wentz began talking. Whatever he said always sounded smarmy and on the make, but I found myself holding in check an impulse of disapproval. As much as I disliked everything about the man, I had to admit that he was as intelligent and facile as could be.

"It is well known that the Chinese are difficult, and they are also very shrewd. They can figure out what access is all about, as can the State Department, which has provided some seed funding. At least that's what they have said. We'll see whether we ever get the check. So, over the last two plus years and a lot of discussions and negotiations with Bryan as the point person and with me doing the inside work we've established the center in partnership with the Chinese as a place for international exchange and dialogue, but also have set the stage for a practical curriculum of study in areas of mutual interest, like engineering. You may not realize it but today China trains half the world's engineers." He turned to me. "The potential for international public relations communications from this venture is vast. Think of the different interest groups who have a stake in knowing the Chinese viewpoint and thinking about different issues in business, medical research, resource utilization, urban and environmental planning, how it melds with, differs from or enhances our perspectives and research. On the political spectrum, think of how these interactions can have a role in helping stabilize international relations, and think of how this new center positions Sessions to attract global support from the business community and foundations, not to mention how it positions us to compete globally for students."

As Wentz continued outlining the scope of the center, its location, plans for programs and admissions, I felt Ursula's leg move ever so slightly and come to rest against mine. Her movement seemed entirely inadvertent but her leg stayed where it was. Suddenly the temperature in the room seemed to go up about ten degrees and the center point of its rise was a fire burning between our two legs, as if high voltage electricity was flowing between us.

I felt my face redden. Zoltan gave me a curious look.

"So, we now have a sphere of influence with the Chinese. Can you imagine what this could mean to the development of an international curriculum and the forwarding of the global university concept? Unbelievable, and all through Bryan's insistence and drive. He speaks Mandarin, you know. Anyway, thanks for listening. We have to go."

He and Ursula rose to leave, and as she rose her hand rested on my arm as if she needed momentary support. For a nanosecond she looked directly into my eyes and smiled.

We watched them walk out of the room, Wentz's stride a disheveled mess, Ursula's with all the right things working.

"So, in confidence," Bernie said, "I think with Frank's permission I can name this donor. It's Melvin Rusoloff. You've undoubtedly heard of him, big developer, built most of our city, has an ego as big as all outdoors.

"For whatever reason, Melvin and I hit it off years ago when I was just some junior schmuck schlepping around in the basement of the administration building carrying cases of annual fund stationery to the printer. My boss at the time, who was a bit insecure and liked me to keep him company, like a valet even, invited me to dinner with him and Melvin. The purpose was to ask Melvin to pony up the lead challenge gift for that year's annual fund campaign, 500,000 bucks. Big ask. I was terrified that I would somehow screw things up. Long story short, Melvin and my boss started hammering Manhattans, got completely shitfaced and the annual fund challenge gift never even came up. I just drank real slow and after two drinks they lost track of the fact that I really was just sipping once every half hour or so. They were just having a great time.

"So, we finish dinner, and by this time they can barely talk, let alone walk, and I shepherd them out to taxis and drive my boss's car over to his house and park it outside and get a taxi home. Next morning, we get a call from Melvin's assistant. My boss hadn't even come in yet, so I took it. She puts me through to Melvin who says, hungover as shit, 'What the hell was *that* about last night?'

"I could tell he couldn't remember anything, so I said, 'We want you to lead this year's annual fund by making a $500,000 challenge gift.'

"'Oh,' he says. There's this long pause. 'You think that'll work?'"

"'Guaranteed,' I told him. 'Plus you will look like a big fucking hero and have the biggest dick in the room.'"

"Another pause. 'I like that,' he says. We got a personal check for the 500k the next week. My boss was super pissed, but ever since then Melvin and I have been actual friends. He invites me to his parties and seeks my advice on most of his philanthropy."

"So, how did we get the $150 million?" I asked.

Bernie took a sip of his martini and stuffed an onion ring in his mouth, talking with his mouth full. "I began talks with

Melvin about his legacy to the university years ago. Well, it turns out that when he was a student here, he was, or at least he felt he was, denied a fairly prestigious engineering merit award because he was Jewish. I kinda discounted that for a while until in doing some research I started going through the alumni yearbooks around his time. And you know what? It's possible, in fact, likely. So, in any case it became apparent that Melvin was not of a mind to donate a gift to the university. Nor was he likely to support the medical campus. His wife died in our hospital about three years ago from leukemia. It's not like Mel is pissed off at the hospital. It's just anything to do with the medical campus brings back a truckload of bad memories. But then Bryan appointed him to the board of visitors for the School of Foreign Service, which is, as you know, one of Bryan's priorities, and he's managed to enamor Melvin with it. So, we've been after the $150 million for a few chairs and to empower an international education fund, allowing us to recruit the best minds around the world to serve Sessions both in research and as part of its growing international continuing education program. All this hooks up to the theme of our becoming a global university and to the Beijing Center.

"So, we asked Melvin to consider endowing the Center, but he kept equivocating, trying to cut a deal that maximized everything in his favor. Anytime something wasn't exactly to his liking and his demands, he'd kibosh the deal. It was getting to the point he was like the runaway bride, except for him it was the runaway ego. I mean he wants national press, talk shows, his name on the Avenue of the Stars—just kidding, but you get my point. And his damn lawyers. They are just all over us trying to maximize the tax deductions on this sucker to where he's getting dollars of tax deductions for every dollar he gives.

"So, I'm in Melvin's office late one day a couple weeks ago and he's just being a complete prick about everything. So finally I've had enough of his shit. I get up and sigh a big long sigh and I say, 'Melvin, I had hoped we could put your name on this center we've been talking about. To me, you symbolize our city. Hell, you built this city. And you, in many ways, symbolize Sessions University. You and your legacy to our city and university ought to be represented prominently in our nation's capital and internationally through its connection to the School of Foreign Service... Now, I don't know, this just doesn't seem like it's going to work out. I'm damn sorry. It bums me out. I love you, man. I wanted to see your name on that center.' I turn and pull on my overcoat and begin to walk to the door.

"I hear a creaking noise behind me like he's just sat straight up in his office chair. 'You got someone *else* who'll do this center?' he challenges, all bluster like there isn't a snowball's chance in hell that I do.

"I slump my shoulders in defeat and turn around. I nod my head. 'Well, yes, but I was hoping it would be you and not the Prince of Morocco who would make this gift.'

"Melvin goes red in the face. 'You'd name that center for an *Arab*?' he shouts.

"I hold out my hands. 'It's not me. It's other members of the School of Foreign Service's board of visitors and our board of trustees. I'm just the broker here.'

"He gives me the longest, most evil stare-down and then says, 'You come here.' And he punches his desk with his forefinger. Christ, I thought he was going to break it off. He says, 'We'll figure this out.'"

At this final sentence Bernie burst into an infectious, long giggle, and all of us started laughing.

"Would the Prince of Morocco have made that gift?" I asked incredulously.

Bernie held up both hands. "I have no idea. We have not actually yet brought it to his attention, although Bryan does have a good dialogue with his staff."

"How many prospects like Melvin are you responsible for?" I asked.

Bernie slumped, took a slug of his drink and popped another

onion ring into his mouth. "One hundred and twelve," he said, his voice muffled by the food in his mouth. "I'm the best friend any of them ever had. And it's killing me. The goose that laid the golden egg is being slaughtered by airlines, hotels and hospitality."

"Wow…" I stood. "I am really late now. Gotta go."

"Yes," said Zoltan, also standing up.

Lusby spoke up. "Before you two leave, we're having a reception at the School of Foreign Service in Washington two Thursdays from now to announce the Rusoloff gift. Bryan wanted to know whether you could make it. He'd love to have your feedback about the event and anything else you pick up on or notice."

"So, we be his spies?" Zoltan asked.

"More like friends, I would say."

"Sure," I said.

We walked down the hallway and out the door into the autumn evening, the smell of burning leaves in the air, the sky a mauve orange, and across the quad toward the parking lot, Zoltan shoving some bills my way to pay for his drinks.

"So, now we know where there's some money to be had," I commented.

"Yes, very interesting. Campaign a very different deal than university budget."

"Sure as hell seems to be."

"You like this Ursula?"

"Part of me likes her a lot."

"That a bad part. No brain."

"Yeah."

"You be careful there. I hear she and president are an item."

"You're shitting me."

"No. Could not be true, but the word's out."

"Fuck."

Zoltan shook his head. "No. No fuck."

I laughed in rueful agreement, "Yeah."

V
Calypso Too

ON SATURDAY AS WE OPENED THE DOORS TO OUR VAN TO GO SPEND A DAY WITH MARK BERGER ON HIS BOAT, I reflected on the odd fact that Janet and I both routinely shook our heads in disbelief that we actually owned such a vehicle. Where had our youth gone? Yet it was our most frequently used car besides my old commuter sedan and her pre-children, sixteen-year-old BMW convertible that now sat forlornly in the garage, covered with dust and boxes because it needed a brake job we couldn't afford.

On Janet's instructions Tommie happily sat in the third row seat with two fire engines he had insisted on bringing along. Sarah sat in the middle row on the forty percent split seat, leaving room for Zoltan on the sixty percent.

"Okay, seat belts?" I asked.

"Yes," everyone but Tommie chimed.

"Sarah, check and see whether Tommie has his seat belt on."

Sarah turned and looked at Tommie.

"Nope."

"Tommie, put the belt on or the fire engines go back in the house."

"Okay, okay, okay…" Tommie whined.

"Did he put it on?" Janet asked.

"Yeah, he did, Mom. You know he'll take it off as soon as we turn around."

"Um, hmmmm," Janet sighed.

"You know, Thomas," she said as I put the car in gear, "I'm sure we'll have a good time today, but I don't really have time for this kind of thing."

"What kind of thing?"

"Blowing off an entire afternoon."

"Um, aren't we supposed to have a life here? Do new and fun things with the kids and our friend? I mean, it's the weekend, isn't it?"

"Sure, but this could go on forever. It's a boat."

"Yeah. Well, let's make an exception to our normal workaholic lives for once."

Janet smiled. "Okay, sweetheart. Just recognize that I'll be in my office most of tomorrow. You have kid duty."

"Sure."

From the back of the van came noises of Tommie playing.

Zoltan rented his room in a dingy white, black-shuttered, ramshackled monstrosity of a wood frame house in an older neighborhood behind the university's stadium, a neighborhood that felt as if it had been in the same dilapidated condition forever, full of similar houses surrounded by ancient gnarled elms, maples and oaks now shedding soft yellow, red and brown leaves on its wide lots, broken roads and uprooted sidewalks.

Zoltan was waiting for us on the large wraparound porch, seated on an ancient cushioned metal chair.

Seeing him come down the porch steps and walk toward us, sporting a new tattersall shirt and corduroy jacket and his regular jeans, but washed, brought a smile to my face.

Zoltan yanked the side door open with too much force, banging it against its stops. "Tommie!" he half shouted. "You been banished to the back, I see. We plot to take over this vehicle!"

Tommie laughed. "Can you help me, Uncle Zoltan, play with my fire engines?"

"Not until you put your seat belt on."

"Okay, okay, okay…"

We heard the click of the seat belt.

Janet and I gave one another an approving nod.

"Hey, this nice car," Zoltan remarked as he sat with neck slightly crooked and his head squashed up against the headliner. "Plenty of room. Hey, put on classical station. At 10 they broadcast *Madame Butterfly*."

I selected the station on the radio and headed downtown.

Zoltan turned to Tommie and Sarah. "So, how is school and what you do there?"

Tommie screwed up his face. "I dunno… It's okay. They make us take stupid gymnastics because we're all spazzes."

"Tommie you must understand that it good for you. Good training. Make you better person."

"I don't want to be a better person. I just want people to leave me alone."

"Yes. That because you special. But look, we all have to go through school and it usually not fun… So, how is it for you, Sarah?"

"Huh?" Sarah pulled at the ear buds she had installed to shut out our palavering. "School?" She thought for a moment and then waved a hand as if she could not be bothered to respond.

"It's passé."

"Ah, you funny girl. We have to get new opera for you to star in when I next take care of you guys."

"Okay. That'd be fun."

"You still getting all A's?"

Sarah shrugged. "Yeah."

"Wow, that wonderful. How come you so smart?"

"I don't know… I just am."

"You like your mother. She smart lady."

"Zoltan," Tommie interrupted from the back, "do you like Dalmatians?"

"Sure."

"Did you know they get along well with horses, so when fire engines were drawn by horses the Dalmatian was used to help lead them to a fire, then they became mascots for fire stations? Did you know that Dalmatians are one of the oldest breeds in existence, going back to even ancient Egypt…"

I looked at Janet and we rolled our eyes as Tommie launched into a history of the Dalmatian breed, which we had heard now daily for weeks, and began working his way into all the reasons we should own one.

Zoltan chimed in the usual appropriate responses as Tommie wound on.

We drove into the city's center and then headed east along the waterfront to a recently developed area where warehouses and tenements had been razed and condo towers, restaurants and shops had been constructed, essentially creating a new community.

Beyond the new development we made a right, and at the end of a desolate, warehouse-lined cobblestone street passed through an open wrought iron gate. A center drive extended out into the harbor with parking spaces on both sides. Beyond the parking spaces were rows of new docks and slips housing a mix of sail and power boats. The drive continued until it reached a boardwalk containing a new marine center and a two story restaurant and shops with coordinated exteriors of natural rough wood, board and batten construction.

"He said to park at the end here," I told everyone, "and that his boat was tied up along the pier toward the bay."

I parked the van and we began walking to open water where the shops ended and the pier continued along the seawall, boat slips and docks to our left and the harbor on the right. Tommie dawdled behind us, a fire engine clutched in each hand.

Simultaneously we stopped.

Tommie said, "Wowwwwww!"

The rest of us were speechless.

Before us was an immense oceangoing trimaran sailboat, its new fiberglass sparkling white in the sun, its port hull along the seawall, tied there with numerous lines that crossed one another to different pilings to hold the boat in check. Massive, evenly spaced fenders cushioned the hull against the concrete and pilings. Taking up several normal boat lengths, it dwarfed its surroundings. The size of it, the intricacy of its equipment, the tree-sized carbon fiber mast with mainsail rolled into it, the roller furled white jib ascending into the bright blue skies of a perfect autumn day, the trash can-sized winches, the airplane propeller-sized blades of a wind generator spinning slowly on a high pole attached to the stern, the grid of solar panels atop a hard bimini over the spacious cockpit, the broad spread of its black trampolines, the sheer rake of its stern with the name *Calypso Too* beautifully stenciled in black and gold, all of it overwhelmed us.

"Thomas," Janet said, reaching out and grasping my arm, "it looks like an oceangoing *Millennium Falcon*."

"Yeah, high tech as hell."

Berger sat in the cockpit in a captain's chair facing us. There was a drink sitting beside him on a sturdy folding table. He was dressed in old jeans, deck shoes and a worn and faded Sessions University hoodie and looked very small and out of place in the midst of his boat's splendor, as if he were an itinerate workman who was taking a break from varnishing and had the audacity to take his leisure in the cockpit of the owner's boat.

"Ahoy," he shouted at us, waving.

A deeply tanned man, silver-bearded and pony-tailed, dressed in a captain's jersey and dark blue slacks stepped out of the main cabin, which extended low and expansively out beyond the cockpit. Wide sections of tinted Lexan surrounded the interior. A younger couple dressed in similar uniforms followed him, the sandy-haired fellow carrying folding tables and the girl, pretty with long, light brown hair, folding chairs.

"Jean Claude will help you on board," Berger called to us loudly. "You see the removable stair on the seawall near the center of the port hull, the hull on the seawall? You climb up that and walk across the strut and onto the deck."

The captain, moving with the quick grace of someone completely adapted to his ship and the sea, came around the outside of the cabin and across the massive strut securing the port hull to the center hull. He descended the stair to help us climb aboard.

"M*es amis*," he greeted, extending a hand toward the stair.

"We have a very good day planned for you."

"*Bonjour*," Janet greeted.

"*Merci!*" Sarah chimed in graciously.

"*Wee wee!*" Tommie half-shouted and began laughing up-roariously at his joke, clutching his fire engines to his stomach.

"*Vous parlez français?*" Jean Claude asked Janet.

She smiled, holding her hand up with the thumb and forefinger spread slightly. "*Un peu.*"

Sarah chimed in, "*Je prends français à l'école.*"

"*Ah, je suis impatient de parler avec vous cet après-midi,*" Jean Claude responded.

"Mom, this is really cool. I can practice my French with Jean Claude this afternoon."

We gathered in the cockpit as the young couple placed chairs and tables around us.

"Let me introduce my captain and compatriot, Jean Claude Gilbert," Berger said. "Jean Claude is a master boat designer as well as a world cruisah. He helps me out here and there as a favor."

Jean Claude bowed to us politely. "Let me in turn introduce you to our crew, Don and Amy. We have champagne, orange juice for the children, or you can mix the two for mimosas, white wine, some hors d'oeuvres I make this morning. We will also provide the children with windbreakers and life jackets. And windbreakers for the adults." He smiled. "It is a wonderful day but on the water with the wind, you may find yourself getting cold." He turned and he and the crew went into the cabin.

"What the hell make of boat is this?" I asked Berger. "It's incredible."

"Well, it's funny about that," Berger said. "Hey, sit down, make yourself comfortable."

We sat on the chairs and on the surrounding cushioned cockpit seats. Tommie sat on the deck near us and began playing with his fire engines, oblivious to our conversation.

Berger continued, "This boat is a one of a kind, so there's really no trademark name. Jean Claude, when he wants to rib me, calls it a 'Bergah 72.' It's always interesting to hear a Frog try to imitate a Boston accent. It's as horrible as my French. Anyway, you are presently ensconced on an oceangoing, electric propulsion, solar and wind-powered, sailing trimaran—one of the fastest cruising boats in the world and completely energy independent. It can sail anywhere without ever needing to stop for fuel. Can cruise comfortably at 15 to 20 knots, cover 250 to 300 miles a day. Produces zero hydrocarbons, no emissions, except perhaps for those nocturnal. Hah! Jules Verne would've loved this baby. We keep her in the Med during the summer, in Miami in the wintah and up here in the fall. With a satellite uplink, I can run all my different enterprises from here."

Jean Claude returned with a stack of cardinal red windbreakers emblazoned with *Calypso Too* on the left front. He handed one to each of us and helped Tommie and Sarah into the windbreakers and life jackets while Don and Amy brought out wine and champagne glasses, bottles of French champagne and white wine, carafes of ice water and orange juice, followed by trays of pate and thinly sliced pieces of fresh baguette, pears and apples.

"Where do you spend most of your time?" Janet asked.

"Around. It's funny, I hate owning things, as I told Thomas and Zoltan, but the accountants keep pointing out the tax and investment advantages of different things like running this boat as a chartah/lease service, and we do rent it out a couple times a year, so long as I have my folks captaining and crewing her. Won't tell you what we charge. It's obscene. Anyway, I also love staying in hotels. Originally that fit in perfectly with my desire not to own things, but then my accountants convinced me that there were tax and investment advantages to actually buying the hotels I liked to stay in. Talk about a contradiction! Anyway, the numbers all made a whole lot of sense, so I went along with it. Now I own hotels in each of the cities where I might be during the year—Boston, New York, Washington, LA, London, Brussels, Hong Kong. And in each one of these hotels I have a private suite. I even have one here at the Intercontinental."

"You own the Intercontinental?" I asked.

"Yeah, actually I do, technically. The ownership of these hotels is set up as a holding company with its own management. One of my other enterprises owns the holding company. So all I really have to do is check the books once a year. Of course, I have one of my own guys embedded in the holding company's management team, so I hear more or less monthly what's going on. Anyway, where was I? Oh yeah. Jean Claude, tell them about the engineering that went into this baby."

"Ah, *merci*," Jean Claude said as he sat facing us on a cockpit cushion. "This vessel has the most advanced carbon fiber and Kevlar construction with a focus on weight saving and strength. A trimaran is a naturally fast design with minimal wetted surface. The decks and hull are cored composite, very lightweight. Even the larger pieces of furniture are cored with honeycomb.

"We have a carbon fiber mast and a retractable mainsail that can be adjusted in or out depending on wind speed, as can our genoa. All our equipment is electric powered but has mechanical back up just in case. The centerboard, which serves as our keel, is retractable, and the rudder, the blade at the end of the boat by which we steer, can also be raised. So, you can put this boat in less than five feet of water. As you will see, she sails almost flat, very sea kindly and comfortable. She is safe, unsinkable. Water tight bulkheads throughout the lower deck and in the hulls.

"Great room here for dining and entertainment, as you will see. Below toward the center of the hull we have our electric power, battery banks and equipment such as our water maker.

The living area has four staterooms and the crew quarters situated around it. There are only the two crew you see besides me right now. Any bigger boat and we would have to have many more crew, and the boss here likes his life simple and his privacy, especially since he often runs his businesses here."

"How you guys know each other?" Zoltan asked.

Jean Claude and Berger looked at one another as if Zoltan had just told a very good joke.

"It, as they say, is complicated," Jean Claude smiled.

"Jean Claude is my hero," Berger said. "Fact is, he saved my life, and that of five other crew members on a totally snake bit chartah cruise I took in the Virgin Islands, what, a dozen years ago? One of our crew, a very attractive member of our crew, met Jean Claude and we began hanging out and sailing together, which was a very fortunate thing. Jean Claude was sailing his own trimaran single-handed, a hell of a boat, in fact, such an incredible boat it inspired me to build this one. Tell them about the original *Calypso*, which he still lives on near Marseille when he's not captaining for me or helping me with other projects."

"Ah, my *Calypso*, she is a beautiful 42 foot trimaran that I worked with designers and a builder to construct over fifteen years ago. She is my home. I have sailed her around the world.

"But to finish the Caribbean story, there was a terrible storm and Berger and his fellow sailors had a derelict boat, and of course their tour leader at that time found a way to disappear. I found them about to be swept by the winds and tide onto the rocks on the east shore of Tortola and we were able to get them onto my *Calypso* before their boat was destroyed and they all got killed. So, I end up saving these bums. Then, oh, years later I am back in the Mediterranean, having lived in Tahiti for six years and completing my around the world trip, cruising the Med where I please, but I must admit a bit bored, and I get this call from *mon ami*. He has in mind this big project, this very boat in fact, and he wants me to use my background in building my *Calypso* to become his project manager in building *Calyp-*

so Too. Now I think, how *magnifique* is this—spend someone else's money, a good friend in fact, to build the best, the fastest oceangoing cruising vessel in the world, and French-built at that. And we did; it took four years. The boat you are on is the result."

"That hell of a story," Zoltan observed. "What the plan for today?"

"I thought we'd take her across the bay," Berger told us, "anchor in a small creek off a river over there and have lunch, blast on back and let you folks enjoy the rest of the afternoon."

"Now children, what are your names?" Jean Claude asked.

"Tommie."

"Sarah."

He knelt to talk with them. "Well, as captain on this vessel I am charged with educating young men and women about this boat and about sailing.

"Now you must obey my commands at all times. Do you understand?"

"Yes sir!" Tommie said, tucking a fire engine under one arm and giving Jean Claude a mock salute.

"Sure," Sarah agreed.

Jean Claude smiled. "Yes, you do understand. *Merci.*"

He stood and addressed all of us. "Now, important thing for you to know. There is a toilet, or 'head' as we call it, in the cabin toward the front of the boat. If you must use it while we are underway the first rule of sailing is 'one hand for the boat, the other for yourself.' He reached out and held onto a handrail. "Are any of you sailors?"

"Just Janet and me," I told him.

"Okay. In sailing we have all these very stoopid terms, but just so you know the basic, port is left and starboard is right. The sail in front is a genoa, the sail above us is the main. It travels out of the mast on this big carbon fiber log right above our heads. What is that called, children?"

Tommie and Sarah stared at him respectfully.

Jean Claude shouted suddenly and leapt toward them. "It's the BOOM!"

Both Tommie and Sarah stepped back laughing.

"You good teacher," Zoltan observed. "You should come to my 8:00am laboratory."

"*Merci.* Oh, one final thing, children. The lines that attach to the genoa and the main to reel them out and in are called sheets. Now that we have a little idea of what is going on, it is time to get underway."

Toward the stern, Berger took his place behind the wheel, extending from a pedestal, which also served as the platform for an array of instruments in front of and on either side of him, the center containing a large GPS navigation screen. He began checking instruments and clicking a few switches while Jean Claude and Don and Amy quickly stowed the chairs and tables and we found seats around the cockpit.

They then loosened the lines holding *Calypso Too* to the seawall, hung them on pilings and pulled up the onshore stair as the boat began to drift away.

Berger reached over to a small joystick beside him. A churning noise came from under the hull and we moved sideways away from the dock.

"Thrusters," Berger commented. "Nice feature to have in a boat this big. Moments like this I feel like I'm piloting a small condo."

He engaged a shifter on the pedestal housing and there was a large bubbling noise from the stern of the boat and we thrust forward suddenly, grabbing onto nearby support to steady ourselves as Berger turned the wheel. We were underway, moving almost silently out into the harbor and a wide, well-marked channel, leaving a clean, shallow wake behind us.

"Electric propulsion's interesting," Berger told us. "No transmission and electric engines are high torque, so you just get up and go. I always gotta be a little careful not to toss everyone onto the deck when we get started. As we cruise out of the harbor here, I think we'll find some wind."

We headed east out the long channel toward the bay, warehouses giving way to factories until the waters widened and the shoreline on either side began to fall into the distance. Heavy industry faded to light industry and then into a distant line of fringe neighborhoods, the air rank with the smell of manufacturing and sewer spillage, the water an unhealthy black-brown.

Berger was right about the wind. As we made our way into more open water a breeze came up from the northwest, ghosting at first and then rippling across the surface. Jean Claude took his place next to the large winch atop the starboard side of the cabin and wrapped the main sheet around it, locking it into the self-tailer at the top. Don and Amy positioned themselves by the starboard winch along the cockpit coaming and similarly wrapped a genoa sheet around it. Berger placed the engines in neutral, then shut them down and the churning underneath us stopped, leaving us coursing through the water that gurgled mildly in our wake as we slowed. He turned *Calypso Too* directly into the wind and Jean Claude pressed the switch controlling the main's winch. The main sail moved rapidly out on the boom, rustling loudly while Don hit the switch for the starboard genoa and we watched it unfurl at the bow, flapping. Both massive sails were out, the noise had become almost unbearable and we had slowed to the point of almost drifting. Berger said loudly above the din, "All right, folks. You ready?"

We nodded at him.

He turned the wheel as Jean Claude and the crew tightened the sails. The boat fell off to starboard as Don and Amy finished bringing in the genoa. The wind caught both the main and genoa simultaneously and with a loud, percussive boom they filled and we shot forward seamlessly. I watched the awed expression on Zoltan and Janet's faces and on Tommie and Sarah's who were sitting on either side of Janet. Our speed built in a heartbeat, as did the noise of the trimaran coursing through the water, beginning to send up spray all around us from the center hull bow and the port and starboard hulls. The port hull lifted slightly. There was a gust of wind and we were flying. Berger's condo was flying on a magic carpet of water. Channel markings zipped by us. We saw other boats in the distance and in a moment we were past them.

"Now you'll notice," Berger shouted, "we're barely heeling. Comfortable as hell, doing, oh…" he looked down at the instruments, "18 knots."

Mon Capitan! Jean Claude shouted suddenly and pointed.

Ahead of us in the middle of the channel sat a small fishing skiff, obviously new, its blue metal flake paint sparkling in the sun. Two fishermen stood on either side of the boat. The one facing us, holding his rod, was slack jawed as it dawned on him that he and his fellow angler were very much in the wrong place at the wrong time. He shouted, dropped his rod, clambered over to the controls and pushed the starter button. Nothing. His friend had now half-turned and stared at us with wide open eyes.

"Bring in the main and the genoa," Berger commanded. As Jean Claude, Don and Amy immediately responded, Berger spun the wheel a quarter turn to the left. *Calypso Too* canted to port, her port bow lifting further, and we surged forward with even more speed. The fishing boat shot by us, perhaps five feet away, the fishermen's expressions frozen in stark terror.

"Fall off," Berger commanded, and almost immediately we were back onto our original course, the fishing boat a speck behind us. "You know, Jean Claude," he said ruefully, "maybe next time, we wait a bit longer before putting up the sails."

Jean Claude nodded and gave Berger an amused and knowing look that needed no translation.

"You'll understand now," Berger remarked to us, "why this boat and its owner and captain like open watah. It's pretty well understood as a rule of common sense that if you're fishing, it's not real smart to be fishing in the middle of a channel. Hell, that's the main channel into the city. Tankers use it. Those guys are probably newbies who drifted into the channel and weren't paying attention. Just gotta be careful in these waters, make sure we don't hit anything and that anything under power gets the hell out of the way. So, now you can sit back and enjoy yourselves."

We headed across the bay at speed. In our *Calypso Too* windbreakers, we felt like we were part of the crew, the bright sun sparkling in millions of reflections on the water, which ran against the hulls in a refreshing rush, leaving scents of vegetation and brine. We amused ourselves and the kids with the sightings of various sail and power boats, deciding which ones would be our personal preference for ownership, gazing with awe at the size of some of the tankers anchored out waiting for a berth to offload their cargo.

The eastern shore soon came into view, a low line the russet color of autumn leaves.

To our port was a distant lighthouse that enlarged rapidly. It was white with a black base and turret, listing slightly to the south in the middle of a large tract of open light brown water.

"You see that," Berger said, pointing to it. "Seems like it's out in the middle of nowhere but if you look way the hell east you'll see that there is actually a point of land, which continues underwater all the way out to the lighthouse, almost a half mile. Behind the lighthouse you've got only a couple feet of water. During the summer, the breeze blows predominantly from the south and holds the water up in the bay, so all the power boats and many smaller sailboats cut the point by going behind the lighthouse to get to where they're headed. Everyone's in such a hurry yah know. Real smart—until the first fall weekend after northwest winds have started cranking down the bay, blowing its water out into the ocean. Happened two weekends ago. That's the day the Coast Guard gets its yearly record number of emergency calls from all the schmucks stuck in the mud behind the lighthouse and God knows in how many other shortcuts. Almost worth coming out to see it. It's a real spectatahs' sport!"

We blasted by the lighthouse and after a time passed by a large red can on our starboard, then a green can on our port, marking the mouth of the river. Almost immediately we turned northeast and passed through a set of red and green marks on pilings and headed up a river. Beautiful woods on our port side protected us from the wind so that the boat slowed to an idling pace. The trees were at peak foliage, glowing red, brown and gold even this late in the year because of their proximity to warm water. On our starboard side were rolling fields of brown earth and freshly harvested corn stubble. In the fields and in the water before us were flocks of ducks and geese.

Berger turned the boat into a sheltered cove while Jean Claude and the crew quickly furled the sails. As *Calypso Too* slowed to a stop, Jean Claude went to the bow. Soon, as he worked a remote control, the huge plow anchor plunged from the bow into the water. We drifted backwards in the wind, then came to a stop, feeling the anchor digging in. There was a churning noise as Berger hit reverse to set the anchor, then shut down the engines. Suddenly there was silence; the breeze whistling slightly here and there off fittings, water playing in small noises against the hulls, the distant sounds of ducks and geese, the wind in the trees.

"My Lord," Janet said, "what a wonderful place."

"Thought you'd like it, dear," Berger said. "Lunch in ten." He stepped out from behind the pedestal.

Jean Claude hurried by us smiling, and Don and Amy joined him in the cabin.

We sat comfortably around the cockpit and enjoyed the scenery.

"Hey kids," Berger said, "let me show you the trampoline."

With Berger leading we all rose and walked out on the port deck. A flock of geese passed overhead in V formation, their honking sounding clear in the crisp air. "They're getting ready to fly south to Boca," Berger commented.

"Watch this!" he shouted at Tommie and Sarah, his eyebrows

raised high over his enlarged eyes and spectacles. With a leap he dove from the cabin top and rolled onto the trampoline. Laughing, the kids followed and in a moment they were all bouncing around as if they were on a real trampoline while we grinned at them and laughed.

"This'll get the wiggles out!" he shouted to Tommie and Sarah who were giggling as they bounced around. He looked at us mid-bounce. "Hard for kids to be on a boat. Have to have a few diversions."

No one will believe this, I thought. I'm standing here on a multi-million dollar sailboat, watching a multi-billionaire bounce around on its trampoline like some Dr. Seuss character.

After several more minutes Tommie and Sarah, not to mention Berger, had let off enough pent-up energy and their bouncing slowed. They wallowed over to us, climbed back onto the deck and we headed to the cockpit. The tables and chairs we had been sitting on were being rearranged by the crew for dining.

Berger told Tommie and Sarah, "You guys will have lunch with Jean Claude and the crew. You can sit out here."

I could see Tommie was pleased with this arrangement because it would allow him to play with his fire engines while they were having lunch.

A lemony aroma was now drifting from the cabin. We followed Berger in.

As we entered, Janet exclaimed in a hushed voice, "Oh my God."

The interior was breathtaking. The surrounding Lexan window let us see the entirety of the outdoors yet dimmed the incoming brightness so that the space inside was cast in a tranquil, even light. A white headliner ribbed with cherry battens muted the sound, as did the open cabin with its beautiful ultra-suede dark green surrounding sofas, striped green pillows scattered around on them. LED spots lit the interior and highlighted the teak and cherry floor. To our left were cherry cabinetry and a navigation

station with an array of instruments, electronics, a large monitor, a satellite phone and a small library, and then the galley with
stainless steel appliances and Corian counters. Oil paintings of
Mediterranean scenes in broad sweeps of color were hung on the
walls between doors that led to surrounding suites.

Jean Claude was at the stove managing several crepe pans.
Beyond the galley was a spacious cherry table set with stone-
ware. Several bottles of unmarked white wine were in holders.
French bread and fresh squares of butter were set between the
bottles of wine. We took our places and began pouring.

"The wine is from my uncle's estate," Jean Claude said over
his shoulder. "I hope you like it."

He shut down the stove and took a plate of crepes out to
the kids while Don and Amy served dishes of crepes stuffed
with fresh crab meat and topped with a lemon sauce, plates of
assorted cheeses, a bowl of greens and a bowl of fresh string
beans covered with butter. We passed the wine and the dishes
around, helping ourselves, and began our meal.

Berger joined us and poured himself some wine.

"Fantastic meal," I told him as he sat down at the table.

Everyone nodded enthusiastically as they ate.

"So, you like our little sail over here?"

"Fantastic," I told him.

"It's a whole different world over here, isn't it?" said Janet.
"So tranquil and beautiful."

"Yeah, it certainly is... What I like about it is that time slows
down quite a bit, so this is a great place to catch up with folks,
discover what they're all about. This may sound a little banal
but where the hell are you guys with your lives? I'd love to hear
what's goin' on."

I don't think I've ever met anyone as charmingly inquisitive
as Mark Berger. He genuinely wanted to know all about us,
and so over the course of the next hour we told him while we
savored Jean Claude's remarkable crepes and wine.

Mark learned all about Janet and my settled life in suburbia, the enjoyment of our family and struggles with the suburban lifestyle, her overwork, my inability to make any progress in academe, Sarah's ascendancy in school and Tommie's struggles. Zoltan talked about his frustration with his projects, workload and the uncertainty of recognition for any landmark work or findings, his weekly pitched battle with Frida. I found myself shaking my head about Berger's fascination with the normalcy of our lives and challenges.

"Okay," Zoltan asked when we paused, "now I must ask you question."

"Sure," said Berger.

"Why you not married or have girlfriend?"

Berger smiled a reasoned and indulgent smile. "Zoltan, in case you haven't noticed, I am one, an asshole." He held up his hand, commanding silence as he saw that Janet was about to protest. "Nope, no objections. Look, I've known me fifty-one years; you guys have known me a few more than fifty-one minutes. I know what I'm talkin' about. Now where was I? Oh, yeah… Point two, I'm too busy for nagging and women after a time always start with the nagging. Three, I have no need for any trophy bitch; I can always rent one. Four, I'm not terribly interested in searching. I like my life uncomplicated. That doesn't mean to say I'm without interaction with the opposite sex." He raised his eyebrows up and down. "It's just on my terms and on my schedule, if you know what I mean. Now having said all that, would I like a companion, partner and friend? Yes. Just the right one has never come along, and it's not like I'm exactly helping the situation. But, you know, no complaints. I like my life just fine, thank you."

"A bit foreign to us," Janet added, "stuck as we are in the middle of overachieving suburban bliss. You had disapproving parents I take it, who set impossibly high standards?"

Berger smiled again, ruefully. "Yes, my dear, you hit the nail on the head. My parents didn't let me play ball even; I had to go to Jew school and piano practice. They wanted me to be the next Horowitz—all angst, guilt and melodrama. But they're gone now and I am a free man."

"Makes sense to me," I said.

"So," asked Zoltan, "Berger, why you even care about us? We just little people. Why you like us?"

"You mean, what's my angle?"

"Yes."

"You'll have to take this at face value. I got no angle. I like genuine folks who aren't on the make. Over the years I've found that friends are where you find them. By that I mean that when you discover people who you have a natural connection with, doesn't matter who, how or why, where they live or what they do, you should encourage the natural development of that relationship. Make sense? You guys are my kind of folks. For some reason I like you a hell of a lot more than my fellow rich folk."

"Well, here's to Mark!" I toasted, raising my glass.

"Here's to Mark!" Everyone raised their glass and saluted the owner of *Calypso Too*. We were all feeling the warmth of wine, the beauty of the fall afternoon and the gaining of a new friendship.

He blushed. "Guys, this is not necessary. Okay. Time to get the hell out of here."

As we blasted back across the bay, I made my way to the front of the cockpit and looked out over the port trampoline and into the distance, watching our progress over the open expanse of water. Here we were, sailing along, faster than perhaps was wise, which seemed the way life moved these days, with the capability of going anywhere in the world, yet we were going back home to all the familiar situations and surroundings that entrapped us. Berger, on the other hand, could sail or travel wherever he chose. Was money the great enabler? I thought about Jean Claude, also free, but here by choice. No, it was not money, it was following one's passion. Berger had done it; Jean Claude had done it, sailed around the world in fact, and now was content to serve his ally and friend. And what was my passion? I had no legitimate answer. I had my profession, my family, friends, a good life. Why this feeling of constraint, of harried imprisonment, frustration, anger? I shook my head.

I realized Janet was by my side. She slipped her arm inside of mine and leaned against me and we stood together watching the water course by the hulls, sailboats and powerboats off in the distance. The air was already growing cold as the afternoon sun went low in the sky and began casting a gold, then orange shaft of light onto the waters. Jean Claude was talking amiably with Sarah, explaining different French phrases. Berger was perched happily behind the wheel, steering his condo/spaceship and our lives to our port of call. Zoltan was beside him, asking questions about the equipment and the engineering that went into the boat. Maybe my prison of a life wasn't so bad after all. I smiled, turned and Janet and I shared a long kiss.

"FIRE!!!!"

The shout was from Don and came from the cabin, Amy shrieking and the odd wailing of Tommie in full distress sounding in the background.

We looked and a small trail of smoke was streaming from the top of the cabin door.

Jean Claude leapt up and dashed into the cabin as Berger steered the boat up into the wind to slow it. Janet, I and Zoltan trailed after Jean Claude.

As we reached the cabin door we heard the short, jet sound of a fire extinguisher, smelled burning plastic and entering the cabin saw Don extinguishing one of Tommie's fire engine's, which had caught fire atop the stove. Tommie sat helplessly on the floor, his other fire engine beside him broken by its impact. When he was truly upset and terrified, he let out this all too familiar wail, remarkably loud and frightening, as if he was dying or mortally wounded, an animal sound, unnatural, ugly and, as much as I did not want to admit it, institutional. Janet rushed to him and smothered him with a hug. He continued wailing. The fire was out. Gradually Tommie quieted as we stood looking helplessly at one another and breathed a collective sigh of relief.

"What happened?" I asked.

Jean Claude looked at me, half astonished, half chagrined. "I thought he was going to the head!" he said. "Instead he must have come in and played with the gas burner and his fire engine. The engine got too close to the burner and caught fire."

"Jesus."

"No problem," Berger shouted at us from the cockpit. "Happens all the time. I mean, that we burn things. You may think Jean Claude is a great cook, but *au contraire*. I know the truth!"

We smiled abstractly, indulgently at his humor, and could feel him turning *Calypso Too* back on course and our speed picking back up.

We were silent on the rest of the sail, lost in our own thoughts, recovering. I wondered at how Janet could deal with Tommie daily, so patiently. Yet I knew how she worried, how his hurt was hers and how she fought for him with different school systems and administrators, ever his advocate and protector. Not that I wasn't involved, but a child only has one mother and there was a special birthright bond between them. So she held Tommie now and rocked him gently and he was quiet, sitting in her lap and holding onto her like a strangely oversized, giant infant. It hurt to watch them. Having a special needs child gnawed at me, brought up in me the all too familiar feeling that he was our fault, that there was something wrong with us to have created him. Then there was Sarah, the antidote explanation of his being a genetic accident, intentionally oblivious to her brother, talking again with Jean Claude. I could see through her act. It was how she coped during those times deviance took him over. Maybe this situation was the root of all my dissatisfaction. Certainly I could feel my anger at the moment, anger at our situation, at having to live with this burden, at Tommie himself, anger that I would quickly bury in the day-to-day, that only showed itself at times like this, but that was in actuality gradually dragging me down.

In the harbor, once the boat was docked and secured and

we were departing, Berger said, "You guys take the jackets. A present."

We thanked him.

"You going to be at that reception in DC next week?" I asked him.

"Nah, I can't be there, gotta be in Brussels to scope out things at the IMF meeting. Look forward to hearing about it. I suspect you'll find it most interesting."

"I suspect."

We said our goodbyes, Zoltan and I shaking his hand, Janet and the children giving him hugs. We made our way to the van. The sun was low in the sky, casting late autumn shadows, the crisp air filled with harbor smell again.

The car was quiet on the way home.

Just before we dropped Zoltan off, Tommie said, "That was fun. Can we do that again?"

VI
The New Las Vegas

WASHINGTON, DC. Dark, cold, rainy, headlight filled, traffic snarled, corridors of derelict early 20th century buildings pressing in from both sides as Zoltan and I navigated the slick streets and confusing circles.

We had left early and so were almost on time when we found the entrance to the School of Foreign Service parking lot just off DuPont Circle. We wound our way down the corkscrew concrete tunnel to the lowest level, noted thankfully that the garage space where we parked was numbered, and walked through the exhaust smelling, dimly fluorescent lit labyrinth of parked cars to the elevator bank. In the elevator we stared at the polished marble at our feet rather than at our murky reflections in the stainless steel door.

At the ground floor we were joined by three Chinese and two Americans who were chatting amiably and who, by their educated and polished appearance and their deferential and pleasant facades, were from the two embassies.

The doors opened at the twelfth floor. We stepped off into a too bright, hot and stuffy hallway opening into a large cafeteria, which had been converted to serve as a dining room for the celebratory dinner and announcement of the new center. At the end of the room was a raised dais illuminated by stage lights. Behind it a large American and an equally large Chinese flag hung at either side of a maroon velvet curtain. Between the flags was a large video screen. Out front, a lectern with the Sessions University seal on it was at the center of a long, white-clothed row of tables with place settings. A dozen circular tables were each set for ten and decorated with a cut glass centerpiece holding arrangements of blossoming flowers.

Closer to us was an area set up for mingling with a bar on either side. Groups of dignitaries, university colleagues and Chinese and American officials were in conversation. The low-ceilinged room reverberated with garbled noise.

Wentz and Lusby stood there, checking the arrivals. Wentz took a step toward us, gesturing with his almost empty martini. "Madam Secretary is here," he whispered conspiratorially with a muffled squeal.

"Madam Sec…?" I began, before I caught on that he was talking about the secretary of state. "Really?"

"Bryan knows her well," said Lusby. He was dressed in his usual funereal suit and held a seltzer water with both hands. "But we weren't sure she'd be here until a short while ago. She's actually going to say a few words. I believe Mr. Rusoloff is about to shit himself; he's so excited. Would you not say that's correct, Wentz?"

"Yeah, this is all way out of his league."

"Grab your drinks and we'll introduce you."

We found them again toward the center of the room. Instead of the big, tough developer I had imagined, Rusoloff was actually standing protectively next to Reve the way a child stands next to its mother. He was a short, stocky, florid, balding, grey at the temples man with a wisp of thin black-grey hair combed up onto and over the crown of his head, feebly trying to represent a hairline. At the moment he looked thoroughly intimidated. As if to offset that, he was wearing the most expensive suit I had ever seen of heavy, beautiful, dark gray pinstriped virgin wool, tailored immaculately. His suit cast an aura so independent of its wearer that I felt it might walk off on its own, leaving Melvin Rusoloff standing there in his skivvies with just a big platinum watch and football championship ring to symbolize his prominence.

Reve, who looked significantly larger around the middle than when we last saw him, was trying to balance a martini and a small plate of hors d'oeuvres in one hand, so that he could gesture with the other, introducing people to Rusoloff.

Rusoloff jumped when Reve tried to introduce to him to Zoltan.

"Who the hell is this?" he turned and asked Reve loudly in a gravelly voice, eyes popping.

"I, Zoltan Vastag, professor at medical center."

They shook hands, Rusoloff's speckled hand limp as it disappeared into Zoltan's.

"Damn. I could use you in my collections department."

"Thank you."

"Hey, glad to meet you guys," Rusoloff said, recovering. "What's happenin'?"

"You big man tonight," Zoltan told him.

"Hey, thanks." Rusoloff took a heavy swig of his straight up vodka with a lime. "Appreciated." He turned to Reve, "So, are we getting hooked up after this?"

Reve looked acutely embarrassed. "Let's discuss that later, Mel. Let's focus on the fact that you're about to meet the secretary of state."

"Maybe some of these Chinese chicks want to party?"

"Melvin, hush!" Bernie scolded.

Rusoloff looked a bit crestfallen. "Okay. Whatever."

Out of the corner of my eye I saw Kravitz talking with a woman I did not recognize.

"Let me introduce you to the provost," I said loudly to Zoltan as a means of getting us away from Rusoloff and more embarrassment for Reve.

Zoltan nodded and we took several steps in the provost's direction when he grabbed my arm and held me back. He had a worried expression on his face. "Thomas, what is provost?"

"You don't know what a provost is?"

"No, I hear name all the time, but don't know."

"You're not pulling my leg?"

"I not want to pull your leg. I want to know what is provost?"
It never ceased to amaze me what Zoltan did not know.

"He's the university's academic affairs officer, high up in the
chain of command, handles all academic policy, has a role in
faculty hiring and firing, oversees curriculum development for
divisions and departments so that they're integrated and progressive. That kind of thing."

"Ah. Thank you."

On our way, John Fein, sweating profusely, hurried by us.

"Hi, guys," he greeted as he passed.

"How's it going?"

"Oh, fine, fine," he said distractedly as he headed toward the
audio-visual equipment.

The woman Kravitz was in conversation with was quite attractive, tall with mid-length blond hair, Slavic.

Kravitz was saying to her, "The language barriers alone are
défi de taille. It remains to be seen how well these difficulties,
not to mention those cultural, may be ameliorated through the
Center's programs and interaction."

"Provost Kravitz."

Kravitz turned and peered at me as if I were panhandling
him, then recognized me from our previous conversation.

"Ah, Professor Simpson, is your daughter going to be available to help with Natalie's children?"

"Yes, as a matter of fact. Janet and I discussed it with her and
she'd like to."

"That's splendid of you to help."

Then he turned his back on us.

I realized that I had left one awkward situation for a significantly greater one. Wrong person, bad timing. The provost
had more interest in my daughter than me. What the hell was
I doing?

Not knowing what else to do, I said, "I'd like to introduce
you to a colleague of mine from the medical center, Professor
Vastag, Zoltan."

Kravitz pivoted, looked at Zoltan in puzzlement.

"Yes, thank you," he said finally, reaching out and shaking Zoltan's hand. There was an awkward pause. Clearly, Kravitz simply wished for us to go away. But seeing that we were not, he sighed and said with faux graciousness, "Let me in turn introduce you to the associate dean of the School of Foreign Services, Kristina Zvereva."

"Ah," said Zoltan, "your name sound like ballerina or ice skater. You Belarusian?"

The associate dean brightened. "Ah, yes! And you?"

"Our family Hungarian, originally."

"Madarak egy toll!" Kravitz beamed.

"Igen!" both Kristina and Zoltan remarked simultaneously and laughed.

"As I was saying," Kravitz continued, now speaking to all of us so as not to lose the stage even as he glanced beyond us to see who of greater import he might talk to, "these Chinese, both students and professors, arrive on our campus unable to fully understand or speak the language, having no inkling of how to navigate in our culture. It's a travesty really. And what is our solution? We bury our heads in the sand. One would hope that this new center can serve as a cultural and language orientation for us and them."

"Yes," Associate Dean Zvereva agreed. "That is part of the plan."

I certainly hope so. Frankly, I don't see where they are getting the money for this venture. It's all a bit suspicious."

"150 million isn't enough?" I asked.

Kravitz shook his head in pity at my naïveté. "My dear young man, first, the $150 million is a pledge, to be paid over ten years. Second, it is a pledge to endowment, which I commend, but that means only five percent of the funds can go toward the center's operation annually. Well, that means that this year their operating revenue, as a result of the Rusoloff pledge, is five percent of $15 million, or $750,000. What other funding there is from private, government or other sources I do not know, but it seems to me that the Center is a risky proposition, at least financially, for at least the next several years. Add to that the Chinese façade of a populace unified by the abiding superiority of communist ideals, regimented planning and sustained economic success versus the reality of great internal division and disparate forces at play, and you have politics surrounding the center that could change in a heartbeat. What happens when their government decides the center is educating their students to emigrate forever to the U.S.? Risky, risky, risky. We would have been far better off to establish our first center in a European venue. Brussels, for instance, would be ideal."

"Very interesting analysis," I observed, thinking to myself that the provost was no one's fool and that I certainly did not ever want him as an adversary.

I watched as Zoltan performed his own balletic side step, as comical as it was adroit, which brought him next to the associate dean. They smiled at one another and began a polite side conversation. I could see Kravitz was now becoming something of a distraction to them.

"Well, at least they won't be invading our campus immediately and mucking things up with their poor language skills and clueless inability to connect with our people. I will say that on one count at least our president has the right idea—keep them over there, at least until they are better acculturated."

"We must see colleague," Zoltan announced politely to Kravitz. "It was pleasure meeting you." He reached out and shook Kravitz's hand, then turned to Kristina and took her hand in both of his. "And you too, my dear. We must talk, perhaps at dinner?"

She smiled. "Yes."

They looked into one another's eyes briefly. I found myself resisting the urge to roll my eyes and shake my head. We walked away toward the bar.

"Colleague?" I asked.

"Yes. Important colleague. Mr. Barman."

I laughed.

"Thomas, I now know what provost is. He academic big it."

"You mean bigot."

"Yes."

"You catch on quickly, don't you?"

"Yes."

"I think the associate dean likes you."

"You think so? Thomas, she like opera!"

"You know, for a big ugly fuck you do okay."

"Yes. Speaking of okay, I see Ursula is here. She just walk in with president and secretary of state.

"Shit."

They came directly toward us. Ursula leading, followed by Fitz-Hugh and the secretary of state who were in conversation, flanked on the sides and rear by Secret Service.

"Bryan wants a word with you," she said as they approached us.

Hearing this, the secretary of state said to Bryan, "I must talk with the Chinese ambassador, my dear."

"Perfect," said Bryan. "Let me introduce you to our associate professor of communications, Dr. Simpson."

The secretary was a large woman, Germanic, with straight brown hair in a pageboy cut and square metal glasses. I thought instantly of a field hockey coach or headmistress at a girls' school. However I also saw not the official visage that the press and cartoonists found so easy to parody, but a powerful woman, clearly brilliant, who also possessed a genial wit.

"My pleasure," she said, shaking my hand. "Yes, we all know that any help we can get with communications is commendable." She turned and with her security entourage walked toward the dais where the ambassador was holding court.

Bryan turned to me, Ursula standing beside him.

"I'm looking for something to hang my remarks on. Have any ideas?" he asked casually.

I smiled. "That's interesting. On the way down here I was thinking about how you might make the most out of this opportunity. It struck me that even with all our interaction with the Chinese we are still often a mystery to one another. Their perspective is grounded in a mindset that takes into consideration thousands of years of history, context and strategic thinking; our perspective is grounded in a mindset that any consideration older than a thousand seconds is no longer relevant."

Bryan beamed, gave me a light punch on the shoulder and said, "Splendid." He and Ursula turned and headed for the dais, Ursula flashing me a slight head nod and congratulatory smile.

"How he going to make something out of your dumb ass comment?" Zoltan asked.

"Beats the hell out me." I shrugged. "He's the genius. I'm sure he'll figure it out."

As everyone took their seats on the dais and at the tables, Ursula came and took my arm.

"I was hoping I might enjoy dinner with the best looking man here," she told me.

I looked around, feigning puzzlement. "Yeah?"

"Ah, self-deprecation," she smiled as she guided me to one of the tables in the back of the room.

As we went, I noticed that Zoltan and Kristina were seated at a middle table and were talking animatedly. With relief, I also saw the Kravitz was sitting at the front of the room, all the better to discover something worthy of caustic commentary later.

We sat and Ursula put her hand on my arm and said, "Our meal tonight is being prepared by the Chinese embassy's chef. Peking Duck is the entrée."

"I'm impressed."

In front of us were small dumplings on a bed of greens, different sauces to the side. Waiters and waitresses came and poured chardonnay into our white wine glasses.

"Bryan has been very keyed up about this event. It should go well."

"Apparently Mr. Rusoloff is also very excited."

"Awk," she scoffed, as we began to enjoy the succulent dumplings, each one with a different fill of beef, chicken or vegetarian puree with hints of spices and onions, scallions, peppers. "That peasant. He doesn't remember who I am from event to event, and so he propositions me at each one."

"A real gentleman."

"Trash."

"Hey, he's one of Bryan's biggest fans and biggest donors."

"Yes," she said and smiled a saccharine smile, "a wonderful man… Trash."

I laughed. "You have a very interesting job."

"At moments, yes. And for long periods of time, no."

"How'd you ever come to work for Bryan in the first place?"

"Ah. It is a long story. The short of it is that we have a great friend in common."

"Who is?"

She waved a hand. "That is not important."

"Okay."

"Who recommended me to Bryan two presidencies ago."

"You've worked for him that long?"

"Yes. He jokes occasionally when he is being bad that I am his groupie."

"Hmmm."

She reached out and placed her hand on my arm again. "This is all in fun. There is nothing between us personally other than a very good and close professional relationship, contrary to what you might hear."

The waiters and waitresses came and removed our first course dishes while others began serving our dinner of Peking Duck, now filling our red wine glasses with a Pinot Noir.

"Okay. So, where are you from?"

"Washington DC and Germany. My parents were in the diplomatic corps. I was born in the states, my parents adopted me and then they were posted to Germany when I was an infant, so

I went to grade school in Germany until they were reassigned here, and so my last year of grade school and high school were here, then college, MIT."

"You're adopted, that's interesting."

"Not very. What about you?"

I shrugged. "Nothing special. Grew up in Baltimore. Went to Cornell, then Columbia for my PhD. Got lucky and got hired at Sessions as an assistant prof and they made me an associate professor a couple years ago."

"And Zoltan?"

"We just connected from the very start. He came to Sessions the same year as me. We're compadres."

"You are the odd couple. It is very amusing."

I laughed. "Okay, if you want to put it that way. I will say life around Zoltan is not boring."

"Yes," Ursula said, deadpanning and imitating Zoltan's usual response.

After a time and more conversation, as our plates from dinner were being collected and desert was being served, the TV lights came on, the room lights dimmed and the university anthem sounded momentarily as a signal for the crowd to be quiet.

The president rose from his seat next to the secretary of state and took his place behind the lectern and microphone.

"Welcome everyone to a very auspicious occasion. We are particularly honored that our good friend and colleague, Madam Secretary Greta Hausler, was able to be with us tonight. Those of you who know Washington know that the attendance of the secretary of state is always a last minute decision given the various troubles facing our world at any given time, so we feel," he turned to the secretary of state, who smiled at him, and then back to the microphone, "very fortunate."

Applause.

"To me, it seems only weeks ago that Greta and I were two starving graduate students at Harvard sharing pizza and a six pack with our fellow classmates. Carefree, stimulating times.

Who knew then what the world would be like today? I am simply glad and frankly comforted that my colleague and friend is now being called upon to help lead our country. Ladies and gentleman, our secretary of state, Greta Hausler."

The secretary of state rose and came to the lectern as Fitz-Hugh took his seat.

"As I recall those pizza sharing days now many years ago," she remarked, turning to Fitz-Hugh, "I also recall that one had to be very competitive with Bryan to make sure you got your share. As in all endeavors Bryan is a quick study, especially in the art of consumption."

Laughter.

She turned back to the audience. "But we are here tonight, thankfully, for a far more important celebration than we had in those times, and with a profound appreciation for the remarkable largesse provided by Mr. Rusoloff." She nodded at Rusoloff, who was sitting on the opposite side of the dais, and he turned crimson.

"At present the State Department daily confronts international crises, war, civil war, sectarian strife, genocide, human rights violations, the worldwide plight of refugees and the strident accusations and demands within our own country that we somehow find a better way to do our job. So you can imagine in this context how pleasurable it is for me to be here this evening to celebrate the forging of a remarkably promising partnership for future world understanding and peace.

"I have known Bryan Fitz-Hugh for over twenty-five years and it comes as no surprise," she turned to Fitz-Hugh momentarily and then back to the audience, "to me that he would be the one to foster the kind of learning and exchange that will take place in Sessions University's new Beijing Center. So, let me, in my official capacity, thank Bryan for his relentless pursuit of this attainment, and let me in turn," she turned again to Rusoloff, "thank Mr. Rusoloff for his confidence in Bryan, in Sessions University and our country's future.

"This is what world peace should look like with the uplifting force of education leading the way. Students, our future leaders from disparate cultures, learning and working together to become part of the Sessions University family and the worldwide family of those who have learned that we all share the same societal needs for progress, peace and stability. We can literally change the world one person at a time, one center at a time, one nation at a time until our global village is populated with those who understand that global learning and interaction are our future, not war, not attrition, not starvation, not contagions of disease but peace, and through peace better understanding. The process renews itself. And that renewal begins here tonight. Thank you."

There was sustained applause.

The president rose and again took his place behind the microphone. Radiant and confident, he spoke with no notes, looking at the audience as if he were talking to each of us individually.

"There is a Mandarin proverb *Wànshì qǐtóu nán*, which translates to 'The first step in a thousand different matters is always difficult,' or, in our own parlance, 'The first step is the hardest.' So we begin a first step tonight, recognizing well that it will indeed be the hardest.

"While we work to forge better relationships and understandings with the Chinese," he gave a deferential nod to the ambassador, who smiled in return, "we discover that the Chinese are to us and we are equally to them too often, given our remarkable cultural differences, a mystery.

"The fact is that the Chinese orientation and views are grounded in the experiences of thousands of years, encompassing a thousand different matters; our orientation and views on the other hand seem too often not able to tolerate thinking on any single matter that goes beyond the last one thousand seconds."

There was a ruffle of laughter from the audience.

"Let me try to put into perspective the importance of our

understanding one another. The Chinese represent one-fifth of the world's population, over 1.3 billion people. China is the third largest country geographically in the world behind Russia and Canada. It has the second largest economy, next to the United States. Its civilization has existed for more than 2,000 years before the birth of Christ. Ladies and gentleman, I would submit to you that it is *not acceptable* in this day and age that we and the Chinese continue to remain a mystery to one another.

"Thankfully, Sessions University is fortunate to have among its supporters visionary world leaders such as Melvin Rusoloff, who understand that our future, the future of world peace, will only be achieved through daily, in-depth exchange, communication and study. Melvin knows not only as a businessman, but as an aware and sensitive citizen and patriot, that the success of our School of Foreign Service will directly enhance the building of a foundation of international accord. As of today, with great thanks to Mr. Rusoloff, I am pleased to announce the founding of the Melvin and Sadie Rusoloff Center for Chinese-American Studies, Beijing China."

As Fitz-Hugh named the center, an attractive rendering of it flashed onto the screen. There was sustained applause. As Fitz-Hugh continued, a succession of renderings followed: the courtyard with students sitting on benches conversing and walking while in conversation, a classroom with a lecturer speaking collegially with a small group, followed by pictures of actual Sessions Chinese and American students.

"The Center exists as a vital partner with the Chinese and their intellectual and civic leaders toward better and more cooperative understanding and will promote cross-cultural learning, exchanges and partnerships between the United States and China for many decades to come."

Applause.

"The Center will be administered by co-directors, Chinese and American. Its curriculum will include not only courses in economics, Chinese and U.S. history and international relations, but will also integrate courses exploring international practicum and problem-solving in business, the environment, technology and productivity. Our hope is to integrate real practitioners into our course work by having visiting lecturers drawn from both Chinese and American corporations and that the Center may help to serve as a real world incubator for future business and government leaders who are grounded in a better understanding of one another and of one another's culture and heritage."

Applause.

"Now, I want you for a moment to imagine with me the invaluable and perhaps charmingly amusing experience of Chinese and American students, our future business and government leaders, rooming together in the Center's new dormitory, interacting together daily, staging events and plays together, visiting different locales in China together. It's exciting to think about such cultural exchange and what it may mean to our ability to understand one another in a hopefully far less mysterious future. Thank you."

There was sustained applause. Fitz-Hugh let it run for a moment. He held up his hand and gradually the applause faded.

"Now let me introduce to you the Chinese Ambassador to the United States, the honorable Zhang Hu."

The Chinese ambassador, a wise eminence in his late sixties, with close cut white-grey hair and a kind, learned countenance, rose and came to the lectern as Fitz-Hugh took his seat at the table. As he did so, a picture of the Chinese embassy came up on the screen.

The ambassador adjusted his spectacles and turned to Fitz-Hugh momentarily and then back to the audience.

"I must tell you something about your president," he began, "that I believe has some bearing on why we are all here this evening."

He paused for effect.

"He is a man of not only great perception but one whom we

have learned with great reverence has an appreciation of the details and subtleties that help to move the larger forces of cooperation forward.

"I call your attention to the centerpieces at your tables. I am sure that those of you here who are not Chinese recognize the beauty of these arrangements and are thankful that they grace this occasion. However, to the Chinese, we notice that without our ever saying a word or even thinking about such a detail, these arrangements are of peonies, which to us symbolize riches, prosperity and honor, plum blossoms, which symbolize endurance and the constant will to become stronger, orchids, which symbolize integrity and friendship and finally the China rose, which symbolizes dauntless spirit. So," he turned again to Fitz-Hugh, "Bryan, I congratulate you on your sensitivity to our culture and your continuing engagement in our partnership with the Beijing Center."

Applause.

The Chinese ambassador returned to his seat and Fitz-Hugh again came to the microphone.

"I've asked Mr. Rusoloff to say a few words," he announced and stood to the side and began applauding. The audience joined him.

A portrait picture of Melvin and Sadie Rusoloff, obviously from years before, flashed onto the screen.

Rusoloff, red-faced and beaming, stood, pushing back his chair with such force that it fell over backwards, the microphone picking up its clattering. He stumbled his way to the lectern.

I turned to Ursula. "He's shitfaced."

She grimaced, "Oh no," then sighed a long, helpless sigh.

Rusoloff approached the microphone, reached into his beautiful suit jacket for his remarks and realized he had left them at the table. Not wanting to embarrass himself by retrieving them, he proceeded to embarrass himself far more seriously with the garbling statement that came from his mouth.

"Bry-yan is the great-test pres-si-dent!" he half stammered, half slurred into the microphone, the sound of his voice cascading too loudly over the audience.

He paused. We sat with a creeping feeling of suspense tinged with dread, waiting for him to figure out what he might say next. "Thank you for coming to-Night! I am happy I could HELP! Thank you!"

With this last utterance, Rusoloff swept his hand across the podium as a gesture to the audience and managed to hit the microphone, which sounded with a loud POW!, dislodging it from its holder so that it vaulted into the air and then, as if it was a World War II bomb just released from a bomb bay, fell from the lectern past the dais all the way to the cafeteria floor below. When it hit, the explosion over the sound system was deafening, women and men instinctively cringing and reaching for their ears, knocking over their water and wine glasses as they did so, the blast so loud that it also caused a waitress to lose control of her tray and dump its entirety of dishes and silverware onto the floor.

Rusoloff shrugged and held up his hands defensively as if to ward off evil spirits, then shuffled back to his chair, which a waiter had retrieved and placed back at the table.

Fitz-Hugh walked rapidly to the front of the dais where one of the waiters handed him the microphone. The screen flashed to the Sessions University crest. He took the few steps back to the lectern, quickly placed the microphone back in its holder and said into it, "Thank you, Mel." He paused for effect. "You have enlightened us."

The audience began to chuckle.

"And scared the crap out of us."

Laughter.

"I want you to know," he said, turning to a now almost purple Rusoloff and then back to the audience, "that there is no greater advocate for this university and the School of Foreign Service than Melvin Rusoloff. He applies the same work ethic to our cause that he has to his business and with equal success.

So, Mel, we are honored that you are here tonight and we all thank you for your remarkable stewardship, and we know, too, that Sadie is watching over this occasion with great joy and approval."

The president led the audience in applauding, his applause sounding heavily over the sound system. Bernie Reve shot up from his seat, followed by Wentz and then Lusby and then more slowly by the rest of us as the entire audience gave Melvin Rusoloff a standing ovation.

Rusoloff began to cry openly, tears of pride, joy, sorrow and humiliation streaming down his face.

For the first time, I liked him.

Fitz-Hugh leaned back toward the microphone and said pleasantly, as if we were on the doorstep of his home, "Thank you for coming. We've enjoyed having you. Be safe on your journey home."

There was loud and resounding applause. The TV lights went off, the screen went dark, the room lights came up and we all stood, the room filling with a great babble. The secretary of state gave Bryan a light buss on the cheek and whisked away with the Secret Service to an obviously designated hallway door. The Chinese ambassador shook Fitz-Hugh's hand, held it briefly in both of his and they smiled gratefully at each other. Then he too was gone.

I looked around for Zoltan and caught a glimpse of him across the room leaving with Kristina through a hallway door now open on the other side of the dais.

Ursula grabbed my arm. "We must take care of Bryan," she said urgently, and we began making our way toward the dais. Fitz-Hugh was now standing in front talking with Reve, Lusby, Wentz and Fein.

As we approached I saw with surprise that he was furious.

Bryan was saying to Reve in hushed and angry tones, "Don't ever let that fucking asshole near a mike again. You understand me?"

"Yes sir," Reve said, his eyes downcast, looking like he was enduring a physical beating.

"He's a walking crass indignity. Get him out of my sight!"

"Yes sir." Reve turned and walked off, catching Rusoloff just as he was about to join us. Lusby and Wentz followed closely behind to assure Fitz-Hugh was screened from any further contact. Fein just stood there, paralyzed.

"Bryan," Ursula said to him, "behave!"

He looked at her in anger and defiance, his own face now crimson.

"Fuck!" he said. "What a great fucking legacy to leave in recorded history."

"It can be edited, Bryan. It will be fabulous."

He paused, gathered himself. "I fucking hope so."

"We will make it right." She turned to Fein. "Is that not right, John?"

"It'll be fine," said Fein, his eyes popping out of his head.

"You make sure it is," Fitz-Hugh ordered to Ursula and then looked me straight in the eye, raised his arm and pointed a forefinger at me. "You too. I want you to review it."

"Sure."

He gathered himself again, another step toward recovery. "And thanks for your idea tonight. It was just the right cue."

"No problem."

Fein looked at me, puzzled.

"I must be going," Fitz-Hugh announced, turned and left us.

Ursula and I began walking toward the elevator, leaving Fein standing there, frozen to the spot. I looked at her quizzically.

She read my look and said coldly, "Madam Secretary's limousine awaits."

"Oh…"

I felt Ursula's arm slip under my jacket and around my waist and turned to see her eyes were twinkling.

"At least now you and I have a moment together."

"Yeah, where the hell did everybody go?"

"Ah, Thomas, your naïveté becomes you. It is part of what makes you so attractive."

"What?"

"Bryan has left with Madam Secretary, Zoltan has left with Kristina, Reve has left with Rusoloff, Wentz and Lusby are off together, Fein, he is fine, and you and I remain."

"Okay. Wentz and Lusby? God damn."

"This is Washington, DC, my dear, the new Las Vegas," she said and looked at me, amused. "Looks like you will have to stay over. As it happens, I have a room."

She now had my full attention. "How is it that in the past you treated me with an attitude so professional it bordered on contempt and now you seem to be interested in me? What changed?"

She looked into my eyes. "I know things you do not know. I hear things; I see things."

"So, somehow that makes me attractive? Nice that it's all so personal."

"You are being silly. I've always liked you anyway. Just couldn't show it. It would look very unprofessional. But now we are going to be in same circles."

"We are?"

"You'll see. I can be a big help to you."

"Yeah. Big help in my personal life too."

"That's no concern of mine."

"Oh, I couldn't agree more, but you'll understand that it just might be a concern of *mine*. For starters I need to text Zoltan and I need to check in at home."

"That's not a problem. I will wait for you in the hallway." She turned and walked away toward the elevators and I watched her from behind with appreciation, telling myself firmly that I should not be going along with this and knowing I was not about to resist.

I pulled out my cellphone and Janet answered on the second ring.

"Hey, I've got a bit of a problem here. I can't find Zoltan. He may have gone out with some other colleagues for drinks. I'm hoping he'll text me. Anyway, by the time we reconnect it'll be late as hell. I'm thinking it would be smarter, especially given the weather, if we stayed down here for the evening and drive back in the morning."

"Okay, honey," Janet said. "Just like Zoltan. It's more important that you be safe. It's a bad storm. Take care. I love you."

"Ummmm, okay… Love you," I said, my intense feelings of guilt overwhelmed by arousal and excitement.

I texted Zoltan, "Where the hell are you?"

There was no response.

VII
Afterglow

THE SHERIDAN CIRCLE HOTEL WAS A FEW BLOCKS FROM THE SCHOOL OF FOREIGN SERVICE. Her room was a spacious top floor suite.

"You administrative types really slum it, don't you?" I asked her as we walked in.

"You do not have the same," she said turning to me, "when you go to a conference?" She reached over and switched off the lights.

We embraced and began a kiss that tested and explored lips, tongues, teeth. Her body against mine felt hot and hard-edged.

Someone pushed the Fast Forward button and our actions became like those in a silent movie, a piano racing away in the background. Clothes flew in all directions as we disrobed with ridiculous gyrations, sheets flew from the bed and we were at it, hard and fast and noisy. No style points were awarded.

I discovered as we went that she had a lithe intensity, an ability to excite me to better serve her, and within moments we plunged into mindless, frantic action, pounding until the first full simultaneous explosion of ecstasy.

After a time of drifting, when we had caught our breath, she told me, "You will do."

"Thanks. Such a compliment to know I'm adequate."

"My dear. You are more than. But then you know that. You just want me to tell you."

"Yeah. Well, I also find you…ummmm…okay."

We laughed.

We basked in our afterglow for a time, the smell of sex surrounding us.

Eventually my mind began to work again. Who was this woman? "Did you like growing up in this area compared to Germany?"

Lying beside me, our bodies visible in the faint illumination of street lights behind closed curtains, she made a small shrug. "It was very different. Germans like control and in Germany to some large degree it is maintained. Here," she rolled her eyes, "everything is out of control. Germans are too direct, say exactly what they think, and that is to them the way the world must be. Here, no one says what they think; it is all a masquerade of insincerity."

"Hmmm... You know who your actual parents are?"

"Yes. I made it a point to find them when I was in high school. We've become quite friendly. Now...where were we?" She turned and our bodies closed on one another.

A reflection ran through my consciousness momentarily that she seemed to have no interest in my life other than our being together here and now, whereas I wanted to know not only about her but about all that went on around her.

"So, you don't have a boyfriend somewhere?"

She drew back. "Think about it, my dear. In my position who is there who I might have a relationship with where it would not become an immediate problem?"

"It would have to be someone outside the university, I guess."

"Yes, or somewhere else. I work all the time. Not a lot of opportunity... And face it, my dear, men are a royal pain in the ass: needy, demanding, thoughtless, inconsiderate, self-absorbed. I have much of that with Bryan. I do not need more of it!"

"Wow. With such low expectations, no wonder I look okay."

"That and you have some other appeal."

"A life support system for a pecker perhaps?"

She laughed. "Yes."

"So, do the secretary of state and the president spend a lot of time together?"

"On occasions such as tonight, other state dinners. They are old acquaintances."

"I just had a feeling that it was more than that."

She sighed. "Bryan has a problem with his zipper."

"A problem with his zipper?"

"Keeping it up."

"Oh."

"Worse, he has no quality control. In fact, he invites all comers." She laughed a surprised laugh. "I made a joke, didn't I?"

"Yeah."

"I do the best I can, but he is impossible. Celeste is never around. I do not think she cares. Maybe she cares about the children in some distant manner. Who knows? But Bryan, I mean, it is very risky what he does."

"How do you mean 'risky?'"

She rolled her eyes. "Oh my God, the New York Alumni Association president's wife, for instance."

"Oh shit."

"That's what I said. Faculty. A graduate student. A board member, female, thankfully. He at least stays on one side of the street. Board members' wives. Donors' wives. Maid service."

"No."

"Yes, I am serious. Whatever and whomever. It's his ego and his love of himself. He is driven to do it."

I shook my head. "Not surprising, I guess, that he's a more complicated character than he seems."

"You do not know the half of it."

"I don't want to."

"And I will not tell you."

"Fine."

"I think we have other things to do here."

"Uh, yeah."

I could say that we woke early the next day but the truth is neither of us slept. Around 6:00am she rose, showered, gathered and packed her belongings, gave me a peck on the cheek and a meaningful, soulful look and was gone, her roll-aboard clanking over the sill and the metal door lock sounding loudly. I checked my phone. Zoltan had texted me a single question mark. I texted him to meet me for breakfast in the hotel cafe, showered and put on last evening's clothes.

In the hallway to the elevator I took a self-assessment. I was elated, mellow, adrenalized and running on empty. I felt fabulous and very guilty.

"You look like shit," Zoltan told me when he slid into the booth I had taken.

"Hey, you're even uglier than usual."

"I do not have to go home to Janet."

"Good point. I have a change of clothes at the office and shaving stuff."

"Yes, and wipe away your expression. You look like dog caught eating out of garbage can. You not teach on Fridays, yes?"

"Right."

"That good. I have teaching assistant covering my one lab today."

"Good. Guess we'll survive. Hey, an important point: Last night, it never happened. We will never talk about it. Especially we will never tell anyone about it."

"Yes. I sphinx."

I breathed a sigh of relief. "Okay, man. Never."

"Never."

"So, let's rehearse what didn't happen last night."

"I talk with colleagues after dinner. Look for you. Can't find you. Wait outside. You never show up. What happen to you?"

"After the event there was a recap meeting with the president near the dais, then we escorted him outside through a different exit to the secretary of state's limo. Then I walked around front. I guess you had already left."

Zoltan raised his eyebrows as he said, "He left with secretary of state?"

"Yeah."

"That interesting."

"Sure was. So, what did you supposedly end up doing last night?"

"Cannot find you so I book room in hotel and watch TV until I fall asleep."

"How come we couldn't find one another?"

"I lose my phone. Have to go to School of Foreign Service to find it this morning."

"Okay. I buy that. Let's eat. I'm starving."

It was a desultory drive back to Sessions, still raining hard, trucks spraying water into an impossible-to-see-through haze. Zoltan had to punch me in the arm a few times to keep me from dozing off. I called Janet from the car and let her know I was dropping Zoltan off at his place and heading back to the campus and that I'd be home as soon as I could clear up grading some papers and taking care of some administrative work, time to stall and get my act together.

I dropped off Zoltan, went to my office, changed into jeans, a shirt and sweater that I kept there, shaved, shut and locked the door and slept for an hour and a half. Then I fixed a cup of coffee and sat and thought for a time.

I surprised myself by scrolling for Berger's number on my cellphone and giving him a call.

He answered almost immediately. "Bergah!"

"Hey, Mark, it's Thomas."

"Thomas, how the hell are you?"

"Don't you have anyone screen your calls?"

"Nah, I don't give this number out to many people, and if someone calls me who's an asshole, I tell them they're an asshole and hang up on 'em. So, how's the family?"

"Terrific."

"So, what can I do for yah?"

"Well, when we last talked, you mentioned wanting to hear about the Beijing Center announcement."

"Yeah. I did hear a bit about that and the flyin' microphone. Melvin's a piece ah work. All and all, the event was a big success I guess."

"Mark, you're a guy who's accustomed to high powered, Washington DC events like that, right?"

"In a manner of speaking, yeah, maybe."

"I need to ask you a question in confidence. Don't laugh."

"Sure."

"Does everyone normally go off and sleep with everyone else?"

Berger broke into a long, howling laugh.

"You said you wouldn't laugh."

"No, you said that. That's hilarious. So, who went off with who?"

"Well, Zoltan and the associate dean for the School of Foreign Service, the president and Madam Secretary."

"Oh really. That's interesting. How do you know they weren't jus' going out for a nightcap?"

"I don't know. Vibes, I guess. I mean, let's put it this way, I tend not to imagine things. That's what it felt like."

"Well, I'd keep those perceptions to yourself."

"Yeah, I will. Just wanted some perspective from someone I knew wouldn't talk."

"Okay. Who else?"

"Lusby and Wentz."

"Grotesque."

"Yeah."

"And what about you?"

"Guilty."

"Let me guess. Ursula?"

"You're a smart man."

"She's a deceptive gal."

"Yeah."

"Don't worry about it."

"You're kidding?"

"Naw, forget about it. Never happened. Just wish I had been around, damn it. Weird things happen in our nation's capital when folks get away from home. I mighta got lucky. Zoltan can keep his mouth shut, I take it?"

"Yeah. No problem there."

"Good... So, on another subject, I think you're up for a promotion, my friend."

"What? I am?"

"Yeah, you didn't hear it from me. That's all I'm gonna say. Just understand it wasn't my idea. They just ran it by me."

"Okay. I'm clueless. A promotion? Okay, we'll see what the hell that's about. When are you going to be back in town?"

"Next board meeting is the first week in December. Let's get together."

"That'd be great."

"Jean Claude's and *Calypso Too* have left the harbah and are off Hatteras right now sailing the boat down to Miami. So in December during the Board meeting I'll be at the Intercontinental."

"Would you like to come over for dinner? I mean, we don't live like you do."

"Fuck that. A home-cooked meal? I'm there, man."

"Well, good cooks we're not, but I believe that with Zoltan's help we could put together something reasonably delectable."

"Yeah. Love to see you guys, plus your kids are great. Look forward to it."

I hung up the phone and sat thinking some more.

My cellphone rang. It was Zoltan.

"Meet me at club."

"No, man, I gotta go home. Fallin' flat on my face."

"Meet me at club. It important."

"Aw shit."

"Half hour."

"Okay. I can only stay twenty minutes and then I have to be outta there."

"Yes."

I walked across campus in a persistent wind and drizzle that had left the walkways glistening black. The leaves had fallen and the gnarled limbs of ancient oaks reached up over roof lines of brightly lit classroom buildings into the leaden sky. The temperature felt as if it were just above freezing and halfway there my guess about the temperature was confirmed. Snow began to fall, heavy flakes being blown sideways by the wind. I rushed along, my overcoat at home, my suit in one hand waving in the wind and my rolled shirt and skivvies under my other arm.

The club was warm and welcoming, Thanksgiving decorations already up. I put the clothes I was carrying in the coat room and as I walked back toward the bar area I noticed that the place was almost empty, which made sense. Anyone at the festivities the night before would not likely be here, and perhaps this was one of those Fridays where people had left early to get out of town.

Zoltan was in our usual spot, hovering over his vodka and trying to extract pretzel loops from a glass bowl.

I sat down. The waiter came with my beer, a benefit of being a regular.

Zoltan looked extremely worried and worked up, a rarity, but a set of emotions that could go over the top if not dealt with quickly. "Something happening," he told me. "Dean and the director of medical center want to see me. I worry they going to take away my lab."

"What makes you think that?"

"I not sure. They never call me into meeting before, not together."

"I thought you were their rising star?"

"That what they say, but you know administrators, speak from both sides of mouth, then stab you in back."

I shook my head. "I don't know. I think it could be just about anything. Maybe you got a campus traffic ticket."

"Not funny, Thomas."

"Okay. Maybe it's good news."

Zoltan looked at me. Obviously this thought had not crossed his mind.

"I don't know," he said, and he sat thinking.

"So, you want to hear my news?"

"What?"

"I called Berger just to say hello and get his take on the Beijing Center event and he told me that I'm up for a promotion."

"To what?

"He wouldn't tell me. Does that make any sense?"

"Maybe they make you Ursula's assistant." He started to laugh.

"Not funny."

He broke into a large belly laugh. "Or housekeeper."

"Way not funny."

His laughter died away and he became serious again. "By the way, you know what Kristina tell me?"

"What?"

"She sleep with president last year."

"She told you that?"

"To us Europeans it not such a big thing as with you Americans."

"So I gather."

Zoltan shrugged. "She say that when he take woman to bed he talk a lot."

"That's not all that unusual."

"Yes, but what he say is. Bryan plans centers like Beijing all over world—Beirut, Rio, Brussels, Moscow."

"Wow. Maybe he was just trying to impress her."

"You know what else she say? They don't know where money come from."

"Money for what?"

"New Beijing center."

"That's interesting."

"Yes. She say it just allocated to center budget account in China from university without going through School of Foreign Service or anyone saying anything about where money come from, like from Rusoloff endowment. No accounting, just big lump sum deposit, millions, bang."

"I don't know what to make of that."

"I do not either."

We finished our drinks. I fetched my clothes, Zoltan paid me for his portion of our tab and we hustled to my car in the descending gloom of oncoming winter, the wind and snow pelting us. I dropped Zoltan off at his apartment and drove home.

Halfway there my cellphone rang. I could see a university number on the screen and pick it up.

It was Ursula, all business.

"Dr. Simpson?"

"Yes."

"Can you attend a meeting with the president in his office this coming Thursday at 3:30pm?"

"Sure. What's this about?"

"I'm not at liberty to say."

"Okay. Who's going to be there?"

"President Fitz-Hugh, Dr. Calhoun, Provost Kravitz, John Fein, Frank Lusby and myself."

"Wow. That's quite a gathering."

"Yes. It will be interesting."

"Oh, thanks for all the background and information...not."

"You are most welcome."

"Have a nice weekend."

She sighed. "You cannot imagine. I will be here the whole time."

"Um, sorry."

"That I appreciate. May you actually enjoy your weekend."

"I'll try. Thanks."

We hung up. I shook my head. This was all getting a little weird.

I drove up the steep hill on the twisting road that bordered our neighborhood and turned onto our street. Snow was already beginning to stick in the yards and on the edges of the roads, the wind also blowing snow and a few remaining leaves through my headlight beams toward the river.

The golden light from our house's windows penetrated the dark, snow falling through it. Its glow warmed my soul. Home. A spasm of guilt hit my stomach. I quashed it by focusing on my need to get indoors.

I parked in the garage. When I entered the family room, Sarah was there watching TV. The smell of stir-fried chicken penetrated the air.

"Dad! I thought I heard something!" She stood and came toward me.

We hugged awkwardly, given that I was still holding my suit and rolled-up clothes.

"Man, Dad, your clothes stink."

"Oh, sorry."

I went into laundry room by the garage entrance, dumped in the offending articles, added detergent and a pour of vinegar, started the load, breathed a sigh of relief, then took my suit and laid it on a chair in the front hall.

Janet was in the kitchen stirring the wok, the table was set and there was a glass of white wine she had poured for me on the counter. I gave her a hug and a kiss.

"So, how was the event?"

"Interesting. I met the secretary of state."

"Really?"

"Yeah. She and the president were grad students together at Harvard. They're old friends."

"That's interesting. Put some water glasses on the table, will you? Tommie's in the basement. You'll need to go get him in a couple minutes."

"Sure. How are you?"

Janet slumped a little. "Not great."

"Really? What's up?"

"Dr. Compton is a mess."

"Oh. How come?"

"He's self-medicating again, and he won't be straight with me about what he's taking. It's making his mood swings worse, and he's getting less and less rational. I mean, to put it in colloquial terms, he's in deep shit and doesn't even know it."

"Time for a shrink?"

"Yes—if he'll go to one. In fact, I gave him some referrals, told him his situation was getting beyond what I could help with, told him I would call and get him an appointment if he wanted. He just shook his head and smiled that damn 'I've got a secret' smile of his."

"Hmm. Very upsetting."

"This is a brilliant man who knows better and he's just hell bent on not listening."

She shook her head.

"So, I've got some strange news."

"Strange?"

"I called Mark Berger this afternoon, just to catch up and say hello, and in the course of our conversation he told me that I'm up for a promotion."

"Really?"

"Yeah. Isn't that weird?"

"Promotion to what?"

"He wouldn't say, just that it wasn't his idea, that they'd run it by him."

"That doesn't make any sense. It's not like Howard's going anywhere."

"The more I think about it, the more I think the president may have something up his sleeve. He doesn't do anything halfway and he's not afraid of change."

"What are you talking about?"

"Well, Bryan's been asking my opinion on university communications here and there and he seems to like what I have to say. So, I think it's something in that arena, but that's just a suspicion. In any case, I've been called into a meeting this coming Thursday at 3:30 with Bryan, Howard, Kravitz the provost, Frank Lusby, the campaign consultant, and John Fein. So, we'll see."

"That sounds serious."

"Yeah, it does."

"Okay, back to reality. Tomorrow, you need to take Tommie to the dentist. I'll take Sarah to ballet."

"Okay. By the way, I invited Mark Berger to dinner."

"What? Here?"

"Sure."

"My God, Thomas. And he accepted?"

"Would love a home-cooked meal."

"Oh, honey. You invited a billionaire to our home? What were you thinking?"

"That he might like a change of pace. Plus, he's a good guy. I told him Zoltan would be helping out. He thought that was great."

"When?"

"Around the next board meeting; early December."

"I can't believe you did this."

"I don't see what the big deal is."

She put her hands on her hips. "No, you wouldn't, would you?"

I shrugged. "Sorry. Seemed like a good idea at the time. Anyway, I'm taking my stuff upstairs. Be back in a minute."

Janet said, "Okay," and shook her head some more in disbelief that I was such an idiot.

I walked into the hall, picked up my suit and headed up the stairs, pausing at the top to let out a long exhalation. What the hell was I doing with my life? None of this made any sense. I gathered myself. Somehow I would make it through.

VIII
Promotions

THE SESSIONS UNIVERSITY ADMINISTRATION BUILDING EXISTS AS A MONUMENT TO THE ATROCIOUS CAMPUS AR- CHITECTURE OF THE LATE 60S AND 70S. In this case, the architects had attempted to merge the dominant Georgian grace of our campus with the functionality of a modern office building. The resulting bastardization created a four-story square building with brick facing, inlaid front and back with four ersatz concrete pillars and a ridiculous short overhang of slate roof. A massive, energy inefficient atrium is at its center, surrounded by offices on each of three stories, a full office complex on the fourth. The of- fices feature large sealed-in-place thermo-pane glass views of the campus, but are otherwise known for their inability to be cooled or heated properly. Plans are underway for a new "green" ad- ministration building, but it has yet to receive board of trustees' approval, pending funding through the Campaign for Progress.

The president's office is on the third floor, shielded purpose- fully by a small cluster-maze of outer offices so that its entry is not readily apparent. I found my way there, where to the side of Fitz-Hugh's closed door, Ms. Bemiss, known far and wide as The Gatekeeper, sat on her ample derrière behind an aircraft carrier of a desk devoid of paper. Her head was shorn. She wore spangled earrings of glossy white ovals that looped almost to her shoulders, a white dress imprinted with massive black triangles and an expression of glacial calm that told me quite specifically that I meant nothing to her.

She placed her long fingers together, each fingertip touching lightly on the side, allowing her dark brown, inch-long nails to cross like swords in a military procession.

She looked through me. "You may enter," she pronounced.

I found myself wondering what she did in the evenings and what would happen should some unfortunate soul attempt to trespass into the president's office. Would they be Wolverined by those nails?

Once inside I saw that his office was quite beautiful with mahogany paneled walls and oil paintings of the campus. The left wall held mahogany shelves filled with university awards, display books, pictures of dignitaries with Fitz-Hugh at ground breakings or other momentous occasions, pictures with corporate CEOs, signed pictures from politicians and one or two Hollywood stars. In the middle was a bar section, glass shelves holding university seal glasses and beverages, under it a small refrigerator.

Given the building's age, the underlayment of its thin parquet floors had deteriorated so that the parquet compressed and creaked hollowly with every step. This accounted for the spacious, thick Persian rug, which took up the majority of floor space.

Fitz-Hugh's massive antique partner's desk fronted a large center window overlooking the lower quadrangle, a windswept expanse of ice patched asphalt, bare trees, brown lawn and dirty, yellow spotted snow. Off to the right side of the room, near the right wall, was a mahogany conference table with comfortably cushioned adjustable rolling chairs.

In them sat Lusby, Ursula, Kravitz, Howard and Fine Fine John Fein. I joined them, and after a few greetings we sat there, hot to the point of sweat dripping from armpits, the sound of dry, overheated forced air as background noise, the chairs clearly the only comfortable element in our presence. I sat next to Lusby and across the table from Kravitz. Kravitz had taken a chair that had been lowered previously so that it appeared as if only his massive head and thin neck were present rather than being accompanied by the rest of his body. He stood with some irritation and pumped the handle at the base of the chair and sat again, now in an elevated, throne-like position that was equally ridiculous. Normally I would have found this amusing but today I was distracted by the very deep and active anxiety tumbling around in my middle.

We sat wondering where the glowing eminence of our esteemed president, Bryan Q. Fitz-Hugh, might be. Tension and irritation filled the air, accompanied by the mild smell of urethane outgassing in the sealed building from the wall to wall carpeting and particle board furniture in other offices. No one made small talk. The atmosphere was ugly, ugly, ugly.

The latch of a side door clicked above the noise of the forced air heat and Fitz-Hugh strolled in, all smiles, all business and took his place at the head of the table. He noticed Kravitz in his elevated chair and suppressed a small smile.

"Good afternoon everyone. Sorry I'm a few minutes late."

We all nodded and murmured acceptance.

Fitz-Hugh took a small breath, smiled and launched. "The future of Sessions University, its destiny, our futures, our destiny will be determined by the success of the Campaign for Progress. Look around you, for instance, at this outmoded building, an anachronistic pustule on the face of a beautiful campus. Its demolition and replacement is a campaign priority, after, I should add, the enhancement of our academic programs, corridor and equipment." He nodded deferentially to Kravitz, who did not acknowledge the gesture. "The point being that as the campaign goes, so go we. To that end, I sense that we have a greater opportunity than we have heretofore taken advantage of to let our supporters, our internal and external audiences, the alumni, our leadership and friends know the unique nature of what we can accomplish with the campaign."

He looked directly at John Fein who looked crestfallen and defeated. "This is no knock on our current beleaguered public relations, marketing and communications effort, John. I know you are understaffed and I know you are doing the best you can. I want you to keep up that effort, John."

"Thank you," Fein whispered timorously, his expression returning to its normal, anxiety-ridden state.

"What I am suggesting is that we need a comprehensive effort over and above our current capability to help power our outreach and communications to creatively make Sessions known to not only our current stakeholders but to the country as a whole and globally. We need to literally put Sessions on the map of national and global thinking. We need to be a domestic and international player. If we can do that, it opens up a world of funding and partnership prospects. It puts us out front, shaping and leading the agenda in higher education, not following prevailing trends. Are you with me on this?"

The group nodded hesitantly. I could see an implacable resistance in Kravitz's barely perceptible nod.

"Accordingly, I have determined that we should create an office of campaign and university communications as part of our Campaign for Progress. Its overriding purpose will be to bring an exponential power to not only our campaign communications, public relations and marketing but to our overall efforts, melding them into a single, forceful program that can communicate a worldwide message about who we are and what we have planned for the future. The office of campaign and university communications will be responsible for assembling a master plan for joint efforts on behalf of the campaign. It will be powered by a separate enhanced budget that will be derived from the Campaign for Progress itself." He raised a hand, forefinger extended to forestall what he knew would be Kravitz's objection.

"Now I know some of you might question the economic and practical, reality-based wisdom of doing this, but the facts are that given our current success with the campaign and our anticipated future success given prospects being approached, the addition of this new campaign expenditure will not cause our overall campaign budget to exceed acceptable standards. Is that not correct, Frank?"

Lusby nodded sagely. "In fact," he said, "we're still under the one percent mark on budget versus attainment with the national standard being five to ten percent. Of course, costs always rise toward the end of a capital campaign because of its roll out regionally and to general constituencies, but I'm very comfortable with where we are at the moment."

Kravitz jumped in. "This is still most irregular. It makes a complete joke out of chain of command."

"Actually, it simply marginally realigns chain of command, and frankly, Samuel, your planning and budget expertise," he said with just the slightest hint of irony on the word 'expertise,' "are not why we wanted you here, but instead we wanted you here to personally communicate with you and Howard about the academic implications of this change."

He continued, unperturbed by Kravitz's open hostility. "I've had the good fortune over the last several months to occasionally seek communications perspective from Dr. Simpson here. I've found his counsel to be extremely helpful, sensitive to the nuance of a number of critical settings and communications. For instance, I surprised him with an inquiry about how I should frame my recent remarks before the secretary of state and the Chinese ambassador and in a moment he articulated exactly the thematic I needed to make my remarks work. So, in this and in other interactions, I find there is a certain *simpatico* and an intuitive understanding between us about where we can and need to go with our communications programming in the future. Accordingly, as of today, I am appointing him to be director of campaign and university communications, heading an office of that title under the Campaign for Progress."

I felt my stomach and intestines drop out of my body and splatter silently on the floor. A single two-word thought formed in my mind beginning with 'holy.'

"Accordingly, should he accept these responsibilities, his academic appointment will be in suspension, at the very least until the campaign has ended. I recognize Howard that this creates a bit of a gap in your department. We will ask Dr. Simpson to finish out his courses for this semester. In the meantime, I want you and Provost Kravitz to work on how to best cover the department's needs during Dr. Simpson's absence. In this new position, all university, medical center and any other division's communications, public relations and marketing programs and personnel will report to Thomas. He will serve as a member of my executive cabinet, meeting as part of that team monthly to plan our university's future. In the next forty-five days, with your cooperation and help, he will devise a coordinated master plan for the university and the capital campaign's programs and present it to me and then to the board of trustees for their approval. Is this clear?"

Everyone but Kravitz nodded, more vigorously this time.

Fitz-Hugh turned to me. "Thomas?" he inquired.

"Thank you," I said evenly, almost pleasantly. I was pleased with the way it came out because the rest of my mind was shouting the four letter F word over and over.

"I will let Ursula brief you on the details of your appointment," he said to me. "Gentleman," he said to our group, then turned to Ursula and said graciously, "and lady. Thank you."

He rose. We all followed his lead awkwardly, avoiding eye contact. The others walked out, Kravitz high stepping in angry arrogance, Howard with a shocked, disbelieving look on his face, Lusby with a glum "another day at the office" expression, looking as if he wanted and needed a drink, and John Fein with his tail between his legs, leaving Ursula, me and Fitz-Hugh together.

The door closed and Fitz-Hugh turned to Ursula. "That *fucking* arrogant bastard," he snapped. "He thinks he runs this damn place. Can't bear the thought that he was not selected president. He's consumed by jealousy. He'll be all over the faculty with this, stirring them up."

"Yes, Bryan, he is a thorn in the side," Ursula commented.

"He's more than that. He's dangerous. Faculty are fine as long as they are asleep in their ivory towers, but wake them up and all hell breaks loose."

"Yes," Ursula said.

Fitz-Hugh looked at each of us, smiled suddenly, indulgently and waved his hand, "You kids go and play. I've got work to do."

"Sure," I said, and Ursula and I headed off to her office, which was just down the hall, a small, square space with a good view of the student center, orderly to a fault—no art, no pictures, a large screen monitor on her paperless desk.

She shut the door, gave me a buss on the cheek and sat behind her desk. I took the chair in front.

"Surprised?"

"Floored. I knew something was up, but I never for a moment expected something so...grandiose. Hell, everyone's going to hate me for starters."

"Um, welcome to the administration, my dear."

"God damn."

"I don't know that he has a whole lot to do with it. We are all just from hell."

"Well, that explains it. Okay, do I have a position description?"

"Yes. When you write it."

"Damn. Okay, I get it. I'm to create everything from scratch."

"Yes. Bryan has a lot of confidence in you."

"Utterly misplaced."

"Don't tell him that."

"You can count on that... So, what does this position pay?"

Ursula mulled this for a moment, shrugged. "That would be a key part of the budget you will create... Why don't you submit three times what you are making currently."

"Three times!" I heard myself exclaim too loudly. "Fuck me! Get outta here!"

Ursula laughed hard. "Um, Thomas, I think we have taken care of the first part of that statement, and as for the second part I have no intent on going anywhere."

"Okay, sorry… Why would you even suggest that?"

"Because Bryan wants you to be bold and that is a good way to start. Once you have finished your budget you can meet with our comptroller, Ken Depew, and also go over your numbers with Frank Lusby before you review them with Bryan. To a large degree, the campaign budget is separate from the university budget. Do not be shy about this."

"Okay."

I could feel my phone vibrating in my pocket. Undoubtedly Zoltan—a thirsty Zoltan. It would have to wait.

"Let me know how I can help you, and, of course," she said with a twinkle her eye, "Bryan will want you to attend some signature events. For starters, our annual board retreat outside of Miami in January that is being hosted by Mark Berger, where you will present your master plan."

"Okay." I could feel a rising sense of interest in this part of my new responsibilities.

"Now, go. You have a lot of work to do given your double duty in the next month and a half. And I have much work to do also."

I walked out of the building into the cold gray of mid-Atlantic winter. The smell of oncoming rain or sleet was in the air. I pulled my phone from my pocket and called Zoltan.

"Thomas," he said, "something crazy has happened. We must talk."

"You don't know the half of it."

"What?"

"I'll fill you in later. I have to go back to the department for a bit, do some damage control. Meet me at the club in an hour."

"Yes."

I walked to Hart Hall on the upper quad and down the hall to the communications department and to Howard's office. His door was open slightly. I knocked once, pushed it open a bit more. "Can I come in?"

"God damn, yes!" was the response. I pushed the door open,

shut it behind me and sat down in front of Howard's desk. It was the same disheveled office I had been sitting in on occasions for the last dozen years, and I immediately had the familiar sensation of my nose beginning to run. But things had changed.

I had rarely seen Howard Calhoun angry—irritated yes, pretty much daily—but rarely deeply, implacably furious. I had never seen that, and I hope to never see it again.

"Can you believe what that overweening punk has done?" he asked me, his voice rising and cracking, his face reddened, contrasting brightly with his disheveled white hair, staring at me through his thick lensed glasses, his eyes darting about behind them as he scratched in quick distracted fury at a swatch of eczema on his neck.

"I had no clue," I heard myself say innocently, defensively. I sneezed loudly and reached for the supply of Kleenex I kept in my jacket pocket in the winter months. "I'm as surprised by this as you are." I blew my nose.

"You should turn him down. Do you realize the risk you would be taking? How can you possibly succeed? Thomas, I think he's setting you up. He's a very Machiavellian and suspicious character."

"Well, I can see why you would say that."

"But you're foolish enough to do this, blinded by pride and ego and his blandishments?"

I thought for a moment, shrugged and laughed lightly. "Yeah, that sounds about right."

"Well, don't come crawling back to me."

"I don't think I'll have to if I get the employment contract worked out right. He did say my current position would be in suspension, correct?"

Calhoun threw up his hands. "I'm not going to argue about that, Thomas. You're a damn fine professor. I'd be glad to have you back, if I'm still here. Hell, maybe I'll just retire, get away from all this." He waved a hand in the air.

"You're still way too good to retire, Howard."

"Well, thank you for saying that." I could see he was beginning to calm down a bit. "You can understand that I'm quite upset by this naked power move of the president's."

"I'm a bit upset myself."

"What are they paying you?"

"I haven't a clue. We'll see… Look, Howard, I still think you're the best. I want you to know how much I appreciate you, our relationship and all that you've done for me over the years. I hope we can still be colleagues and friends."

"Okay, Thomas, enough. You always were politic, but I hear you and I appreciate your sentiments. I also know they are genuine."

I breathed a large sigh of relief, blew into my Kleenex again. "Thanks Howard, that means a lot."

"I know you'll do your best to finish out this semester with the same degree of competence you have always shown. After that, we'll stay in touch. Now go."

"Thanks," I said, rising.

The club was just beginning to fill up when I arrived. Zoltan was at our normal table, vodka in front of him, pensively waiting for me.

"Ah, there you are!" he blurted loudly as I sat down and the waiter brought my beer, the few other patrons present looking over at us as if they suspected Zoltan was about to stand up and start throwing furniture.

"A little less loud, huh?" I asked.

"Thomas," he said, now in almost a whisper, "the most amazing thing has happened. I meet with dean and hospital director. They give me my own laboratory."

"I thought you had your own lab?"

"No, no, no. I supervise a lab, yes, but all the research protocols are teaching protocols for students to learn how to work in lab. They are now making me a lead researcher with my own facility, my own staff. I do not teach anymore; I research; I set protocols; I design research; I boss people around; I can take my research findings outlined in my last paper and start clinical trials. They pay me a lot more. I big man on campus."

"You're a schmuck."

"Yes, but I now very big schmuck! I like that word. It is a good word. Let us celebrate!"

"Yeah, let's celebrate."

We drained our drinks, clinked glasses and ordered another round.

"I cannot wait to tell Kristina!"

"How are things going with her?"

"We going to alternate weekends here and then there. We also visit one another every Wednesday."

"What's she think about your bureau drawer?"

"Ah, I have locksmith come and install lock. Safer that way. Keep money out of sight. So, how about you and young lady?"

"Ah, turns out lunch hour is a good time. Her apartment is only a couple blocks off campus."

"Free lunch is the best. Very dietetic."

"I don't know whether it's free exactly."

"Best to ignore those thoughts."

"Yeah. Maybe." I thought of my overriding impression of her apartment. It was as if no one lived there: impeccably presentable, like her office, no pictures or personal mementos anywhere to be found.

"So, what is this damage control you talk about?"

"When Bryan Q. Fitz-Hugh decides to do something, he doesn't go halfway. He calls this meeting of Kravitz, Howard, Lusby, Ursula and Fein and slam dunks in their face my appointment to be director of campaign and university communications as part of the Campaign for Progress in charge of all university, medical center and other divisions PR, marketing and communications programs. I have to have a master plan for university communications to him in forty-five days with a complete budget that I'll create from scratch. He put my current appointment in suspension. I'll finish out the semester and he charged Howard and Kravitz with figuring out how to make up for my transfer over to administration. Kravitz was fit to be tied. Howard's royally pissed and a bit heartbroken, but I think I've got him calmed down."

Zoltan stared at me. "You now part of administration?"

"Yeah."

"You run whole campaign and university communications?"

"I not only run it; I've got to design a whole new paradigm."

"My God, Thomas. You in deep shit."

"Yeah."

"That great news. What they pay you?"

"I have no idea. I have to figure it out. First thing I have to do is consult a number of salary surveys. That occurred to me as I was walking here. Then I've got to review the marketing survey the president's office had conducted two years ago by that outside firm, then absorb the follow-on strategic plan adopted by the board and see how that flows into the campaign plan. Then I ought to have some sense of how to proceed. But I can tell you one thing."

"Yes?"

"It's got to be top drawer and cutting edge and a bit out of the box."

"Yes, you are fucked. I glad to know you. Who is schmuck now?"

"Oh, undoubtedly I am."

"Here is from one schmuck to another. *Egészségére!*" Zoltan toasted.

We looked one another in the eye meaningfully, drained our glasses and set them down.

It went on that way for a while, Zoltan reviewing and thinking out loud his plans for his laboratory and its research, me doing more of the same regarding my new assignment.

Eventually, aware that our words were beginning to slur and that a great deal of time had passed, we surveyed our empty glasses and the empty bowls of snacks on the table philosophically.

"I better go. I don't want Janet to get pissed."

"Yes."

I dropped Zoltan off at his apartment, found my way to the expressway and called Ursula at her office. She picked up on the first ring.

"I just learned from Zoltan that he's been given an entire lab and research program by the dean and director of the hospital.

"Yes."

"You don't seem surprised."

"I was aware of it."

"Does this have anything to do with Bryan?"

She paused. "I do not know. Bryan does like to help those he likes and respects."

"And those he doesn't?"

She paused again. "It is not pretty."

"Ohhhh-kay. Just wanted that clarification. Good night, my love. Wasn't there a movie by that title?"

"You are being silly."

"Yeah. Catch you later."

"I hope so."

I laughed and hung up.

It was after ten, the house was quiet, the kids were upstairs and I stumbled on the doorstep coming in from the garage.

Janet said from the family room, "I take it things went well?"

"Unbelievable," I heard myself say, and was pleased that I no longer seemed to be slurring words.

I went into the family room. She had a glass of white wine and was curled up on the couch, a blanket drawn up around her, reading a novel, the latest deep and meaningful historical novel selected by her book club.

I sat down heavily on the couch beside her.

"It's been an amazing day. Zoltan got a research lab of his own and was made a lead researcher for the medical center and I was promoted to director of campaign and university communications in charge of all PR, marketing and communications at the university, med center and all other schools and divisions. Everyone reports to me. I have to have a master plan and budget on the president's desk in forty-five days. I'm to continue teaching through the semester, then I become a member of the administration."

Janet looked at me calmly, but as if she were seeing me in a different light. "That's remarkable."

"Yeah, Zoltan and I did a bit of celebrating at the club. Sorry I'm late."

"We missed you. Joan Kravitz called this morning and wants Sarah to babysit her grandchildren, Natalie's son and daughter, on Saturday. They're here on Thanksgiving break."

"That's interesting."

"What do you mean?"

"The provost was not at all happy with my new appointment, felt it made a mockery of the chain of command and that the capital campaign is running the university, not academe."

"Hmmm..."

"Obviously, Joan called you before Bryan announced my appointment at the cabinet meeting."

"Or they just need a baby sitter and Joan is not nearly as deeply troubled as the provost, or they'd call and find some excuse not to have Sarah work for them, don't you think?"

"Yeah..." I considered her observation. "You're probably right."

"And you missed endless Tommie yammering about a Dalmatian."

"Wow, will he ever give it a rest?" I moved over and put my arm around her and we hugged.

Janet shook her head. "I doubt it. Once a notion has taken root, it's impossible for him to stop obsessing about it. Plus, Christmas is just around the corner."

"Oh no... I hadn't thought about that. What's Sarah's take on all this?"

"Oh, she's above it all as usual."

"Yeah... You know, back to the situation at Sessions, it's going to be a hell of a ride from here on in."

"No doubt."

"I don't think I'm through celebrating."

"You smell like beer."

"Yeah."

"Maybe you'll get lucky."

IX
The Library

SATURDAY MORNING WE HUSTLED THROUGH BREAKFAST—waffles from the freezer heated in the toaster, not half bad as long as they were slathered with squeeze bottle margarine and fake maple syrup. Orange juice. Milk. Coffee. Small sausage links that Janet was frying in the electric frying pan—tasted better than they looked. Tommy dawdling, half-asleep, a fire engine hanging out of his bathrobe pocket. Janet cajoling him to eat his oatmeal. Tommy required breakfasts that had as little sugar in them as possible, but his medications often left him with no appetite.

Janet was bustling about, getting ready to go to the grocery store with Tommie as a cross to bear. She had to get out early to avoid the crush of Saturday traffic and crowded stores, a strange phenomenon in workaholic suburbia. All week between rush hours stores and roads were deserted, and then on the weekend a total claustrophobic, cluster fuck traffic jam of cars and shoppers. My assignment, drop off and pick up Sarah at the Kravitz's for her inaugural baby-sitting job. In between I was allowed to go to the office.

"Dad, what are the Kravitz's like?" Sarah asked as I stood to get another cup of coffee.

I shrugged. "Dr. Kravitz is the university's provost, chief academic officer, very learned, loves languages. Try your French out on him. He might find that charming. He takes himself a bit too seriously. Joan, his wife, seems lovely, but I've only met her in passing at events. They live in a big house in Hampton Park. Been there forever."

"Oh, Hampton Park, la-de-dah. All my friends call it Hamster Park. What about their daughter and her kids?"

"Natalie? I've never met her. The kids neither."

Janet chimed in as she gave the electric frying pan a quick wipe, put it in the sink, filled it part way with water and dish soap, "I talked with Joan about them yesterday. Natalie's a concert pianist. Her children are Ben, who's nine, and Molly, who's seven. They're from Chicago. Joan said the kids are in the Laurel School there, which I take to mean they're among the 110% of kids from the upper income brackets who are 'gifted.' Apparently they're well behaved. Grandmothers of course think their grandchildren are wonderful and beyond compare, so I asked her how you could best treat them. Apparently they are pretty self-motivated and like their space, so just find out what you have in common and what they want to do. Of course, also see what Natalie has to say."

"Okay. Thanks, Mom. That sounds pretty okay."

"Just be very nice to them. You want to make a good impression so the Kravitz's can be a reference for your next job."

"Duh, Mom. Enough already. I've got it."

The weather as we drove there was cold and blustery. Snow from the day before had partially melted and then frozen overnight to a slick, glazed sheen.

Sarah and I were quiet for a while, lost in our own thoughts, the car's heater gradually warming up the interior while the wind blew assorted bits of trash and an occasional plastic bag across the road in front of us.

Given the cabinet meeting and Kravitz's clear antagonism to my new appointment I was anxious about whether we might see one another today. On one hand, the timing of this baby-sitting gig couldn't be worse. On the other, perhaps there was an opportunity here to set things right with Kravitz the way I had with Howard. Doubtful, given that he and I had no real prior relationship. Maybe we wouldn't even see one another today; maybe he would even avoid me. Nevertheless, I steeled myself to our meeting and rehearsed what we might say to one another. It always helped to be prepared.

Sarah asked out of the blue, stream of consciousness, "Why is it, Dad, I mean, Tommie, I love him, he's my brother, but, Dad, he's a disaster. Does he get any better?"

"Yeah?" I remarked, surprised. Clearly she had been giving this subject some serious thought. I always found it interesting how the car freed us to talk about subjects we would never address in our home. "Over time, with a lot of help from us, maybe he can live a more or less normal life. At least that's the hope that's held out to us."

"But he causes a lot of stress. I can see it in you; see it in Mom. I feel it too. It's like every day, all day everything revolves around Tommie and trying to keep him straight. Don't you feel like it's dragging all of us down?"

I thought for a moment, sighed a long sigh. As usual, she was dead right. Sometimes Sarah was so damn sensible I felt as if I might as well be talking with Janet's twin sister. "Well, that's very perceptive. Yeah, you're right, but I haven't a clue about what more we can do about it except to try to raise him in as supportive and normal an atmosphere as possible, which is our home. Sending him away is just unacceptable. I mean, it might destroy him. Our thought is that he needs us and will do better being with us than not—at least for now." I paused, thinking my way through my response. "So, I guess we'll have to find a way."

"Yeah Dad. You know, some colleges have tracks for under-age admissions for gifted and talented students. I want to look at them, see whether it would make sense to go to college early. No offense, Dad, it may do Tommie good to be with us but for me our house is a stress. Plus, let's be honest, I'm not getting anything out of school at this point, at least academically."

"Well, yeah…" I replied, downplaying the shock I was feeling and thinking fast. "Sessions wouldn't work for you? I mean, there's a gifted and talented track for younger students. You could possibly even dual enroll and transition into it."

"And where would I live? Don't you get it? Sessions means I'm still at home...*forever.*"

"Not necessarily."

"Yes, necessarily. You and Mom will give me all these assurances and in the end I'll still be living at home. Trust me. I know you guys."

"Okay... Let's continue this conversation...at some other point when we have more time and we've all had a chance to think about this. We'd miss you but I understand where you're coming from. Have you talked to your mother about this?"

"No. She'll just freak out."

"Hmmmm... I don't know. She might end up being a big help and a resource."

Sarah considered this. "I'll let you tell her. See what her reaction is."

"Oh, thanks."

Sarah smiled. "But you'll do it, right?"

"Yeah, but... well... I'll let you know what she says."

"Thanks, Dad. You're the best."

I might be the 'best,' I thought, but somehow all this made me feel a profound sense of loss as I confronted for the first time the real possibility of my daughter leaving home. A freshman in high school, she seemed much too young for this. Time had a way of accelerating, but even when you knew that, it continually took you by surprise. And now this new notion of Sarah's she had ambushed me with? I found myself shaking my head.

Hampton Park is a venerable neighborhood. Its houses were built in the early 1900s by wealthy families as country estates, places of respite from their owners' downtown residences—this was in times when a trip from the outlying valleys, which today took perhaps thirty minutes outside of rush hour, took an entire day. So, now, of course, in a world of ever-expanding suburbia, its location was viewed as being closed in. Given this, its presence near the university, the solidity and style of its architecture and construction, the size of its lots and its remarkably attractive, mature and well-kept grounds, Hampton Park continues to be a prime address.

As we turned into main drive, I found myself again admiring the neighborhood, which was impressive even in the dead of winter.

Large, beautiful brick colonial houses with slate roofs as well as mansions of granite or limestone or of Tudor design graced spacious, manicured lots and were flanked by massive, now bare rhododendrons and azaleas, tall oaks, maples and beech trees, the main drive winding in two opposite lanes with a small stream, path, dormant gardens running between them. There was a feeling to the place that spoke eloquently of upper crust living. Every spring it was the favorite location for garden tours.

How had the Krazitz's come to live here? Must be some family money, I thought, and made a mental note to ask Lusby. Must be family money and a willingness to ignore the history of the place. Only a few decades before, Hampton Park had actually had, as part of its neighborhood covenants, a clause forbidding Jews, and even in relatively recent history several Jewish families had made accusations of realtors steering them elsewhere. I found it telling that these same covenants had made no mention of blacks or any other ethnic groups, no doubt because it was beyond comprehension decades ago that such minorities would ever have the financial capability to live there. Jews, on the other hand, were a different story.

But today the world had changed. Samuel Kravitz and his family could live in Hampton Park not because he saw himself or his family as pioneers of religious or ethnic equality. Rather, given his academic attainment, he would feel that he was above it all and deserved the best. The funny thing, given changing times and his status as a provost at our university, he was and did. Status was increasingly a function of attainment and wealth, not of social standing or family connections. The old order of society had passed. Would Sarah and I ever talk about all this? Did it even matter going forward in today's changed world? Was it a sad fact that many of the lessons I had learned and things I knew and had experienced had no bearing on, or relevance to, the society that Sarah would inhabit? Probably.

The Kravitz's lived in a large Tudor house built at the top of a rise overlooking the main drive, its stream and gardens. An unobtrusive black wrought iron fence surrounded the property, the drive leading to a center courtyard fronting the main entrance and then trailing off to the back of the house to the garages.

I pulled up front.

Sarah looked at me and said, "Dad, you have to come in with me," a sign she was feeling a bit insecure.

"Sure."

We rang the bell, a dog began to bark, a large dog by the sound of it, and after some delay we could hear someone approaching from behind the thick, mahogany door, the sound of paws hitting it in anticipation of company.

The heavy door was opened with a creak by Joan Kravitz, clearly expecting us, nevertheless a bit befuddled, obviously her permanent condition, trying to rein in a beautiful but overly enthusiastic standard poodle.

"Down Marcel! Behave!" she scolded the dog who was now sniffing Sarah and me vigorously.

"A French poodle named Marcel," I said to her, smiling. "After Proust, I take it."

"Yes, yes, of course," Joan observed. "Our own little inside joke… Well, Thomas, Sarah, do come in!" She had unruly steel-grey hair, was wearing tan slacks and a grey cardigan sweater. She peered at us through thick trifocal glasses on a woven lanyard—the perfect picture of a literature PhD grandma.

The entry hall was a tall, wood paneled half-hexagon with a coated flagstone floor, doors on either side and high windows, European cottage diamond-patterned lead and glass, with a stained glass center featuring heraldic crests.

"You're so nice to do this," she said to Sarah.

Natalie walked in briskly, brightening the room. She was pale, a youthful brown haired version of her mother, especially her eyes.

Her radar was on, I could see. She took one glance at me. The word 'acceptable' flashed in my mind. And then she looked Sarah over in one quick, intense glance, thought she was fine. Natalie turned back to me with poise.

"Hello," she said pleasantly, reaching out and shaking my hand, her long fingers strong in a brief grip. "Thank you so much for making Sarah available for this afternoon."

"You're very welcome."

"I understand you've just had a significant promotion, heading up university communications."

"Yeah, it's going to be quite a challenge." 'Okay,' I thought, 'she's direct and even-keeled. Good.' I looked at Joan. There was no indication from either of them of disapproval or hostility. Obviously, our family and my promotion had been a dinner or breakfast topic of conversation for them just as they had been one for us.

"I can't say I envy you that. Having grown up in the Sessions world, I've always thought that it was comprised of so many different interpretations of reality. No one's ever on the same page."

"True. I guess I'm impossibly tasked, but" I shrugged, "a lot of it is tailoring the message to fit those different perceptions."

"Nice trick!" She laughed, a lovely laugh.

"Yeah." I laughed with her.

"In any case, thanks for Sarah's help today. I'm sure she'll do well."

Ben and Molly had followed her and stood behind her, both

children overdressed in the way children are when visiting their grandparents, Ben a solid lad with close cut brown hair, in gray dress slacks that looked uncomfortable, a white dress shirt and blue sweater, and Molly, a willowy girl with fly away, curly dark blond hair in a flowery dress that I guessed she had picked out with great pride.

I watched all the telepathy going back and forth instantaneously between Sarah and the kids and could tell almost as quickly that everything would be fine.

"Sarah," Natalie said, shaking Sarah's hand politely, "this is Ben and Molly."

Sarah and the children nodded at one another. Clearly, they wanted to get out of our company.

Joan turned to me and said, "We're going to the Saturday matinée broadcast of the London Philharmonic Orchestra at the Majestic, Brahms, Symphony Number 1. I quite enjoy seeing the orchestra in that venue. Almost like you were there, and quite a bit less expensive! A bit much for these younguns. They'd much rather sit around with their iPads." She turned to the kids. "Why don't you all get acquainted? Natalie can show you to the family room." Then back to me. "Thomas, Samuel wanted to see you in the library, I think to show it off, frankly. If you just go through the hallway here past the living room you'll find him there."

"Thanks," I replied pleasantly, while I felt a sinking feeling inside. I looked at Sarah, who gave me a quick 'I'm fine' glance, turned and walked away with Natalie and the kids.

While I was aware of the Kravitz library from conversations around campus, I was in no way prepared for it. It turned out to be a separate wing added onto the original house.

There was a change in the humidity and temperature as I opened the door and surveyed what I quickly estimated must be a forty by sixty foot, two-story room lined with books.

Kravitz stood in front of me, his prominent face in his large head relishing my open amazement and admiration of the place, his large black eyebrows bobbing, rubbing his hands together in front of his small torso.

Behind me, as I turned to look, was a first level of books extending from the parquet floor to a second level with a metal walkway that gave access to small corridors of books, which I calculated must extend over the original house. A metal ladder on wheels attached to the bottom of the walkway by a metal runner gave access at its center to the second story as well as to the first level's collections. On the three exterior walls floor-to-ceiling books were accessed by similar two-story ladders on rails, passing by large palladium windows with tinted glass so that the interior was in subdued light. Mahogany tables for laying out large folios, glassed-in mahogany display tables and accompanying chairs were placed on Persian rugs. Red leather overstuffed reading chairs with adjustable brass LED lights were toward the outside wall.

"Good morning, Thomas. Good of you and Sarah to help us in this manner," Kravitz greeted me pleasantly. I felt a guarded sense of relief. He continued, "I thought since you were here, you might enjoy seeing a major *préoccupation* of mine. Joan would probably refer to it as an obsession.

"I've always been interested in books and their representation of their time, nationality and culture. In fact, I began collecting books at a very young age. In a very major way it was my interest in books that led to my engagement in the humanities.

"As time went on, I became more sophisticated, but the problem with this is that as I became more sophisticated my interests and relatedly my collections became ever broader and larger. So, would you like to see a signed copy of *The Canterbury Tales*? I have one. Would you like to see an original folio of *Don Quixote*? I have one. Original Audubon prints? Of course. Signed first edition of *The Great Gatsby*? Why yes, we happen to have two.

"It got to the point that our house, lovely as it might be, was taken over by cluster OCD piles of my collections. So, could I find these treasures at any particular time? Doubtful. At Joan's threat of divorce we had an architect who specializes in collections come out to examine how to better catalogue and organize and then remodel. One glance and he brought in a structural engineer who after a quick study informed us that our house was in imminent danger of collapse from the weight of these 70,000+ books and documents.

"What you see here is the solution to our dilemma, brought about thankfully by a cooperative arrangement I made with Sessions' former administration, which was far more interested, I must say, in the pedagogical and research treasure trove of our collection than the current administration ever would be. To wit, Sessions helped with the cataloging, organization and imaging of what is now our joint collection so that it is now a formal part of the university's computerized library system. Graduate students and other researchers can access copies of much of what is here from the library's website or come here at prescribed intervals to view the documents themselves.

"Joan and I, out of appreciation for this partnership, have left our collection to Sessions. In fact, as part of our estate plan, our residence will become a named university library facility. The kids all live elsewhere and fully approve of this arrangement. The university's legal department has cleared the way with the neighborhood association and zoning approval. Not that Joan or I intend to go anywhere near the land of the departed anytime soon."

"Wow," I said, commenting on the arrangement, "I had no idea."

"Yes, we have not broadcast this, for a variety of reasons, privacy being one. We're happy to have academic researchers here but would abhor rubberneckers. Garden tourists are bad enough. You know, on occasion they will even wander up, ring the doorbell and want to ask questions."

We had begun walking around the perimeter of the library as he spoke. I admired the snow covered views of the large yard and its oak, maple and elm trees amongst different gardens, a white, painted gazebo toward the back of the property overlooking a small pond with an arched oriental bridge to a miniature island in its center.

"But on another subject," I heard Kravitz say, which brought me back to full attention from what had become the pleasant mumble of his tour, "you know the primrose path of our current leader is inevitably one of overextension, mission degradation and self-destruction?"

"Um, hmmmm," I heard myself half utter, a sound that carefully expressed neither agreement nor disagreement.

"Look," Kravitz said, turning to me, "I understand that a young man in your position must have an attitude of *carpe diem.* We have all been through those times. Never easy trying to make one's way in the world. So, Thomas, please understand. I in no way blame you for accepting this new position that our charlatan, carpetbagger, carnival barker of a leader has offered. But the facts are that he has no interest in advancing the pursuit of knowledge. He's in the game just for the pursuit of his own fame and fortune, his own glory, not for that of our esteemed Sessions University. Surely you see that? Accordingly, you should also understand that he has no interest in you. You are simply a means to an end. Make a mistake and you'll be gone."

"Ummm, humph," I neither agreed or disagreed, feeling like a total chicken shit but not knowing what else to do, how to avoid commitment.

"There," Kravitz nodded his oversized elegant head, "I knew you'd agree with me." He held up a hand. "But don't worry, your secret's safe with me."

"Okay," I replied in a mildly puzzled manner.

"I'm glad we had time for this little chat. I knew that as a fellow academic you would understand my viewpoint. The dark side of the administration has yet to fully corrupt you."

"I guess not." I looked at my watch. "I better be going or I will definitely be in trouble on the home front." I didn't want to mention to him that my next stop was the office.

I walked back through the house. Marcel joined me, trotting alongside, seemingly hopeful that I would stay, the adults now dispersed to their rooms, readying for the trip downtown, and the kids off somewhere, undoubtedly preoccupied with one another. I petted Marcel goodbye and left him in the front hall.

In the car, once I started it, I paused for a moment. Curiosity got the better of me and I called Lusby on his cellphone, then put the car in gear, made a U-turn and began my way down the drive.

Lusby's voice came over the line, smoky, slightly slurry, almost as if he had just woken up, "Yessss... Thomas? What can I do for you?"

"I hope I'm not bothering you."

"Nope. Just sitting here watching the build up to the game."

"The game. Which one would that be?"

Lusby responded with a put-on aggrieved tone, as if half astounded by my stupidity, half insulted, "Notre Dame, of course."

"Oh."

"Former client. Hard not to adopt the team once you've experienced the awesomeness of the place and the culture. I learned a lot on that assignment, including that those Catholic boys can be tricky, particularly the Jessies. But it was a great campaign, very successful."

"Interesting... Say, I got a question for you. I'm just leaving the Kravitz's house where Sarah is babysitting for their daughter."

"You mean, Natalie. Quite something, isn't it?"

"Unbelievable. Where'd they get the money to do all that?"

"Haberdashery, on Joan's side."

"Haberdashery?" I pictured a couple of old Jewish men conducting a meaningless back room argument amongst racks of suits.

"Where did your father and where do you occasionally buy your suits?" Lusby asked.

"Jeremiah Blank and Sons?"

"The one and only. Joan's a Blank, only child. Truth is there were no sons. Her father ruled it with an iron fist, took no prisoners, fought his way to the top in a remarkably cutthroat business. You may remember that he sold out about twenty years ago, ostensibly to retire. But guys like that never really retire. Beyond the clothing business, he liked investing in real estate. So, after the sale he parlayed the proceeds into signature properties in a couple of big cities, places that with their location and clientele minted money. When he died, Joan had the estate lawyers sell it all. Didn't want to be bothered. Interfered with her Seven Sister's, PhD lifestyle. Didn't hurt that she sold out when the market was at its peak. So, in general terms, she inherited a fortune. A lot of it is in generation skipping trusts, but there was plenty in direct trusts and investment and cash accounts for Joan and Samuel to blow during their lifetimes. Fact is they got cash flow out the wazoo. If they like Sarah, tell her it's okay to ask for a raise."

"Wow. Small wonder the university is so interested in a partnership."

"Well, the library collection alone is worth it. Given the provost's current relationship with our president, however, I don't think we'll be seeing much else. I've been hammering Bryan repeatedly to make peace with him, but he's as willful and stubborn as the provost. As you've seen, Kravitz cannot get over the fact that the board didn't hand the presidency over to him. In some ways, I suspect, Joan's money has given him delusions of grandeur."

"Yeah."

"So, what are you doing today?"

"On the way to the office."

"Yeahhhh," Lusby sighed empathetically, "figures. I'd tell you to take it easy, but you won't listen. You'll do fine, just gotta get through the next couple months."

"Don't I know it."

"Okay, see you. Game's getting ready to start. Gotta find my golden helmet. Brings 'em good luck."

"Golden helmet? You are a sick mother."

"Yes, it's true. But the helmet sure beats the Leprechaun outfit I wore last year. Made sudden trips to 7-11 or the liquor store very awkward. At least with the helmet you can take it off readily. You're welcome to come over after the office. I think Wentz may stop by in a bit."

"I don't buy the Leprechaun story, Frank."

"Aw shucks," Lusby said languidly. "Well, you're welcome to come over."

"Nah, I gotta get home. Thanks."

"Okay, I get it. Know you and Janet have some challenges."

"Yeah, thanks."

Driving to the office I thought of Lusby sitting alone in his apartment with his golden helmet on watching the Notre Dame game, no doubt a case of lite beer in the fridge for refreshment, eating God knows what, extra spicy buffalo chicken wings, jalapeño nachos, stuffed crust pepperoni pizza, whatever else unhealthy, while the Kravitz's took in the Metropolitan Opera and I went to work. I thought about him and Wentz and felt a small shudder. I thought about his comment about Janet and my challenges and had to tamp down a flash of anger. It was just a fact that people talked behind your back, even when it was none of their Goddamned business. Lusby meant well, I knew. But he'd crossed the line. While his invaluable knowledge of the politics and personalities of Sessions meant I needed to maintain our business friendship, in no way would I ever be a buddy. Why was it, I asked myself, of all the strange things that Berger could be our friend and Lusby could not? After some reflection, it occurred to me that everything Lusby did, no matter how genuine or sincere, it all eventually one way or another turned into manipulation. Whereas Berger? Somehow he was instinctively, sincerely, flying by the seat of his pants genuine, just doing what the hell came naturally, trusting his instincts and not giving a shit what anyone else thought. I was convinced that regardless of the circumstances, Berger hoped for and wanted the best for us. Lusby? He was playing a far different ball game.

In the office I took care of back emails and continued to review and mark up relevant headings or sections in a collection of materials I was using to help guide the master plan: the Sessions University marketing study done two years previous; the university strategic plan; the Campaign for Progress operating plan, other universities' communications and admissions strategies and plans; corporate communications strategies; international education programs, particularly those with global, multi-campus orientation.

In what seemed like a short time, I realized three and a half hours had passed. I emailed my progress on the master plan outline to myself so I could pick up the trail at home.

At the Kravitz's Sarah bounded into the car, excited.

"Dad, they paid me!" She held out the bills proudly.

"Wow, that's great. How'd it go?"

"Oh, those kids are really nice, and smart."

"Yeah, that would figure."

"Ben is like gifted in mathematics, like gets to take classes in their upper school. He's a little weird but okay, and Molly is already speaking French better than I can."

"Wow."

"Yeah. They said they'd call me next time they needed some help."

"That's great. What are you going to do with the money?" I asked.

"College fund, Dad."

"Oh."

We walked into the family room at home to the sound of Tommie upstairs in his room wailing.

Janet came in from the living room, dust cloth in her hand, which signaled she was upset. Our house got cleaned in a more or less therapeutic manner.

"What's the noise all about?"

"Tommie discovered at the grocery store that they sell matches."

"Oh shit."

"I thought he was right behind me and the next thing I know a couple clerks run by and grab him. He'd just struck a kitchen match. To say the least, they were quite unhappy. Tommie didn't even seem to get what was wrong until we got home and I explained the facts of life to him, which made him very upset. So, now he's up in his room, hopefully not trashing it."

"Jesus…" I looked at Sarah, who looked back at me, held up both hands and shrugged.

"How was the Kravitz's?" Janet asked her.

"Oh, it was great. Kids were nice. Really nice house and dog. They paid me, Mom."

"That's great, honey."

"Kravitz showed me his library," I told her. "Exceptional. I'll have to tell you about it. In fact, we've got a lot to talk about."

"We do?"

"Yeah, but let's settle down for a bit. We can talk after dinner."

X
Lunch on the Edge of Town

THE FOLLOWING WEEK, Thanksgiving week, I was in my office working on the master plan, fleshing out different sections, making notes on how each would be represented by a Power Point slide.

My cellphone rang. Berger. "So, how yah like the new position?"

"Uh…it's a challenge."

"Hey, it ain't no rose gahrden, but then again, you ain't no rose."

"Thanks. Where the hell are you? Brussels, Bangkok, Rio de Janeiro?"

"I'm right here, at the Intahcontinental. Just thought I'd check in, see how you were doin'."

"Oh. You're here early."

"Yeah, board meeting next week. This seemed like as good a place as any to hang out."

"What are you doing for Thanksgiving?"

"Nuttin'"

"You're kidding?"

"Nah, family's mostly gone. Those that aren't gone are strangers. Modern day dilemma. These days your friends serve as your family and your actual family are distant acquaintances, most of whom you don't particularly care for. And most of my friends are scattered all over the place. I may go out and get some dim sum."

There was a brief pause while I thought about the appropriateness and possible consequences and then decided to go for-ward. "Why don't you come over to our place for Thanksgiving?"

"What? Nah, I couldn't do that. That's your time to be with your family."

"Friends are family, right?"

"Yeah, but I would just be in the way."

"Zoltan will be there with his girlfriend, Kristina. In fact, he's helping us cook Thanksgiving dinner. We talked about you getting together with us for dinner. This would be as good a time as any."

"Let me think about it, okay?"

"Sure. No problem."

Ten minutes later my phone rang. Berger.

"What am I thinkin'? Would I rather be sittin' around here poundin' my pud and going out for dim sum or having dinner with you guys? You guys won out, narrowly. So, what time?"

"Say three?"

"Sure."

"You have our address?"

"Sure."

"Okay. That'll be great. Look forward to it."

"Same here."

I hung up and looked out my office window and saw snow-flakes drifting by and a scraggle of windblown bare black tree branches moving against the grey sky, checked my watch, found that I was shaking my head, stood, put on my overcoat, turned off the light and locked the office door behind me. Time for lunch.

The university, being on the edge of the city, has a periphery of shops and well-to-do apartment buildings, wide boulevards, small parks and lots of green space. Off campus students usu-ally lived to the east in what's known as the Sessions' ghetto, where the edgier sections of the city meet up with the bet-ter parts of town. Ursula's apartment was in a small modern building a few blocks west. I walked there under the now perpetual gray skies and let myself in the back entry with her key to avoid establishing any identity with the front desk.

She was waiting for me, dressed only in a silk robe, open in the front, which was all the encouragement I needed.

Afterwards, we lay there for a time in silence watching snow drift by her window.

Eventually I asked, "So, what are your plans for Thanksgiving," knowing that were I not to ask, she would volunteer nothing.

"Ah, very busy," she sighed, looking to the ceiling to put the list of activities in order. "First, the secretary of state is having a party at her office and, of course, Bryan will be there with bells on and, of course, Bryan wants me to come along to track his conversations and send follow-up thank-you notes and other communications. That is fine because I can spend the next two days at my parents' and celebrate the holiday with them, but then I have to be back here to attend Bryan's Thanksgiving Day reception at Stewart House."

"Couldn't you skip that?"

"It is a command performance. Even Celeste will be there. You should come too."

"What time is it?"

"One pm. It's set up as an appreciation and thanks giving for everyone at the university should they choose to stop by, particularly for those students, graduate students, fellows, faculty and others who cannot make it home for the holiday. You know, many cannot—too far and too expensive to travel for too short a time."

"I can't make it. Zoltan and Kristina, his girlfriend, are coming at noon to fix dinner. Then Berger's coming over at three, plus Janet will want me to help get the house in order, keep the kids out of her hair and get everything ready."

Ursula turned away from me and was silent for much too long a time while I looked with appreciation at the fine lines of her shoulders and back and her smooth taut skin.

"Something I said?" I asked.

She turned and faced me. "You should not have told me that."

"Okay. Forget I said anything."

"Mark Berger is coming to your house?"

"Yeah."

"For Thanksgiving dinner?"

"Ummm, yeah. That would be the occasion."

"We did not even know he was in town."

"Maybe that's the way he wanted it."

"Yes, I'm sure it is." Another long pause. "Bryan will want to come."

"To our house!"

"Yes."

"No, no, no, that will not work. Janet's already going to be upset with me for inviting Berger. Now you're talking the circus is in town and it's coming to our house? I don't think so. Plus, he's got his own reception to attend."

"He would find a way… She doesn't know he's coming?" I noticed that Ursula would never call Janet by her name. It was always 'she.'

"Just invited him an hour ago. Why don't you just not tell Bryan."

"I have to."

"No you don't."

"You have no idea what you are talking about. You are making everyone's life more difficult."

I reached over and stroked her shoulder. "What could I do to make it up to you?"

"Ah, I have an idea about that," she said, moving to embrace me.

"Good."

Back at the office, I completed my outline of the table of contents for the master plan. I then put the finishing touches on a draft budget I would review with Ken Depew, the comptroller, and Lusby to be sure it was acceptable.

Darkness was already closing in when I walked across the deserted campus to my car. On the drive home worries rolled through my mind: the plan and its budget, Ursula and my dalliance, Berger coming to our house for Thanksgiving and Janet's reaction, Fitz-Hugh's relationship with the secretary of state, Kravitz, the lump sum funding of the Beijing Center, the campaign and its discretionary budget. I had a growing sense that it was all wrong.

Okay, there was the obvious truth of my infidelity. It could harm my family, even ruin it. I needed to come to terms with and end the relationship. Yet there was no way that was going to happen, at least for the present. I was in over my head. There was something going on with me that I had to have Ursula and wanted her much more than made any rational sense.

But there was also a significant undercurrent of facts and perceptions about the university administration that did not add up and that felt…what was the right word? I thought for a few moments. Malfeasant. That was the word. I felt like I was beginning to know too much and yet remained ignorant of what it all meant and that to know what it all meant might even be dangerous.

I parked the car in our garage and walked into a quiet family room. Janet was reading her book. The kids were out of school. Sarah was at a friend's house and Tommie was undoubtedly in Tommie Town.

"Hi, honey," Janet greeted, looking up from her book.

"Evening. What's up?"

"I ordered pizza. Tommie will need some attention in a bit. How's your plan going?"

I sat beside her and we hugged. "Slogging through, outline done, initial draft of the budget complete. Now I have to write the sucker and recast the budget as I go along."

"Hmmm… What are we going to do about Christmas?"

"Christmas? It isn't even Thanksgiving. Your brain fried by the early advertising?"

She shook her head. "No. I mean about Tommie and his Dalmatian."

"Oh, hell. I don't know. I hate capitulating to him all the time. A dog, no matter how wonderful, is a royal pain in the ass. Plus we're not here during the day, so that means fencing the backyard, dog door in the back or someone to walk the dog. I'm even afraid of what Tommie might do to a young puppy—overdo playing with it. There's probably a rescue league where we could adopt a dog. What does Sarah think of all of this?"

"Hard to know. An interesting idea for her but pretty abstract, almost like she doesn't care one way or another."

"Let's wait until after Thanksgiving to think about this. Let's talk to his school about the advisability of having a dog for a kid like Tommie. Do our research on the breed. I mean, it wouldn't be us if we didn't overthink and overcomplicate a situation like this. You know, torture ourselves."

Janet laughed. "Okay. Some wine?"

"Sure. How's Compton?"

She shrugged. "Disappearing act. Typical. I hope he's okay."

"Damn… So, I invited Mark Berger over for Thanksgiving dinner."

"You did *what?*

"Invited Mark to have Thanksgiving dinner with us."

She rolled her eyes in disbelief. "Have you completely lost it?"

"Not really. We were talking about what each of us would be doing for Thanksgiving and he said he'd be, and I quote, 'pounding his pud and going out for dim sum.'"

Janet laughed. "He said that?"

"Yeah. What else could I do? He's like damn Zoltan. Where else would he go? Stewart House for the President's reception? I don't think so."

Janet let out a long exhalation. "As if my life were not already out of control."

"Look, it might be fun. The kids like him. We all like him."

"I certainly hope you're right about this."

XI
A Don Giovanni Thanksgiving

THANKSGIVING DAY, a day to sleep late, give thanks for all one's blessings and celebrate family, friends and good fortune with those closest to you and, of course, I woke at 5:30am worrying about the master plan.

I located my bathrobe and slippers, carefully closed the door to our bedroom and then to Tommie's room and Sarah's, made my way down the carpeted stairs, stepping over the one that always creaked.

The house was silent, gloomy. I fixed a pot of coffee, put bread in the toaster and fetched jam and butter. Glancing out back, I could feel more than see that the skies were overcast, the yard a dim white from an inch or more of fresh snow.

My office was a small room with cheap paneling and book-shelves located toward the front of the house off the family room. I turned on the lights, shut the door and sat in my leather recliner with my laptop and worked. The silence and the cold surrounding me created a pleasant sense of isolation and I became lost in the plan until the kids' voices sounded from the upstairs hall. I rose and opened the blinds. The sun had risen and the day was brightening, the sky clearing, snow already melting on the street.

In the kitchen I found some instant waffle mix, pulled out the waffle iron, plugged it in and turned it on. No frozen, freezer waffles this morning.

Janet padded in wearing her slippers, a wool sweater pulled over her pajamas.

"Good for you," she said, nodding at the waffle iron. "You got up early."

"Yeah. Work anxiety. Had some ideas I needed to get into the plan."

Tommie and Sarah wandered in, Tommie half-awake in his bathrobe and PJ's, a model fire engine sticking out of each pocket. Sarah was already dressed in brown corduroys and a heavy green turtleneck.

"Okay, guys, how about waffles for breakfast? And then we build a snowman?"

"Cool," Sarah said. "It looks nice out."

Tommie sat at the kitchen table, looked at me sleepily. The lids of his eyes fluttered, his face ticked slightly. "I don't know, Dad," he said. "I got plans."

"Plans?"

"Yeah, downstairs."

"Let's get outdoors for a bit, huh? Get some fresh air."

He screwed up his face. "Okay. But Dad…"

"Yeah?"

"Think about how much fun it would be if we had a dog to play with while we built a snowman."

"A dog? You softening your position, Tommie?"

"You know I mean a Dalmatian, Dad. You know that."

"Okay, just checking."

After breakfast, there was just enough snow to make some-thing of a half-assed snowman that we could see would melt in no time, but it was fun being outdoors in our front yard in the sunlight and active, although the encouragement from the few neighbors who walked by had an undertone of being glib, insincere and a touch derisive. I was pleased the kids didn't pick up on that and wondered how long it would be before they did. It was moments like these that I fought the impulse to move. Not that I had the first clue about where we might go.

Janet made a quick trip into the house and rustled up the requisite carrot nose, raisins for his smile and an old snow hat and tattered scarf from the bottom of our hall closet. In a quick trip to the backyard we found oak leaves for his ears, acorns for his jacket buttons and sticks for his arms. We were putting the finishing touches on the snowman when Zoltan and Kristina rolled up in a taxi van.

Zoltan bounded out of the passenger seat in a jubilant mood. "Hey," he said, his breath reeking of vodka, "I know costume and set person at the theatre and she lend us old costumes. We lip sync opera scene after dinner—final scene from *Don Giovanni*."

Janet said, "You're not serious?"

"I am very serious person, like always," he said expressionless, and then let an ugly, savage smile burst onto his face.

"With Mark Berger here? No, Zoltan. Not in our house."

"We leave it to him. You see, he get right with it once he have a drink or two. Be fun time. Memorable!"

The side door opened and Kristina stepped out. "Hello, Thomas," she greeted, giving me a hug, "so glad to see you again." She turned to Janet, "and even more pleased to meet you, Janet. Zoltan is a great admirer."

Kristina had a brisk but shining and pleasant personality, the perfect antidote to Zoltan's foreboding presence. In some small aspects she reminded me of how Sarah might be as a grown woman. Unfortunately her taste in clothes, a white knit, high neck turtleneck, blue slacks and a tailored angora coat, more resembled Ursula. So, I could see that I would need to be repressing that thought for the rest of the afternoon.

We went around to the back of the van, opened the lift gate and saw two huge cardboard moving boxes, another smaller box with a fresh turkey in it and several pizza boxes stacked atop one another.

"You brought pizzas?" I asked, puzzled.

"No, no, no. I just get those boxes from place around the corner where they know me. We spend last evening preparing hor d'oeuvres, put them in the boxes."

"Ah…"

Zoltan grabbed each costume box, one in each hand, and lifted them clear of the car while I retrieved the turkey. Kristina and Janet picked up the pizza boxes and we all headed into the house.

Once everything had been put in the kitchen I was pleased to see that Janet and Kristina hit it off, Janet showing her around our place.

We began our preparations, talking all the while, Zoltan stuffing the turkey with a special mix of different breads, apples and seasoning he had made the night before. Kristina and Janet set the dining room table while I vacuumed the living room and family room. The kids were assigned to pick up and straighten up, most of which was accomplished by Sarah while Tommie walked aimlessly from place to place, pantomiming the chore but in actuality accomplishing nothing. Eventually the house began to look presentable, the smell of turkey penetrating the air, mashed potatoes and vegetables ready for the microwave, biscuits set on a pan for the oven, a pecan pie in the fridge, cranberry sauce on a plate to be passed around. The doorbell rang.

I opened the front door and Berger stood there. He was wearing a red *Calypso Too* foul weather jacket, deck shoes, faded jeans, a new red sweater with *Calypso Too* stenciled in dark blue over the right breast. He had his hands in his pockets and a brown and beige Eskimo hat on his head with ear flaps pulled all the way down so that his appearance was that of an Eskimo hat with glasses, an orange mustache and sideburns.

I began to laugh, turned and shouted inside, "A visit from the Abominable Boardman!"

A limousine was parked at our curb, the engine still running, the driver standing dutifully behind Berger holding a case of wine and on top of that a large bag of carry out that could only be dim sum.

"Hey, howareyah!" Berger greeted, his eyebrows moving up and down under the hat.

"Great. Come on in."

"I been shoppin'!" he said loudly as he crossed the threshold, the driver following him in and dutifully placing the wine and dim sum on the hall table and left as Berger said, "Actually, I got the sommelier to raid the Intahcontinental wine cellar. I think he came up with some good stuff. We'll have to see. Plus I couldn't resist and brought a bunch ah dim sum. Thanksgiving is now officially a Jewish holiday. All I'm missin' is a hot blond chick in a short skirt and a Jersey accent and my life would be complete."

From the kitchen Zoltan half shouted, "You the Lone Ranger, stranger!"

Berger and I exchanged glances at this boisterous and slightly off key greeting as a sign of the kind holiday good cheer only alcohol could produce.

Zoltan came into the hall wearing a large white chef's hat and apron, his face red and glistening with sweat.

Berger and I began to laugh.

Zoltan looked at us disapprovingly. "Obviously you scum have no respect for fine dining," he told us. "I decant your sommelier's best choices." With an air of disdain he took the wine and dim sum into the kitchen.

I walked Berger through the downstairs, showing him around, and when we got to the family room, Janet and Kristina brought out glasses of wine.

We toasted one another, taking a sip simultaneously.

"Wow!!! This is spectacular!" I told them.

"It certainly is," Janet added.

"Yeah, the Chateauneuf-Du-Pape is good stuff," Berger observed.

We went into the kitchen and helped bring the hor d'oeuvres out to the family room and set them on the low table we had in front of the couch, pulled up chairs, brought in bottles of wine and fruit juice drinks for the kids and everyone joined in our pre-meal feast on deviled eggs, Virginia ham on buttered biscuits, oyster sauce with potato chips, sharp cheddar cheese and crackers.

After a time, Zoltan, Kristina and Janet left us, and within a short time announced dinner.

The turkey was already carved and sat steaming and fragrant in front of my place at the head of the table, bottles of red and white wine at each end, dim sum on plates that could be passed around. I took orders on turkey preferences and passed plates to everyone while the other dishes made their way around, helped myself and then picked up my wine glass.

Holding it up, I toasted, "To my family, to our friends, we have much to be thankful for, beginning with one another and extending to our lives together and the many blessings we enjoy."

We raised our glasses, drank and then began our meal, compliments being passed around about the turkey, stuffing and the side dishes.

After few moments when the only sounds were silverware on the plates Sarah asked Zoltan and Kristina, "Do you have a holiday like Thanksgiving in your country?"

They looked at each other a bit bemused and at the same time puzzled, thinking about how to respond.

Berger commented, "If I'm not mistaken, knowing something about the history of your countries, there's not necessarily a lot to be thankful for."

"What do you mean?" Sarah asked.

Kristina put down her knife and fork. "Our countries have histories that go back thousands of years and are full of invasion and suffering. Most recently, our countries not only suffered World War II and the Holocaust but also were invaded numerous times since then by other countries. Millions of our citizens were murdered either in concentration camps or slaughtered in their own towns and the countryside—exterminated really. So given our history we may not have as much to be thankful for if we think about the past. But…that is not a subject for this day. Hopefully, you will learn about it in school. I can tell you, however, that we always look ahead; we try to never look back. It is too depressing and there is nothing about it we can change. It is always with us. We must live our life in the present or we will perish, drive ourselves mad at the horror of our past, of our history."

"That's really sad."

Tommie piped up, "In Hungary and Belarus the fire departments have rescue dogs." I could tell he was reciting a text from something he had undoubtedly searched on the internet. "In Hungary they are Vizslas, but I'm not sure what kind of dog they use in Belarus. Do you know? Here in the U.S. many of the rescue dogs are Dalmatians…"

Zoltan interrupted, as if Tommie had not spoken, and said to Sarah. "All countries go through periods of turmoil at one time or another. To some countries it is a way of life, never stops. You too, in America, had your Civil War, your great tragedy that is still with you today. You had 9/11, but at least your country has not suffered a mass invasion and been subjected to tyranny like ours. So, we are thankful for this: to be here in your lovely home with good friends, to be free to say what we want, to dream, to work hard and be rewarded. That is a wonderful way to live one's life. We are all thankful for that."

"Here, here," Berger saluted lifting his glass. "Well spoken, Zoltan. I could not agree more."

We drank to the future, a murky silhouette against a backdrop of human atrocity past and present, and hoped for the best while a sense of uneasiness ran through us.

"So," Berger asked, "how did we all get here?"

"Taxi," Zoltan responded as he prepared to shove a large piece of dark meat into his mouth.

We all laughed.

"No, I mean, how did we or our ancestors come to the U.S.? I can tell you my story, as far as I know it, which isn't very far. My grandparents escaped Germany just before World War II. They owned a bakery, had relatives in Switzerland and the U.S. Closed up shop one afternoon before the borders closed to Switzerland, most likely sometime in 1938, told no one about what they were doing, left everything."

"Ah," Zoltan said. "My parents escaped Hungary in 1957

when borders open during period of chaos. They do much the same. They tell no one, leave everything. They hike out with just the clothes on their backs and my father have his medical diploma sewn into the lining of his jacket. Friends meet them at farmhouse on other side of border. That medical diploma worth its weight in gold. They come here. He work as orderly in hospital, get to know the docs. They help him get established here. First thing he do when he pass his medical exams here is buy tickets for us to go to opera. Family tradition."

Kristina said, "I came to America as part of UN scholarship in international studies set up by U.S. foundation. But now our country does not allow this foundation to support such programs. They have had to leave our country. So, I got lucky because when I graduate the Sessions School of Foreign Service, it offer me internship and then a job so I continue to be able to live here. How long that lasts," she shrugged, "I do not know."

"Yes," said Zoltan. "We must think of plan for this."

I realized that everyone's attention had now shifted to me. "I really don't know." I shrugged. "I mean it's so long ago, so many generations ago, that I don't really have any idea about the particulars."

"Well, give us the basics," Berger said.

"Originally, our family came over in the 1700s. I'm not even sure why or how. The last two generations before me were involved in any number of businesses. That's what brought them to Baltimore originally. They owned mills there." I shrugged. "That's all I know really."

Janet said, "Our family was Southern, ran a shipping related business in Norfolk. My parents moved from there to Philadelphia when I was a child. My dad worked for electrical utilities and that's where I grew up. But, like Thomas, everyone's scattered, there's no real family connectedness and when you meet them at weddings and funerals there's no real feeling that these are people you want to know better—just the opposite. We've just lost any sense of identity with our roots."

"Yeah," Berger observed, "it seems like all we do in our lives is become more and more disconnected. Part of it is technology, we're all living in little silos of texts and emails, part of it is we don't have appreciation for our individual history or our families' history, so we don't have any real sense of self beyond the everyday, no real sense of identity or awareness of history in general as an advisory resource to the future. It's like there begins to be no history, no connectedness, no attention span, no nothin'. I see it in business; more and more shortcutting. We fight against it, particularly in the hotel business, a people business."

"Mark," Janet commented, "these are the issues that I see in my practice over and over again, of people trying to cope with the isolation they've brought on themselves and not knowing the first thing about how to deal with it except through addiction of one kind or another. They have no perspective, no grounding in a greater sense of who they are and where they came from, no judgment. It's sad."

There was an uncomfortable pause before we all began to talk animatedly with one another. Tommie absently pantomimed eating his dinner while playing with a small fire engine from his pocket.

New bottles of wine seemed to keep materializing from the kitchen, each seemingly significantly better than the last, which only accelerated our consumption. We became louder and more boisterous, our stories getting ever more animated and hilarious. The kids crept off to the family room to watch TV. Eventually pieces of the pecan pie with freshly whipped cream made their way around the table and coffee was served and a bottle of cognac appeared from Berger's stash. In very high spirits we toasted one another.

Zoltan stood, swayed slightly and made a motion to tap his fork on the fine crystal Janet's mother had given us—until Janet shouted at him and took away the glass. She retrieved the kids from the family room for desert and Zoltan's instructions.

"Okay everyone," he told us, "time for our opera. Let me explain how it work. Who is familiar with opera *Don Giovanni?*"

Only Kristina raised her hand.

"Peasants!" Zoltan spat.

"This opera is a story about a great womanizer. For you, kids, that is a person who think it is fun to get as many women as he can to fall in love with him, and then he is unfaithful—just goes on to make the next woman fall in love with him, breaking the heart of his most recent conquest. This opera is about his downfall, and we are going to play the last part of the opera on the big screen TV and dress up in the parts being played and imitate the person playing them, acting out each part.

"I have costumes from theatre where a friend work. I borrow them. Now we do the final scene, very dramatic, where Don Giovanni burn up in fires from hell. We all get to act and sing. Well, not sing, because I will play opera performance on the television, but you can pretend to sing and imitate the part that is happening on TV and I narrate so we all know what is happening. This like big reality show, yes?"

"Great," said Berger. "I love reality shows. Sounds like a blast. Who do I play?"

"Oh, I have very special part for you. But first, the plot:

"Don Giovanni is a very bad man. Not only has he made all these women fall in love with him while he keeps scorecard of his conquests, but he's fought with and killed the Commendatore, the very distinguished father of his lover Donna Anna.

The Commendatore has now come back to life, a living statue from his mausoleum, for vengeance on Don Giovanni. Don Giovanni has the audacity to invite him to dinner and that is where we pick up opera. The characters will be as follows: I will be the Commendatore because I'm like a big ugly statue anyway, Thomas will be Don Giovanni, Berger will be Donna Anna, Kristina, Donna Elvira, another two-timed lover, Janet will be Don Ottavio, Donna Anna's new boyfriend, the kids will fill in here and there, imitating everyone else. Okay?

"I have opera on your TV recorder set at that scene where

we begin. And of course we need to turn on fireplace to imitate hell. Now we all change into costumes and act out and lip sync parts. You women take Berger upstairs and help him dress for part. Men go to other bedroom and dress for their part. We meet in fifteen minutes. Okay. Take drinks with you. Help put us in right frame of mind."

I was not thrilled with Zoltan's casting decision and planned to give him an earful the next time we were at the club. In any case, the women and Berger went up to our bedroom and the men and Tommie headed upstairs to our guest room and rummaged in the cardboard box.

Zoltan put on what appeared to be a Civil War Union military dress jacket, three sizes too small so that it bunched at the armpits and had no hope of ever being buttoned, and a British naval hat. I found a doublet that more or less fit and a hat with a feather plume. We both strapped swords around our waists.

We dressed Tommie in an oversized doublet and three cornered hat, dropped off a doublet, plumed hat and sword for Janet to play Don Octavio and then went back downstairs and waited and waited, Zoltan looking at his watch in frustration while giggles and uproarious bursts of laughter cascaded down to us from the master bedroom.

Suddenly there was a commotion and we heard their voices louder as they came down the stairway, Berger's words slurring a bit. I raised my eyebrows at Zoltan and shook my head. Could this end in any way that was good? I really doubted it. My friend was planting seeds of my destruction. My employment a week from now would be in Sessions University animal control. Tommie would be very pleased.

Berger turned the corner at the bottom of the stairs and flounced into the family room dressed in a billowing maroon filigreed Victorian hoop skirt, something out of a British drawing room drama. The women had smeared ruby red lipstick over his lips. He sported an unkempt harlot blond wig with a profusion of curls that hung to his shoulders. He curtsied to us, held out both hands and said in a falsetto voice, "Tahhh-Dahhh."

"Ohhh shit," I heard myself say though my laughter.

"You PERFECT!" Zoltan shouted. "I knew you would be!"

The women and kids were beside themselves giggling, Tommie in particular. Janet looked interestingly androgynous in her Don Octavio costume.

Zoltan took center stage. "Okay, so Sarah, get remote, turn on TV and when opera come up, hit Play."

The opera appeared on the screen frozen then came to life, the words of the Italian singing appearing in subscript English.

"Okay, here's where we are: they are in the midst of a wonderful dinner, but it has been interrupted by a knock at the door, Leporello—that be you, Tommie—you and I go out to the front door and you scream in horror just like is happening in the opera and come back in here."

I could see Tommie warming to the task. He and Zoltan went into the hall and a moment later Tommie screamed and the timing with the opera unfolding on the TV was almost on cue.

Zoltan peaked into the room. "Now, what is he screaming about? Ah, it is the arrival of the Commandatore. Okay, Tommie, you come back into the family room and act out what you see on screen, which is Leporello telling them that the Commendatore, the statue, has appeared as he had promised."

Tommie came back in and mimicked the scene on the television reasonably well, pretending to be singing and copying the hand and body motions of the on screen Leporello while I stepped in and took on imitating the Don Giovanni and we all began to imitate the parts being played on the television. I felt like a complete fool; however, everyone seemed totally amused and immersed in our performances. It struck me that the acting here played into Tommie's strong suit—he spent a good deal of his life mimicking behavior he didn't really understand or even care about.

Zoltan peeked back into the room. "Okay, so now I come back as the Commendatore, a big ugly fu… uh, person. And Don

Giovanni, you meet me as I come in the room. In this scene the Commendatore offers Don Giovanni a last chance to repent and Don Giovanni, being the charming pig that he is and an egotistical hard headed fool, he refuses."

The scene played out and Zoltan came back into the room, walking stiffly like a Frankenstein character, mouthing his recrimination and offering of a last chance to repent while I resisted and repulsed his offer.

"Now," said Zoltan, "we all become a chorus of demons who drag Don Giovanni over to the fireplace, that is hell, and he shouts and screams as he burns up."

As everyone surrounded me and began to lead me over to the fireplace to my imaginary banishment to hell, fire and brimstone, the doorbell rang faintly in the background.

An image flashed through my mind immediately. Bryan Fitz-Hugh. Shit!

Berger who was closest to the door said drunkenly, "I'll get it!" and before I could say anything, before anyone could move, he reeled and flounced in his dress, his lipstick even more smeared onto his face, into the hallway. I heard the door open.

"Oh, Bryan," Berger slurred, nonplussed. "Oh, hi, Ursula, come on in. Have a drink. We're just finishing up our little rendishion of Don Giovanni."

We heard Bryan demurring.

I slapped Zoltan's hand away from my arm and beat it to the front door, but everyone was already headed into the hallway so I became a witness rather than a player to what followed as we all pushed through the front door and stood on the flagstone steps.

I had never seen Bryan Fitz-Hugh look embarrassed, but there he was on our walkway at the base of the steps, red-faced and bug-eyed, holding a wrapped present, a cocktail table book by its appearance. Ursula stood behind him. Her expression was grim.

Fitz-Hugh began talking, a little too rapidly. "We were on a quick errand, taking a present to the former head of the alumni association and thought we might stop by here also and say hello and offer some holiday cheer to our new director of campaign and university communications and his family... But, um...at any rate I really can't stay. Just wanted to wish you all the best of holidays."

"Damn nice of you, Bryan," Berger said too loudly.

"Well, thanks Mark..." He handed the present to Janet. "We'll be going now."

He turned on his heel and he and Ursula walked rapidly back to his Mercedes and drove off.

"He's a bit uptight, isn't he?" Berger observed. "Heart's in the right place though, I guess. Seems kinda strange to come out all this way given his schedule."

"I think it was you he came out to see, Mark," I observed.

"Oh? Yeah..." A rueful and knowing smile came to his face. "Money makes jackasses out of us all, doesn't it?... Hey, speakin' ah jackasses, let's get out of these damn costumes. It was fun, Zoltan. Great party, you guys. Best Thanksgiving I've had in a while, but no wonder Bryan was acting a little weird. I usually only put on tha lipstick when we go dancin'."

"Was that his wife?" Janet asked as we crossed the threshold.

"No, his assistant."

"Oh... Well, she's a predator, isn't she? You should stay away from her."

"Yeah, that's good advice."

When we got inside, the phone was ringing, which startled us. Who could this be? Janet rushed to pick it up and then stood there listening while we watched her. After a few moments I saw a tear run down her cheek. We looked at one another, suddenly apprehensive. Obviously, something had gone very wrong somewhere and I could only think that it must be with a family member or friend or a patient.

"Yes," she said, finally, "no, I understand. There's nothing that could have been done... Okay, good. Thank you for calling."

She hung up the phone.

"What happened?" I asked.

"That was Dr. Compton's former wife. She and I talk once in awhile. Dr. Compton hanged himself this afternoon."

"Oh my God." I reached out and Janet came to me and we embraced, no longer Don Ottavio and Don Giovanni. I wished everyone else would go away, vanish.

XII
Confession

COMPTON'S SUICIDE HIT JANET HARD, and over the next weeks all she could do was barely cope with everyday responsibilities. Our evenings were silent and perfunctory. Trying to come up with something to break her out of her funk, I had her Bimmer flat bedded to the dealership for brand new brakes and full detailing, racking up a large credit card balance in the process, a vote of self-confidence that my new position would come through. She seemed to appreciate the gesture, but after a moment or two of nostalgic reflection and a ride in the cold with the top down and the heater and stereo blasting, the car quickly became an afterthought, took its orphaned place in the garage and began to collect dust and cardboard boxes again.

From what I could tell from the few times Fitz-Hugh and I crossed paths, his visit to our house on Thanksgiving had never occurred. He was his genial, charming and pleasant self. I knew better but was happy to let appearances become reality and have the incident slip quickly into the past.

The university board meeting came and went.

As I understood it from Ursula, during his opening remarks Bryan announced my new appointment, the rationale for it and my upcoming presentation of the communications master plan at the January board meeting. The news was received with a general reaction of approval and no questions.

The fact was that the board was solidly behind our president and inclined to indulge his interests and direction, confident that his leadership was moving Sessions University in a progressive, considered and savvy direction. After all, university admissions were expanding, the Campaign for Progress was successful, the faculty, at least by all appearances, the usual herd of cats and the medical center prosperous and on the cutting edge of numerous research discoveries. Compared to the rest of the college and university world, which seemed increasingly under siege, Sessions through Bryan Q. Fitz-Hugh's tenure seemed to be enjoying both a renaissance and a movement to the cutting edge of academe that was propelling it up the ranks of competing institutions.

I attended my first executive cabinet meeting in the president's office the following Wednesday. Participation was mandatory and of course the weather that morning brought blizzard-like conditions. Not wanting to miss my first meeting, I slalomed to campus in our van and, with the university officially closed, parked directly outside the administration building.

The deserted lower quadrangle was beautiful in new fallen snow as a light breeze continued to blow heavy flakes across the landscape. The air was crisp. A peaceful, muffled silence gathered around me as I walked from the car, every footstep making dry crunching noises in the snow.

I looked at the unwelcoming visage of the massive block of the administration building, forlorn holly wreaths side by side on the metal and plate glass door entrance, wondered yet again what the hell I had gotten myself into and went inside.

I still had until the end of December to complete the communications master plan. I had set meetings with Ken Depew, the comptroller, and Lusby later in the day to review the budget so that I could be assured that the scope of what I was doing was acceptable. Then I could flesh out the content knowing the ballpark in which I was playing.

Apparently these executive cabinet meetings in the president's office were think tank oriented, so I would be spared having to make the kind of interim report that could be picked apart by someone like Kravitz. While that was a relief, I didn't need this meeting, I needed more time.

Ms. Bemiss was there, wearing a jade green overcoat, fake fur hat, gold loop earrings and jade green nails. She permitted me to enter.

In attendance were Harold Ramis, director of the medical center, Lusby, Kravitz, Wentz, Ursula, and Reve. Depew entered the office close behind me.

Kravitz looked up as I came in. "Ahhh, the neophyte," he sneered to those at the table.

"Good morning," I replied, businesslike and even keeled, thinking, 'This is interesting. In private, Kravitz befriends me. In public, he subjects me to ridicule.' The hell with him.

Wentz, in a humorous, inappropriate gesture, wore a Rudolph the Red Nose Reindeer tie whose red nose flashed whenever he touched a hidden button at the tie's end. He flashed me, smiled and nodded hello.

Harold Ramis sat next to Wentz. He was a 60-something-year-old clinician with a glistening clean skull, massive grey eyebrows and titanium wire rim glasses, exuding rigorous intellectual competence. He was dressed in a heavy gray flannel, well-tailored, three piece business suit, heavily starched white shirt and red bow tie.

Not only had I never met Depew before, in all my years at the university I had never laid eyes on him. He shook my hand diffidently, not looking me in the eye, and said, "Hel-woe," in a strange voice, as if his throat was constricted.

He had stuck-out ears, a pendulous lower lip and an insouciant frown, a thin build with an ample little bowling ball of a gut. A buffalo red plaid hunting cap with ear flaps was pulled down on his head and he wore a lined canvas overcoat, grey acetate slacks even in this frigid weather, a worn-out gray mismatched jacket peeking out from the overcoat and a white shirt so thin I could make out his sleeveless t-shirt underneath. Wrap around aviator glasses with yellow lenses were perched on his nose, the lens color I guessed to ease eye strain from the continual reading of fine print—that or he had just come from the shooting range or from hunting rabbits.

He took a seat beside Kravitz, Ursula on his other side, next to Fitz-Hugh's place at the head of the table, Reve sitting across from her. I sat next to Lusby in part to size up Ramis and Depew as the meeting went on. Lusby glanced at me, gave me a cynical half smile.

There was the usual in air tension while we waited for Fitz-Hugh. It occurred to me that perhaps he liked to keep everyone waiting to emphasize that the meeting could not begin without him and to make an entrance.

I looked across at Ursula. She looked splendid as usual, frowning in concentration at documents she was scrolling through on her iPad. I thought about lunch in her apartment, snow falling outside her window. My momentary daydream was interrupted by the force of the building's heat coming on with a rush that blew hot dry air around us.

The metal door catch sounded and Fitz-Hugh strolled in. "Good morning everyone," he said, heading toward his desk. "Thank you for taking the trouble to be here. It's slippery out there." He picked up his leather portfolio and joined us at the head of the table.

"And how is our esteemed provost this morning?" he greeted Kravitz genially.

"A bit cold. Looking forward to your warming presence."

"Ahhh, Samuel, I don't know that I can help you there. But I am sure our lovely HVAC will rise to the task."

Kravitz smiled, as if indulging an idiot.

"Lovely tie," Fitz-Hugh observed to Wentz.

"'Tis the season."

"On some other tasteless planet perhaps."

Wentz shrugged and let Rudolph blink twice. Reve began to chuckle. There were some repressed smiles around the table, except for Kravitz and Depew.

Bryan turned to Lusby. "When do you go home?"

"Three days from now," Lusby replied. "Back on January third."

"Good, a nice long stay."

"Yeah. Hope I can handle it," Lusby said, shaking his head.

"I am sure you will."

He spoke to the rest of us. "Celeste and I hope we have the pleasure of seeing the rest of you at our Christmas reception on the 21st... I trust you know or have met Thomas."

The group gave the barest indication that they had.

Fitz-Hugh turned to business.

"As you know, the president's executive cabinet is about envisioning how our university can operate more creatively and effectively in the future.

"In this context let me outline some thoughts I've been having about how we might better encourage synergy between those faculty, researchers, scholars and fellows who have ideas, discoveries and inventions they would like to promote and external stakeholders who would have interest in either supporting their work or entering into entrepreneurial partnership with us.

"How do we foster an exchange among ourselves? And then how do we engage external stakeholders? To answer the first question: we have a medical campus; we have a university campus. We have distinguished faculty and researchers at each, and too often never the twain shall meet, or at least there are not any regular opportunities for communication and exchange.

"I would propose that where we have allied or aligned disciplines there ought to be a regular series of departmental peer exchanges—university faculty with the medical center, medical center faculty, researchers, clinicians and scientists with the university. This would provide a natural exchange of ideas and techniques and encourage team or partnership approaches to problem solving and innovation.

"As well, I would propose that there be a voluntary seminar for university and medical campus faculty, researchers, scholars and fellows in how to bring innovations and discoveries to market. This could be organized by our School for Continuing Education under Dr. Wentz's aegis and involve our corporate supporters as well as venture capital alumni and university aligned entrepreneurs."

From Wentz's ample gut Rudolph flashed his approval.

Kravitz began shaking his head and frowning in disapproval.

"Building on this, we might host an annual Innovation and Discovery Conference in which the local, regional and national business community is invited along with university and medical center faculty, fellows and scholars to hear speakers on key research, discovery and innovation subjects of the day as a way to share and cross-pollinate between university, medical and business interests. This takes our natural confluence of interests such as biomedical engineering and broadens the context to produce novel solutions to pending questions of the day. All and all these programs could involve over 45 different departments at our university, medical center and hospital.

"Finally, we could form an Entrepreneur Center in which faculty, researchers and others can team with postgraduates and entrepreneurs to pursue developing business products, plans and initiatives in concert with local, regional and national companies. Pharmaceutical companies in particular are likely to have a great interest in these businesses and partnerships. Now, I should add that none of these ideas are particularly original; they are all in one form or another in existence at other universities. It's simply time for Sessions to get with the program.

"Harold, your thoughts?"

I could see immediately how all this worked. Fitz-Hugh and Ramis had been planning these initiatives for many months. It was all a slam-dunk. The proposed initiatives were already fully conceived, budgeted and ready for launch. I looked around the table. Ramis contemplating his remarks, everyone else with eyes downturned, except Kravitz whose countenance was beginning to screw into obstinate fury.

Ramis commented, authoritative yet friendly, "This all

sounds well-conceived but very ambitious. Over time, however, these kinds of initiatives could very well be phased in and make quite a difference. Let me assemble a team of our faculty and researchers to work with the administration, Dr. Kravitz, Dr. Wentz and select department heads to see how we might best pull this off and come back to you with a workable timetable."

There was a pause. Heads lifted and we all turned and looked to Kravitz for his response.

"My dear Mr. President, my esteemed colleagues, Dr. Ramis," Kravitz said, his hands before him, fingers touching, "we are an institution of higher learning, *not*," he sniffed, "slavish enablers of the military-industrial-pharmaceutical complex."

Wentz rolled his eyes, and with an imperceptible movement flashed Rudolph's nose twice in disapproval.

Lusby's glum, stoical face reddened as he suppressed the hint of a smile. Reve looked down and away to hide his expression.

Kravitz continued, "Let me sum up the present situation from many of the university faculty's point of view.

"With further reductions in state and federal support, we in the humanities endure cutbacks while unfathomable largesse is dumped in the laps of those on the medical campus and those here whose research is technical, scientific or business oriented. In other words, the humanities are being pushed aside in favor of the pursuit of the almighty buck. The worship of mammon has become our modus operandi and we lionize all who possess it.

"Look at our board of trustees. How many educators, how many academics, how many professors are contained in its membership? How many members are women, how many of ethnic, racial or gender diversity are there? It is an old boys club of businessmen with a few members who are stereotypical, symbolic nods to political correctness, the minimum required to blunt criticism.

"All this while the combination of related tuition hikes and increasing student indebtedness have created a parent and student body basically indifferent to the real intrinsic value of higher education, focused instead on jobs, jobs, jobs. These same forces have led to a frantic self-justifying search on behalf of administrators for value in education related only to resulting employability, completely ignoring the true, timeless values that higher education might impart—for instance, the ability to think independently and analytically and to understand current events in the context of historical lessons learned.

"We are an institution of higher learning, of intellectual pursuit and academic attainment. Sessions University is not some mongrelized community college employment machine, nor should it exist as a tool for philistine, monetary gain. You're trampling on a centuries old role. We are the preservers of culture, the above-the-fray force for the higher forms of civilization. Learning for its own sake has value. We're not some career college pawn of business. Our job is to keep the barbarians from the gate!"

Heads turned toward Fitz-Hugh, who smiled, relaxed, friendly, seeming to welcome this dialogue. I looked at Ursula—grim expression. Depew—no expression. Wentz—neutral, no flashing of the tie.

"Samuel," Fitz-Hugh said, "as always, I deeply respect your logical, erudite and well-reasoned thinking. In fact, I applaud it.

"However, as you point out, we do face a fiscal dilemma, which is how to best support higher education and specifically the humanities. The fact is that we are in the business of creating the university of tomorrow. If we stick to the old school, so to speak, we will no doubt see, as we have seen elsewhere, our own demise. Surely you recognize that. We must move forward to survive. That does not mean we have any intention for you to be eclipsed but rather that you come along with us on a rising tide. The fact is that our success in these other endeavors creates the funding to assure the continuation and advancement of the departments whose value is in the cultural, moral, intellectual and analytical capability that will be imparted to future generations of students.

"The university of the future's model is the best opportunity for us not only to survive, but thrive. It will be one that is able to serve multiple kinds of students from traditional, nontraditional, adult, part time, ethnic, international through different educational formats. Gone are the days when we could focus almost exclusively on one kind of student and offer one kind of education.

"Further, we will succeed educationally and monetarily through establishing multiple alliances and partnerships. For instance, what we are doing in the international market not only diversifies and strengthens the institution, its exchange and intellectual discourse but it brings in a far more diversified revenue stream not to mention further opportunities for fundraising.

"The facts are that some significant portion of the funding we receive in other areas is unrestricted and can benefit the humanities. Plus, an increased focus on strengthening the very departments and programs you cherish are part of the Campaign for Progress, which can make all the difference in their future. But we need you as a partner in these efforts to be successful."

Kravitz now had his arms folded and an ugly scowl on his face. "All these inspiring and soothing and uplifting words, Dr. Fitz-Hugh, cannot disguise the fact that you are building a treasure trove and allocating the humanities a yearly pittance. How many more times will I be forced to deny tenure, will we have to cut our departments, laying off good scholars, earnest and hardworking people with families to support, cast them aside because there are insufficient funds? How many more times do I ruin people's lives and degrade our academic product with short term adjuncts and underqualified hourly minions? How many more times? We need money now!"

Bryan put his hands out, palms open. "Samuel, you yourself have seen the Campaign for Progress plans. Only small amounts are to go to the endowment, much of it is for current programming. Let the campaign unfold. You are being too impatient."

"All I know is what I see, which is money being allocated to all these new ventures and none of it coming our way. How can

Sessions afford to do all that you want it to do? How can the center hold here on this campus? All I see is expansion, bastardization, *abomination*. I will not stand for it! I will not! I will take this to the Faculty Senate. I am prepared to take my opposition to your high-handed, self-aggrandizing, so-called leadership to my esteemed colleagues. You may think you can act like a Fortune 500 CEO but I have news for you: you are answerable to us, the faculty of this institution. I have drawn up a list of grievances. I will propose to the Senate that there be an outside audit of the university's finances."

Kravitz stood, grabbed his scarf from the back of his chair, threw each side of it defiantly around his neck, grabbed his overcoat and stomped out of the room, his unfastened galoshes making loose rubber and odd metallic sounds.

When the door had clicked shut, Fitz-Hugh held up his hands in a 'what-can-you-do' gesture, shrugged and said, "Our esteemed colleague has, unfortunately, left, along with his best friend, his inflated sense of himself. We wish him well. Now, can I get some input from the rest of you concerning about how we might best implement the concepts I outlined earlier?"

The meeting was reasonably productive after that, with Ramis agreeing to convene the dean of the School of Medicine and key department heads at the medical center to meet with Wentz, Ursula and select department heads at the university. At the end Fitz-Hugh said that once all the preliminaries were out of the way and a final plan, timetable and budget were in place, he would meet with Kravitz and bring him up-to-date. I thought, 'That'll be an interesting meeting.' I found myself glancing furtively around the table to see how this statement was received: downcast eyes, neutral expressions, except Reve, whose expression resembled that of someone who had just heard the news of a particularly interesting prize fight.

Afterwards, as Ursula and I were walking toward her office, I asked, "Are those meetings always like that?"

She sighed. "The provost is getting much worse."

"Yeah. Should I be concerned? I mean, can Kravitz actually upset the apple cart here?"

She shook her head. "He has a smaller following than he knows and not many new converts. He could make some very troublesome noise however. But we will take care of it," she said with a grim smile.

I nodded.

"I am too busy to see you today," she told me.

"Okay. I get it."

"I am sorry."

"Me too. See you soon, I hope."

"Yes."

Outside the sky was now clear and the air clean and moist. I moved my car to the parking lot, walked to my office, worked through lunch fueled by a couple power bars and coffee and trudged over to the administration building to meet with Depew, then Lusby.

I took the elevator to the fourth floor, where I had never been before.

The doors parted and I was back in time to some 1960/'70s designed, windowless office space with cubicles and a low ceiling with a lattice work of cheap acoustical tiles punctured by nasty, bright, faintly humming florescent lights extending into the distance to a horizon of a far wall that might actually be in another dimension. The place had the smell of new carpet and overheated stale air.

At the first inhabited cubicle I asked the gum-chewing woman perched in front of a large monitor where Depew's office might be and in a local accent she told me to go around to the right and look for the door with his name on it about halfway down the hallway.

I found him in his office sitting behind his grey steel case desk. He was staring at the doorway, his mind a thousand miles away in who knew what realm. His gaze then focused on me and a flicker of recognition flashed across his features.

"Have a seat," he said in his strangulated voice, hand involuntarily pushing his yellow-lensed wraparounds up to the bridge of his nose.

I sat down, pulled the master plan budget from my portfolio and handed it to him. "Any advice you can give me on this I'd appreciate. Not like I do this every day."

He scanned it, expressionless.

"Okay," he said finally, laying the budget on his desk and pushing it back in my direction. "It looks in line, but it's a one year budget."

"Yeah."

"It's a five-year campaign; one year done. Make it a four-year budget. My guess would be that you need to factor in communications planning in line with the regional, national and international roll out in years two and three and in the last year, should the Campaign for Progress succeed as planned, there will be a large celebration and a lot of publicity. Factor all that in. It will look more realistic."

"Good thinking. Thanks. But you realize we're talking now about an overall expenditure of over 5 million bucks?"

"Yep. That'll work. It's the capital campaign. It's all fungible."

"What do you mean by that?"

Depew looked at me levelly, watery blue eyes behind the yellow lenses. "It means that as long as the campaign is being run responsibly and keeping within commonly accepted guidelines for expenditures it can more or less fund any viable program."

"Viable meaning?"

"Whatever Bryan wants."

"That's helpful. Thanks."

"Think nothing of it. I mean that," he looked me square in the eyes, "literally. We never had this conversation."

"Sure," I said, thinking, 'What a strange little man.' "Well, in any case, thanks. I appreciate your help nonetheless."

"Okay. Check it out with Frank. He's the guru."

"My next stop."

Lusby was down on the third floor in an office similar to Ursula's in layout and space, a cubicle with a nice view, but very different in its décor. The left wall was covered with grip and grin photos, signed with congratulations or appreciation by several college and university presidents and by leading board members at those institutions, several Fortune 500 CEOs, a few U.S. senators and members of congress, a governor or two, several billionaires. The right wall was covered with a massive university seal flag. It was all very impressive. I glanced behind me and caught a glimpse of family portraits and a small table with family vacation pictures.

Lusby sat behind his mahogany desk on which were nick-knacks from his various assignments. His swivel chair was turned toward the window and he was staring out at the pastoral snow scene on the lower quad, I presumed with the same distant expression I had just seen on Depew's face.

I recalled the story that after one particularly well lubricated reception at Stewart House, Lusby had stumbled his way back to his office where Reve, Wentz and others had found him in his chair, feet propped on his desk, snoring peacefully, hands folded corpse-like across his chest.

They had draped him in the university flag and Reve had snapped numerous cellphone pictures. Fortunately, being clever, he had resisted the impulse to share pictures with anyone except by passing his phone around at certain key moments of after work camaraderie. Of course, there was implicit blackmail involved, but no one seemed to care.

"Frank?"

Lusby jumped and swiveled around with such velocity that he almost crashed over.

"Oh, sorry," he laughed. "You startled me!"

"Sorry."

"No problem. What can I do for you?"

He seemed to have forgotten our appointment, so I said, "I wanted you to review a draft of the first year budget for the master plan. Just had Depew look at it. He more or less passed on it but said to extend it for the remaining four years of the campaign with emphasis on the communications required by its roll-out in years two and three and a bump at the end to take into consideration all the publicity for the campaign's success."

"Good thinking. Yeah."

I pushed the budget across his desk and waited while he examined it, glancing around at the left wall and the snow scene outside his window.

Lusby looked up at me from the budget. "I see we're creating our own television studio."

"Yeah. How else do we best control Bryan's foray into the world's consciousness? You think that's a bit over the top?"

"Hell, Bryan will *love* it."

"That's a relief."

"Look, Thomas, think of it this way. The university runs as a non-profit entity. As we heard so painstakingly eloquently from our pain in the ass provost, these are very tight times. A capital campaign, on the other hand, while it is part of the university, runs very much like a business, and in business one has to take risks and spend money to make money. One of the most important parts of the campaign, next to the education, cultivation and solicitation of donors is raising the profile and brand of the university so that its perceived value is significantly enhanced. All this works hand in glove as a part of its success. That's why Bryan chose you, to get us out of the same ol' same ol' box that university communications has been in for about twenty years." He glanced back at the budget. "You know what I really like about this budget?"

"No?"

"Your salary. That shows you get it. Plus I like what it says about the whole program—that it's being run by a pro. I think Bryan will like it too." He pushed the budget back at me. "Go for it, Thomas. Lead us. We need it."

"Thanks, Frank."

"Now if you don't mind, I've got a shitload of other things to worry about. Glad you're not one of them."

"Thanks. I'll finish up the entire draft and get it to you and Ursula for review and to give to Bryan."

"Good plan."

I walked out of his office feeling like I was walking several inches off the ground. I checked my phone and found that Zoltan had called.

I called him when I got outside.

"What are you up to?" I asked him.

"Ah, Thomas, no one is here. The lab is deserted. I am not sure why I came here. Where are you?"

"On campus. Had to be at my first executive committee meeting, plus work on the plan."

"How it going?"

"I'll tell you about it. I've got to go back to the office and make some changes to the master plan budget. See you in about two hours, okay?"

I trudged through the snow across the lower quadrangle to the marble stairs that climbed to the upper quad and Hart Hall. The wind was picking up and there were now signs of life around the campus, mostly maintenance crews manning snow-clearing tractors, others with shovels to begin clearing stairs and walkways. The sounds of their activity echoed sharply in the cold, moist air.

The outer door to the building was unlocked but I had to open up our office suite, the still silence of all that empty space ghostly lit by reflection from the snow outside made me hurry back to my office so that I could distract myself with my work as soon as possible.

I extended the budget out to four years and altered the numbers in various categories to reflect the budget requirements of the three additional years, thought of some cues to drop into the evolving master plan and pulled that up. When I was done, there was still a half-hour to go before I'd meet Zoltan at the club, but by then I was fed up with work and the isolation of my surroundings so I went over to the club early.

The temperature outside was falling, the light fading as I hustled along.

The club was deserted but filled with Christmas decorations, an actual real Christmas tree in the front hall, plastic fir trimming and lights running the length of the hallway, an electric candle in each window. As I walked through the tables in the bar, I saw Lusby sitting by himself not at his usual table, but off in an unlit corner.

On impulse I turned, walked over and sat down. The waiter came with my beer.

On the small table in front of Lusby were two empty martini glasses, a half full third and untouched bowls of bar snacks.

"You okay?" I asked.

Lusby looked at me, frowned, then pulled himself together. "Sure," he slurred slightly. I was struck by the change that had come over him since seeing him in his office just hours before.

"Uhhhh, okay. To be honest, you look like somebody just died."

Lusby laughed hollowly. "You may be right."

"Come on, Frank. What's going on? You're scaring me a little."

He considered my statement, shrugged.

We sat silently for a time, Lusby sipping occasionally on his drink, the atmosphere spooky.

"You know," Lusby said suddenly in guarded tones, apropos of nothing, "Who does God talk to?"

"What?"

"It's a rhetor-hical question...to illustrate a point."

"The point being?"

"I have one thing only in common with the big guy. I got no one to talk to."

"Geez, Frank. You sound friggin' pitiful."

"I *am* friggin' pitiful!"

He paused for a very uncomfortable amount of time, then said, "Thomas, you're a good guy, and I know you can keep your mouth shut." He held a forefinger aloft. "We have a bigggggg fucking problem."

"Yeah, I know, the provost…"

"It's *not* the provost. The fucking weasel."

"Oh… You can't talk to me about it?"

"You'll wish I hadn't."

"Well, can't you talk about the problem to your colleagues at your company?"

"Nah. Sessions is our biggest account; these are tough times in the fundraising-consulting business. At headquarters they look at me almost as the savior of the company. I come to them with this problem. Panic. Kill the messenger. I don't think that's an option."

"You're beginning to worry me."

Lusby took a swig of his martini and stared me straight in the eye. "Thomas," he said in his soft and smoky way, "I take great pride on these assignments, in learning and/or discovering everything there is to know about the organization, secret or not secret. I am always the one guy who knows it all. But in all honesty, I don't know the answer to this one. All I know is who does know the answer."

"Bryan?"

"Yeah, and one other."

"Who would be?"

"Depew."

"So, why don't you ask him?"

Lusby looked at me like I was stupid. "Already did."

"His answer?"

"Stonewalled me. Just shook his head. Wouldn't say a word… There are things happening here that I can't explain, that I'm very concerned about."

"Such as?"

"Gifts, large wire transfers of money are coming into the

campaign. They just appear more or less out of nowhere. Usually over the weekend."

"Have you asked Bryan about them?"

"Sure. He told me I've got more important things to worry about. Practically patted me on the head like you would a twelve-year-old. Very patronizing. I'm a good soldier. I say okay, if that's the way you want it. I once kidded him about it being drug money."

"How'd he like that?"

"Told me to shut the fuck up and never bring it up again."

"Oops."

"Yeah. Was not my best day here."

"How much we talking about?"

"Millions and millions. Never from the U.S.; always from some foreign account. No traceable ID. Central Europe. The Middle East. China. Latin America."

"Wow."

"I'm having bad dreams about this shit. On one hand, I really do not want to know. On the other, I better find out. I like my job, like Bryan, like Sessions, you, a lot of other good folks. I don't want to be complicit in something that could hurt everyone around me, cost me my job, ruin Bryan, Sessions. I've just got a very bad feeling about all this."

"Could it be Berger or another board member?"

"I thought of that, but all the little signs just don't add up to that. The whole thing has more of a covert smell to it, not like someone trying to be anonymous. I'm thinking maybe friends in high places, acronym agencies that no one knows about."

"Shit...the secretary of state?"

"Not directly, but maybe somehow through other untraceable sources."

"How can I help?"

"I don't know. I haven't clue. That's what's so scary. I'm baffled. But we've got over $17 million of this shit in the coffers. Occasionally large sums are transferred out and no one says anything about where the money went. I don't know what to do."

"Is it designated at all?"

"Nope. Comes in as wire transfers with no designation, unrestricted; when it goes out, same thing. Where it goes, who knows."

I thought for a few moments. "Is Kravitz on to any of this?"

"Oh, hell no. He's blind, deaf and clueless. But I'm concerned because with his current tact he may be getting himself in way over his head, maybe playing a game that's much more dangerous than he knows."

"Jesus. Should I ever hear anything, I'll let you know."

Lusby exhaled loudly. "Damn, I'd appreciate that. You're a good man, Thomas."

"No I'm not, but I try."

"Okay, I gotta go." Lusby stood unevenly.

Instinctively, I also stood. "Where are you going?"

"Downtown with Wentz."

"Oh. I'll walk out with you. Doesn't Wentz know what's going on with these anonymous gifts?"

"I don't think so; he would have said something and he knows everything. This is deep shit."

As we walked down the hallway we passed Zoltan walking toward the bar. He took one look at us, raised his eyebrows and passed without a word. Lusby did not even notice.

Outside it was almost dark, the temperature was dropping rapidly, our breaths surrounded us in large clouds. It occurred to me that there would be icy patches everywhere on my drive home.

Lusby turned to me. "Not a word to anyone. Even Zoltan."

"Sure," I told him and watched him saunter unevenly toward the parking lot.

I went back inside and sat down with Zoltan as the waiter brought my second beer.

"What that all about with Lusby?" he asked. "It all look very serious."

"It was and it is," I told him. Then I told him everything that had happened that day. It took a while. Zoltan said little but listened carefully with an expression of deep concentration and concern.

When I had finished, he said, "Thomas, my friend, we do not know any of what you just said about these gifts, nor do we want to know any more about it."

"Yeah. There's something going on here way bigger than Sessions University or the two of us."

"Yes. You must promise me something."

"What?"

"You never mention any of this to Ursula, nor ask her anything."

I thought for a time. "Yeah, you're right. She would be obligated to then tell Bryan that I knew. Plus she wouldn't tell me a damn thing."

"Yes... Well, now we know how Beijing center get funded."

"Damn. This is a tricky situation."

"Maybe dangerous too. You best let your fun with this Ursula go away, but slowly, over time, so as to not raise any suspicion."

"Yeah. Easier said than done."

Zoltan said nothing, pulled out a roll of bills he kept in his jacket pocket, paid me surreptitiously for his drinks and rose. "I have to go catch my train to Washington."

"It's your night for that, isn't it?"

"Yes."

"Perhaps Kristina will shed some more light on this situation."

"I doubt it...because I not say anything to her about this."

"Yeah."

XIII
Bryan's Approval

THE NEXT THREE WEEKS FLEW BY, Janet a Shakespearian ghost, my courses on autopilot, the master plan filling in and the kids involved with pre-holiday tests, Christmas pageants and parties until finally the holidays arrived and they were out of school.

Usually the week before Christmas was a time of blessed tranquility, with no classes and the university all but closed. Time to catch up and spend time with Janet and the kids, take in some movies, see friends.

But this Christmas there was no tranquility. I had been at the office all week and over the weekend putting final touches on the master plan and had emailed copies to Lusby and Ursula several days before. Their feedback had been positive and Ursula had set a meeting with Fitz-Hugh to review it.

The Tuesday before Christmas I drove to campus and again it was deserted. A cold snap had arrived the night before with high winds and temperatures in the low 20s. The university roads were caked with salt, sand and patches of ice and the grounds were a flat white of old snow with a few brown bare spots showing through. I parked my car outside the administration building and hustled to get inside, a heavy wind from the northwest pushing me from behind the way a teacher pushes an errant child into the classroom.

The administration building was dimly lit and empty. I took the elevator to the third floor, walked past vacant offices and desks and glanced in at Ursula. She was dressed in a loose fisherman's knit beige sweater and blue jeans and was frowning at her monitor. She brightened when she saw me, blew me a kiss.

"It will go well," she smiled.

"Good to know. Thanks."

"See you afterward."

"Yeah."

I walked down the hall. Ms. Bemiss was not at her desk. Even she took holidays. I knocked lightly on Fitz-Hugh's door.

I heard, "Come on in, Thomas," and pushed the door open.

Fitz-Hugh rose from behind his desk, his blazer on the back of his chair, the sleeves of his open, pale blue shirt rolled up, revealing his platinum Rolex and arms tanned from weekends golfing in Naples. "Glad to see you, Thomas," he said and shook my hand, putting a hand on the side of my shoulder to steer me. "Let's sit at the conference table, a bit less formal."

Two copies of my master plan had been placed on the table.

We pulled out chairs beside them so that we faced one another.

"You know," he said, "as you might have suspected, I asked Fein for a master plan about eighteen months ago. Three months after the thirty days I gave him as a deadline for the plan I received a dozen pages of useless derivative drivel. Since then I've been on a mission to identify someone who could do things right. I deputized Frank to see whether there was anyone on campus who was up to the job. You know, you can hire outside help, but they rarely get it right, too tone deaf to the different cultures and nuances of our many constituencies, how the history of the place plays into present branding, that sort of thing. So, Frank found you and I liked you immediately, could see that we were very much on the same page. And damn it if you didn't do it, Thomas. This is the plan I was looking for. Congratulations."

"Thanks," was all I could muster. "I'm really glad you like it." I was semi-paralyzed by his enthusiasm and good will. My words sounded idiotic to me, because they were.

Smiling at me, he picked up my plan, hefted it admiringly and placed it back down on the table.

"Some things that I would point out that I greatly admire about your work:

"First, it addresses the whole university yet is constituency targeted. By that I mean you have figured out for each constituency how to best promote our core mission as a global university, paying special attention to admissions, which is of course the financial engine that powers the entire university enterprise.

"Second, you have placed the emphasis for communication on the most direct, user-friendly means of delivery for each stakeholder, social media for applicants and recent grads, a multiplicity of approaches both generational and by discipline targeted for alumni of the university, the medical school and our faculty and medical staff with the message on point for all of them, articulated by the president, endorsed by division and department leaders, board members and luminaries here and abroad.

"Third, through the website, surveys, social media, podcasts and the president's forum you've brought interactive communication to the forefront of our communications process.

"Finally, through organizing our media approach, I can now see my calendar filling up with national press, television, radio interviews here and abroad, so that I can literally take our message to the world. I cannot tell you how pleased I am by this plan. Now we need to act on it. I want you to present the basics of it by Power Point at the next board meeting. Just superb."

"Thank you, Bryan," was all I could muster again in response. "Is the budget okay?"

He waved a hand dismissively. "Lusby and Depew have signed off on it."

"Okay."

He stood. "Thanks so much for coming by, and, again, wonderful work."

I followed his lead, stood and said, "Thanks," walked to the door and let myself out.

Down the hall I walked into Ursula's office and carefully shut the door behind me.

She turned in her chair as I sat in front of her desk. "How did it go?" she asked

"Unbelievable. Just fantastic. He loves the plan."

"Good. Are you ready for the board presentation?"

"Yeah, now that I have his blessing. I'll send over the Power Point to you and Lusby in the next few days for your review."

"Good. I have made all the arrangements for the board meeting at Berger's estate. Your room is across the hall from mine."

"Ah, you think of everything."

"Yes, except all the things that happen around here that I do not know about beforehand."

"Yeah, that's probably quite a bit."

"Speaking of this, there is a big problem on the horizon. Kravitz is putting a demand for an independent audit of university finances to vote in the Faculty Senate."

"Uh oh."

"Yes. This is serious, perhaps more from a public relations standpoint than anything else. They have not a clue what they are asking and no proof of anything. It would be largely a vote caused by Kravitz's hostility and suspicion. So, we will profess innocence, probe their ignorance, make them look foolish if possible, sow seeds of doubt and stall while we work on the politics of the situation. It is not like Kravitz is universally supported, and we too have our allies."

"Sounds like fun."

"It is the way things work."

"Yeah. Unfortunately."

"Yes."

"Okay, so tell me about the board meeting. All I know is that it's at Berger's place."

"Yes. We and most of the board are flying in Sunday evening. The board meeting takes place the next day. Berger's place is very private and exclusive, on its own peninsula. When he is not there, it functions as a hotel. In the winter he keeps his sail-boat there and his yacht."

"His yacht?"

"Yes, it is over 150 feet long. From what we understand he charters it except for occasions like this. We spend the night at his estate, which has been vacated for us, and hold the board meeting aboard the yacht. Quite the show."

"That's for sure," I said, shaking my head in disbelief. "There's always a bit of a disconnect between the guy I know and all his businesses and possessions."

Ursula smiled. "He is a man full of surprises."

"So, we've discovered." I stood. "I have to get back to work."

"I will see you for lunch?"

"Sure."

She smiled. "Good."

XIV
The Sweetest Smell

BEFORE DAWN ON THE FIRST SUNDAY IN JANUARY I LEFT
JANET AND OUR WARM BED AND HOUSE, drove in the
dark in pelting sleet to the airport and boarded a plane
for Miami.

In the air, at 36,000 feet with growing anticipation, I watched
stark snow covered vistas and iced over lakes give way to brown
countryside and muddy tributaries, then to the winding rivers of
the low country and onward over a wide expanse of sparkling
ocean. Finally, as we banked to the west and landed, the bright
sand beaches and lush green of the barrier islands and lagoons
of south Florida appeared, high-rises lining the beach, beyond
them residential neighborhoods amongst palm trees.

The jetway leaving the plane was hot and humid and my
winter khakis, long sleeved shirt, shoes and socks suddenly
hung heavily on me and begged to be tossed off.

At the bottom of the escalator at the terminal's exit there
was a small, silent Cuban American driver in a white guayabera
and black slacks holding up a sign with my name on it. He
brought a smile to my face; I never thought I'd be one of those
people being fetched at the airport. We shook hands, he flashed
me his best smile and I followed him outside and down a long
sidewalk and was surprised to see a new stretch limousine. This
felt a bit ridiculous. I took off my coat, settled into the back,
glanced at the mini bar and television, the various papers and
magazines, took a quick video with my cell phone and texted it

to Janet with exclamation points then turned my attention to the scenery.

Thankfully Christmas had been uneventful, Zoltan in Washington with Kristina, the master plan put to bed, the Power Point completed. Janet had seemed to recover a bit from her post-Compton depression. Perhaps it was the distraction of our new year-old female Dalmatian rescue, Sparky, and the attention and, frankly, mothering she required. Tommie of course had thought up her name months before and there was no persuading him that Sparky was a male canine name. He spent most of the day yammering about and playing with her, even neglecting Tommie Town for the time being. The dog had an immediate attachment to Janet, was happy to have any attention from any of us, happy to join me in my den when I worked, happy to hang out with Sarah, playful with Tommie, remorseful about her few toilet training accidents that had carried over from her previous, no doubt neglectful ownership.

For New Year's Janet and I and the kids had enjoyed a quiet evening at home, the dog the center of our attention. Quietly I congratulated myself on our decision to go ahead with the inquiry and adoption process, desperate at the time for some change in our lives. Luckily it had been a very good change. The Rescue League had recently posted her and we were able to adopt her in short order.

The traffic surrounding the airport was dense and chaotic. The surrounding bad roads, parking lots, warehouses and cheap store fronts all seemed covered with a thick layer of tan-gray dust. Over the next miles we wove in and out of lanes exiting onto different highways. Eventually we left the cluster of low-lying city for suburbia and beyond into the countryside, then took an exit onto a sparsely populated two-lane road and after a time took a left turn.

We slowed and made our way down a seemingly endless, winding, landscaped sand road, palm trees high on either side. Lush flowering pink and white oleanders, pink and coral hibiscus and other flowering plants whisked by the window. Small lakes with white and gray herons, white, brown and gray ibis, flocks of flamingos, each formed a small oasis, until we came to a very high white stucco wall capped by red Spanish tiles with an entryway through a thick archway, its end blockaded by two massive dark red painted wooden doors, a small guard house and office built into the wall to the left. The driver spoke in Spanish to a uniformed guard who cleared us in. It felt like we had just crossed the border into some Latin American country.

The interior was a combination of a nature park and golf course, acres of clear vistas of lawn under tall palms, crushed shell paths winding around gardens of blossoming flowers, ponds and lakes, profusions of flamingos, ducks, spoonbills, ibis.

In the distance was a white stucco Mediterranean revival estate house—now hotel—with a red tile roof and gables fronting the Atlantic, lines of palms trees along the shore. The hotel looked as if it had perhaps fifty plus rooms, large terraces and gardens surrounding it. I wondered about the history of this place, what famous people had graced its hallways and terraces, how Berger had come to own it.

We pulled up under an archway. I tipped the driver goodbye and a bellboy picked up my carry-on and suit bag before I could and led me inside. The lobby was refreshingly cool and high ceilinged, white stucco with massive exposed dark brown beams, a broad blade ceiling fan turning languidly in its heights. Dark red tile floors led to doors opening onto a large terrace overlooking the ocean and the beach below, salt and vegetation scented air and the sound of breaking surf pulsing through to the open entrance.

As I approached the check-in counter, the man in front of me, who had just finished registering, turned on his heel and ran straight into me.

It was Kravitz.

He looked at me indignantly.

"Ah, neophyte. How is your *pathétiquement petite et ignorants* communications world?"

"No complaints."

"Communications? Is it not just another word for *connerie*?"

"Just another discipline under the larger cow pie of the humanities, isn't it?"

Kravitz spit out, "*Connard* discipline."

"Suit yourself, Dr. Kravitz.

"I shall, I shall." He smiled at me with wicked contempt and walked around me.

"I'll give your regards to Howard when I next see him."

"Oh do, do, by all means do."

"Fucker," I heard myself saying under my breath.

I turned to the counter and found the staff staring at me.

After checking in, the bellboy and I took a small metal cage elevator to the third floor, made our way down a clean white stucco and tile hallway to my room at the end, which featured sliding doors opening to a balcony overlooking the ocean. I freshened up and changed into summer slacks, a short sleeve dress shirt, summer tie and blue blazer. I stood on the balcony for a time to take in the ocean, the sound of the surf, the beauty of the shoreline and beach and then went downstairs.

The cocktail reception on the terrace was just beginning.

A waiter approached me and took my order for a beer.

Wentz, Lusby and Reve were standing off to the left. Reve, by the look of the unhappy roll of fat puffed out over his black alligator belt, had gained another ten pounds.

To the right Fitz-Hugh, with Ursula by his side, was talking to a small group of board members, including Mark Berger, who saw me, grinned, moved his eyebrows up and down significantly and motioned for me to join them.

"Thomas," Fitz-Hugh said as I walked up to them, "let me introduce you to our board chairman, Fritz Johnson."

Johnson was a very large man, at least six feet, six inches tall and probably weighing around two hundred and fifty pounds. I had read his bio and knew his bulk was by no means all flab; in his college years he had been a four-year starter at tight end for Texas. His hair was black shot with grey, slicked back. He had a big face and a big, fleshy nose and was every inch a Texan, from his string tie to his tooled black boots and hand crafted silver belt buckle with a large turquoise center.

"Thomas, glad to meet chew, son," he told me with a heavy Texas accent as my hand disappeared in his. As we shook I realized that he was being careful not to crush my hand, a subtlety I surely appreciated. "You've written a mighty fine re-port. Glad you're here. Look forward to your talk."

"Thank you, sir."

"And this is Father Lanier," Bryan said, "who serves as university chaplain and as rector of the university."

Father Lanier shook my hand with a limp diffidence as if he were loaning me his hand temporarily only to take it back again. He was difficult to read, his pocked complexion either deeply tanned or debauched—or perhaps both—his eyes lizard green and shifty.

"It's fine work you've done, young man. Our national church could certainly use some of what's in here. Mind if I share it with them?"

"No, not at all." I sensed that this occasion was an introduction only and glanced at Ursula who confirmed it. "Good to meet both of you."

I walked over to Wentz's group. "Is Fein here?"

"He's over in the marina," Reve told me, "setting up the yacht for tomorrow's meeting."

"Okay. I just want to see the room, make sure my presentation's loaded and ready to go. Where's the marina?"

"It's over on the other side of the peninsula. You'll see it tomorrow. Too far to go now; you'd be late for dinner. So relax. Get there early tomorrow. There's a small shuttle that can take you there anytime."

"Okay. How're you guys?"

Wentz motioned at me with his usual martini in his fat hand. "So, Thomas, you smell anything?"

"You're not that close, thankfully."

"Ah," Reve commented, "you picked up Zoltan's shtick. Good. I love it when people insult Wentz… It seems so…right."

"Thomas," Wentz observed, ignoring both of our comments, "I smell the sweetest scent of all. Other than the occasional pussy, that is."

Reve and Lusby grinned.

"What would that be?"

"Money! Money, money, money. Take a deep inhale, Thomas. It's all around you."

I looked around. "Really?"

"The net worth of the individuals on this terrace is greater that the GDP of Nicaragua, not to mention the fifty plus other countries ranked below it."

"Jesus." I looked at the board members gathered there and wondered whether any of them might be behind the rogue gifts being sent anonymously to the university. I glanced at Lusby, who gave me just a hint of a look that indicated he was reading my mind.

"Hey, Bernie," Lusby said to Reve, "give our friend a tour of the board members, will you? He needs to know who they are."

"Yeah, sure. Let me introduce you to our greatest champions, at least by profile," Reve said, reaching out and guiding me to the corner of the terrace to be sure his lesson would be unobserved. He motioned to the different people there with his Manhattan.

"You just met Fritz Johnson, the board chair, obviously a Texan, not an oilman, a lawyer. They say the lawyers end up with all the money and in the boom and bust of Texas it seems that he has ended up with a good bit of it. Shrewd motherfucker, Washington ambitious, which makes him and our president soul mates of a sort. Around here we call him "Big Johnson," not only because of his size but because clearly he's also got a big one litigation wise. Runs a tight board meeting, doesn't suffer fools gladly."

"Well, I'm fucked then."

Reve looked at me evenly. "I wouldn't say that. Bryan thinks you're the goose who's going to lay him a world class golden egg."

"No pressure, huh?"

"You said it, not me. Father Lanier? I don't trust him at all. We had a VP here with an alcohol and infidelity problem. Lanier went to his wife in the guise of a pastor and she confided in him. He took the info directly to the former president and the VP was gone the next day. Three kids. Good guy in my book. Needed counseling and AA. Didn't need to get canned.

"Maggie Garnet, there, is an alumna, former bank CEO, now head of the Federal Reserve in Kansas City. Frank, her husband, who is not here, owns Garnetvision Communications. You've undoubtedly read about them given all the consolidation going on in that industry and the FTC and FCC getting bent out of shape by it.

"Tyson Wiggins, there, might look like a geeky black kid but he founded three successful tech companies before he was 26. Now he's in VC in Silicon Valley.

"Mark Berger. Great host. Has given Sessions some incredibly good investment advice. Keeps his distance. Throws an occasional 50k at us here and there. Can't get to know him well enough to know his interests. I understand you guys hang out occasionally."

"Yeah, but it's just friendly. He doesn't say much about his businesses or even his interests for that matter."

Reve nodded. "Not surprising... Morris Ortiz, there, founded Ortiz Capital, a conglomeration of mutual funds. You've undoubtedly seen their ads in *Fortune*, *Forbes*, *WSJ*. He and Berger get into polite and not-so-polite disputes on investment policy on occasion. Fascinating stuff. God, these guys are sharp. Way over my head.

"Tunstall (Tunny) S. Slingluff V, there, local boy made good, media empire he inherited from his family. Selling it off piece by piece because that's about the only way to go these days. Interesting how fortunes ebb, like with the Slingluffs, and flow, like with the Garnets.

"Beatrice Fontaine, there. Ms. Fontaine. New York City. Billionairess. Inheritance. Likes her men socially prominent, slim and mean and her martinis dry. Divorced three times. Now I think she just hangs around with the gardener. Saves money.

"Allan Gunderson, there, former owner of a bond trading company. Total wild man. Funniest and most creative thinker in this room, but watch him. Just when you least expect it, he'll grab your ass, my ass, particularly Ursula's ass. There is no stopping him, especially as the evening and the drinks go on. He thinks that's funny. He's the only one.

"Over there Senator Egon Maxwell looks the part, doesn't he, with the swept back mane and those big eyebrows? A complete cypher. Say whatever you want; he'll agree with you. He is very helpful with our federal relations, however. Very crafty in regard to our sponsored research grants.

"Jonathan Melfur, talking with the president, is the board president of the Melfur Foundation, grandson of the founder, chairman and CEO of Melfur Inc., the insurance conglomerate that ol' granddad started in his great grandparents' attic bedroom.

"Oh, and there's the honorable provost, Dr. Kravitz, talking with Ms. Fontaine. Not a Board member but here to report on things academic. What a prick. The provost, I mean. Ms. Fontaine may have one for all I know, or something down there with teeth."

I looked at Kravitz and saw that he was working hard, so hard that his natural charm had turned unctuous, his head bobbing and his hands moving as if being worked by an invisible puppeteer for an act that was all about ulterior motives. Clearly Ms. Fontaine was not suffering him gladly as she smiled a saccharine smile and glanced around the room for other company.

I wondered what was driving him. Self-importance certainly, jealously, yes, moral outrage, yes. Justified? Hard to know. His whole presence gave me an uneasy feeling.

Bernie continued, "We have a couple presidents and CEOs. See those two gentlemen over there talking with one another? The one on the left is the chairman of Oxyidite Pharmaceuticals. The guy he's talking with is the president of Allogenic Technology. Both of them and their wives are absolutely charming, intelligent, well-read, cultured, love you so long as you have some business or social value to them. Otherwise you're dirt. Personally, while they all think I'm wonderful for the prestige and connections and just plain suck I can bring to them at Sessions, I find them to be cyborgs with Machiavellian programming. Hearts of stone—or maybe titanium. Cold, mechanical motherfuckers."

"Wow, Bernie, that's pretty harsh."

"Yeah? Is it? I don't think so."

"Okay."

He downed the remainder of his Manhattan. "Well, let's get the hell to dinner. I feel a sudden spasm of charm coming on. There are about five to seven more board members arriving in the morning but these are the mainstays."

We walked from the terrace back into and through the hotel to another terrace on the south side overlooking the ocean where a tent had been installed under tall palms. Tables were set with linen cloths, napkins and heavy silverware, crystal wine glasses for white and red, centerpieces of orchids, hibiscus, bougainvillea, birds of paradise, place cards at each setting. The sun was beginning to set, casting an orange light over the ocean and beach below us. Lights on poles came on as I began looking at each table for the place card with my name on it.

I found my seat and glanced at the first course salad of fresh grilled Mahi glazed with a macadamia and orange dressing on a bed of small spinach leaves and stood by my chair while the others walked in.

Looking at the place cards on either side I saw that Ursula had placed me between Allan Gunderson and Ms. Fontaine.

Gunderson arrived, bourbon on the rocks in hand, flush-faced and in a jovial mood.

"Good evening!" he greeted cordially in a flat and nasal southern accent. "And whom may I have the pleasure of dining with this evening?"

"Thomas Simpson," I said. We shook hands. His grip was firm, aggressive. He looked me straight in the eye, a look of filial camaraderie, as if we were blood brothers who shared a very amusing secret. I could see how Gunderson had been a success.

"Now Thomas, what brings you into this august company of egomaniacal twits?"

"I'm the incoming director of campaign and university communications. Doing a presentation of the master plan for communications at tomorrow's meeting."

"Ah, yes! Pleasure to meet you, young man. Looking forward to your presentation." He reached out, cupped a hand behind my shoulder, pulled me closer and said conspiratorially,

"Promise you won't put me to sleep!"

"Uh…not my intent. I've stashed a nude halfway through. See if you catch it."

"Hah! I like it!"

A mischievous expression came to his face and suddenly he reached around me and grabbed a substantial piece of my right butt cheek in his hand and gave it a hard squeeze.

I jumped in surprise. "Jesus!" I exclaimed, looking around to see whether others had witnessed my assault. Apparently not. "God damn! Whatdayah think you're doing?

"Ah, no big deal," Gunderson said, laughing hard. "Let's have some dinner."

I found myself glaring at him as he sat down, but after a moment of consideration it seemed that there was really no option but to do the same. It was not my place to challenge his behavior, which was probably, I reflected, why it continued.

At some point, somewhere, in a less prominent setting, the re-doubtable Allan Gunderson was going to get punched out.

"So you were in the bond trading business?" I asked Gun-derson to make conversation as we waited for the table to fill.

"Well, yes, we was small potatahs..." he paused, "but we was good potatahs." He began to laugh at his own joke, his face turning crimson. I found I was laughing with him, hoping too that he was not about to stroke out or infarct. "But then we got gobbled up by Morgan Stanley and it made me a very rich man."

"Congratulations."

"Thank you, Thomas."

Bryan Fitz-Hugh stopped behind us as he walked by on the way to the head table and put his hand on Gunderson's shoulder.

"Allan is totally out of the box. But we need that."

"Well, Bryan, at least I ain't outta the closet!"

"You've got to love this guy," Fitz-Hugh said, slapping Gunderson on the back, "but I live in fear of what the hell he's going to say next." He shook his head in mock disapproval and left us.

Kravitz approached our table but thankfully he sat on the other side. A few moments later Fein arrived in his normal state of barely contained panic and took his place next to Kravitz. Then Ursula arrived to sit on his other side. As she sat she gave me a meaningful glance that conveyed the sacrifice she was making. But then she greeted Kravitz with great enthusiasm as if she was delighted to be his dinner partner.

Gunderson leaned over toward me. "You know the pro-vost?" he asked in a half whisper.

"Yeah."

"He strikes me as the kinda guy whose skivvies are maybe a couple sizes too small; like he should be wearin' 36s but's got on 30s." He began to laugh uncontrollably at his own joke, his eyes watering.

I looked around the room.

Bernie Reve was sitting between the two CEOs, the three of them laughing uproariously at a joke he had just told. I found myself shaking my head.

The president, at the head table, was sitting next to Berger having what appeared to be a flirtatious conversation with Maggie Garnet on his other side. Of course, I thought, Celeste would not be here. Berger caught my eye and gave me a shrug with his hands up, conveying the sentiment of 'What the hell am I doing here.'

I felt a hand on my left leg and turned to see my other dinner partner, Ms. Fontaine, had arrived and was regarding me predatorily.

Her face was hawkish, her eyes small, active, flint-like. She had close cut light gray hair, large jade-encrusted earrings and a promiscuous, red lipsticked mouth, a power necklace of agates and platinum and a slithery and sparkling jade colored dress.

"Hello young man," she pronounced in a husky baritone as she removed her hand and searched fruitlessly in a small glittering handbag looking for a light. She found a silver case and pulled from it an impossibly long and thin almost black cigarillo, tapped it on the table and looked back to me hopefully.

"I don't smoke."

She gazed at me flatly with a 'What good are you?' expression.

"Beatrice," Allan Gunderson said from my other side, "be my guest." He tossed a book of bar matches across to her.

"Ah, my love, you are a life saver! Thank you!" she exclaimed, and then whispered to me, "And a terrible misogynist and homophobe."

She lit her cigarillo and blew a heavy wad of blue smoke away from the table, then turned back to me.

"Yes, darling" she said, "a vile habit but I must admit one that I can't seem to get rid of. I hope you don't mind."

"Of course not."

"Well, you may say that, but it's clear that you do, and frankly, I must tell you that I don't give a shit. Get over it, love."

"Okay."

I felt Gunderson tugging at my arm and turned toward him.

"How'd you like to come home to that gargoyle every night?" he whispered. "Seriously, though, one smart lady. You'll see. Just lock your doors this evening. She's on the prowl."

"I can see you two get along famously."

Gunderson snorted in surprise. "Actually we do."

I felt Ms. Fontaine's hand on my leg again and turned to her.

She nodded slightly across the table to Kravitz.

"*O, beware, my lord, of jealousy;*
It is the green-ey'd monster, which doth mock
The meat it feeds on."

"Very good," I said.

"Othello, but you wouldn't know that, would you, darling?"

"No."

"Communications is an odd discipline. Devoid of culture, isn't it?"

"I'm afraid so."

We were finishing the first course and Berger's tapping of his fork against fine crystal brought our conversations to an abrupt halt.

He stood, white wine glass in hand. "Yah know, as I've told many of you, my accountants keep making me buy these places. I always resist. But in this case, they flew me down to Miami, drove me out here and I took one look around this property and I called my main numbers guy, Ziggy. I said, 'Ziggy, where the hell do I sign? This is paradise!!!' So, welcome! You'll now understand why I'm often absent from some of our winter board meetings, hidin' out as I do in the meager confines of the boathouse. It's tough to leave this place!... Our staff stands ready and willing to assist you, so please do not hesitate to ask them for anything at all. I hope you enjoy your stay here." He raised his glass. "To Sessions University and to our remarkable president, Bryan Fitz-Hugh, to my fellow board members, our academic team and the dedicated professionals who work tirelessly to help our university and to our successful meeting tomorrow."

We applauded.

Berger turned to Fitz-Hugh. "Bryan…" he queried and sat down as Fitz-Hugh stood.

"My commendations, Mark. You've been holding out on us. Henceforth I shall recommend that we designate your winter residence here as Sessions University South and hold all winter board meetings here."

"Great idea Bryan," Berger smirked, "but we're booked! You're always welcome on the yacht however."

"What a unique property," Fitz-Hugh continued, "and how good and generous of you to host our board meeting. This is a place where we can relax and get to know one another a little better than we can in faster-paced circumstances that normally surround these meetings. As well, we can take the time as a board to focus on the opportunities and challenges ahead. Let us raise our glasses to our beneficent host!"

With this final toast, dinner was served and the noise rose under the tent. Evening spread across the ocean, turning it into a mauve pastel, stars beginning to come out and a cooler breeze moving through the tent.

It was not that I did not know the trick of dinner table conversation was to get those next to you to talk about themselves, but, unfortunately, no matter how deftly I tried to turn the conversation around, Gunderson kept grilling me in a very pleasant and inquisitive manner about our family and Ms. Fontaine managed to do the same about the communications master plan. I barely touched my dinner before it was whisked away and a replaced by a lemon parfait, which looked wonderful, but by this point of my inquisition was completely unappetizing.

As for Kravitz and Ursula, he actually seemed to warm to Ursula's blandishments. I felt a small, distracted pang of jealously but was too busy dealing with the conversations to either side of me during the rest of dinner to give their exchange much further thought.

Finally, we all rose to leave. I watched Ursula and Kravitz walk toward the president's table.

"I must go," Ms. Fontaine said importantly and then placed a hand on my arm and looked directly into my eyes, "but I do hope we can spend some time together tomorrow."

"Sure."

She turned and strolled back into the hotel.

"Thomas," Gunderson said from behind me.

"Yeah?" I turned.

"Pleasure meeting you, young man." We shook hands. "Don't worry about tomorrow. I'll have your back. I know Berger will too. We've been talking."

"Thanks, Allan. That sure beats you having my ass."

Gunderson laughed. "Oh, I don't know about that, son. Good ass is hard to find! I'm headed to the bar. Care to join me? I believe Frank Lusby and Bernie Reve will be there."

"No, I've got to get some sleep."

"Suit yourself. See you in the mornin'."

"You got it."

Later, I lay in bed in the dark looking out of the balcony's open doors at the moonlight on the ocean.

The handle on the room door made a faint sound as its knob was turned carefully. Ursula entered the room silently, undressed, slithered under the sheet and we embraced.

"I thought I would never get free," she whispered in an exasperated tone.

"Yeah, I wondered."

"Our president is with Mrs. Garnet. That is the only reason I could get away."

"Oh, Jesus. A supreme sacrifice for our alma mater."

She laughed ruefully. "Oh yes."

"Why did you put me between those two? Lord, Gunderson got me in the ass and Ms. Fontaine about devoured me for dinner. I think she wore a hole in my pants from stroking my leg."

"I thought you would find them interesting."

"Bullshit. You thought it was funny. And then you sit across from me flirting with Kravitz. I thought I was gonna puke."

"Yes." Ursula began to laugh. "And it was very funny to watch you have to deal with them while I was entertaining the provost, man eater on one side, ass grabber on the other."

"Hilarious."

I got out of bed, closed the balcony doors carefully and pulled the curtains closed.

"We'll need to be really quiet," I said getting back into bed.

"Yes."

XV
Dream Maker

WHEN MY CELLPHONE ALARM WENT OFF THE NEXT MORNING AT 6:00AM, Ursula was gone. I rose, opened the curtains and sliding doors to the almost imperceptible beginning of dawn and breathed deeply cool, fresh, ocean air.

By first light a staff member drove me in the shuttle over to the marina. The lawns and vegetation were covered with dew. In places a light mist hovered near the golf course and tree line. In a long sleeved dress shirt and tie, holding my blue suit jacket and portfolio on my lap, I felt out of place and constricted.

We took a sand path around the periphery of the golf course, birds chattering and singing to one another, then traveled into the palm trees and native plants covering the ridge fronting the ocean. The view coming over the top of the ridge took my breath away. The great apricot crescent of the rising sun illuminated the sparkling ocean and the sky. Low, soft cumulus in slate and white, tinged with orange drifted in the distance. A fresh breeze cooled us and any feeling of humidity was whisked away. The shoreline below us curved into a horseshoe bay. At its center was a green metal-roofed, gray board and batten boathouse, actually a residence over top of four boat slips, and beyond it the yacht, as Ursula had described, over 150 feet long, gleaming white and modern with a swept back design featuring large areas of tinted Lexan that made it look as if it were underway. It was tied to a bulkhead that ran at great length along the shore, the name *Dream Maker* on its bow. Off to the right beyond the yacht was a small cove in which *Calypso Too* was drifting peacefully on a mooring, looking a bit deserted.

The door to the slips inside the boathouse was open, no one yet there to direct board members, so I walked through, along the dock inside and outside to the bulkhead and the ramp leading into the lower deck of the yacht where there was an elevator.

It opened at the top deck to a large conference room surrounded by a sweeping panorama of ocean on the port. On the starboard was a view of the shoreline, *Calypso Too* in her small cove and part of the boathouse. Linen covered conference tables forming a square had been set up for the board. At the front of the room an audiovisual projector had been lowered from the ceiling and displayed different icons for the various presentations on the screen. A lectern was off to the right.

Hotel staff were setting the conference tables. A buffet breakfast and coffee were on a long table across the room.

Fein was scurrying about putting packets of materials at each board member's place.

Ursula was at the breakfast table, dressed in her most serious pinstripe dark blue pantsuit with a royal blue scarf, talking with Jean Claude in his captain's uniform, laughing at something he said.

Jean Claude saw me as I walked over to them. "Ah, *mon ami*," he greeted amiably. "So good to see you again. How are you today?"

"I'll know better after this meeting."

"Ah, yes."

Ursula said, "I am learning about Jean Claude's many adventures, how he knows Berger."

"It's an interesting story. Are you here for the winter?" I asked, grabbing a quick croissant and a cup of coffee.

Jean Claude gestured with a back and forth wave of a hand. "*Plus ou moins*. I just returned from Europe where I spent the holidays with the family in Marseille. I'll travel for some of the boss's business here and there and then toward the spring time take *Calypso Too* down the Bahamas chain and then onto the Virgins before heading to the Med."

"You're a very busy guy."

"*Ah, oui.*"

I went to the lectern, picked up the remote, highlighted the icon for my Power Point, brought it up, clicked through a few slides, breathed a sigh of relief and closed it, giving a thumbs-up to Fein who nodded back at me like a bobblehead doll.

Board members began to arrive.

Mark Berger came in, dressed in a perfectly tailored dark brown pinstriped business suit, walked up to us, looked me straight in the eye and shook my hand.

"Damn," I told him, "you look almost respectable."

"Yeah, long as I don't open my trap I should be good. Unfortunately, it opens by itself sometimes." He turned to Ursula. "You look terrific."

"Thank you."

To Jean Claude he said, "What's happening?"

Jean Claude smiled indulgently. "I am here. I am ready."

"Good."

Ursula and I looked at one another. What was this about?

Fitz-Hugh walked in, talking animatedly with Maggie Garnet.

"Thomas," a soft, ever so slightly slurred voice said from just behind me. Lusby took a step forward and appeared by my side. I had not even seen him come in.

"Yeah?"

"You've seen the agenda?"

"Same as the one sent out earlier?"

"More or less. The provost reports right before you."

"Yeah?"

"If his remarks seem a bit, say, disruptive, I want you to promise me that you'll simply go forward with your presentation as if nothing had happened."

"Ohhhh-kay."

"In other words, whatever happens, don't let it rattle you."

"Got it."

"Good man."

We looked one another in the eye and shook hands.

Chairs were set up for staff along the wall on the right side of the room and Lusby and I went over and sat down. I picked up the agenda that had been placed on each seat and sat there to review it and my hard copy of the Power Point with my notes scribbled on it.

My presentation was right after the approval of the minutes, the president's report, then Kravitz's report. Once my remarks were finished I was to take my leave and was free to pack up and head home.

Fitz-Hugh sat at the head of the table with Fritz Johnson, Ursula to Fitz-Hugh's immediate right taking minutes and recording the meeting on a small handheld recorder. Johnson asked Father Lanier for his blessings, which he gave with obsequious piety, called the meeting to order with his no nonsense Texas drawl and turned to Fitz-Hugh.

As expected, Fitz-Hugh's report was quick, upbeat, a review of recent highlights at the university and abroad, a brief report on the Campaign for Progress, a reference to my upcoming presentation and an introduction of the provost.

Kravitz rose and went to the lectern. He carried no notes.

"Over the last 23 years," he began in a strong and forceful voice, "I have been proud, indeed blessed, to serve Sessions University. Sessions is my and our home, not only from an academic, career standpoint, but my family has been part of the Sessions family, has grown and prospered at Sessions with our two children now off in early successful careers. Further, given this, it is an even greater honor to have been chosen by this administration to serve as provost and by my fellow faculty members, to represent them as chairman of the Faculty Senate.

"I take these responsibilities very seriously, wishing selflessly for the best for our university. And so I am very glad that I can play a role, for, after all, what are we, what is Sessions University, without an exemplary faculty?

"It is for these reasons, with this background, that I stand before you today troubled by what my fellow faculty members see as what might best be termed as a lack of transparency in our university's finances. Is this intentional? It is difficult to know.

"But here is what we see: A new center in Beijing for which there seems to be only partial support, yet it is funded.

"Secret plans for other centers worldwide being assembled clandestinely.

"A Campaign for Progress garnering ever greater hundreds of millions of dollars—and at the same time severe economic constraint being leveled upon our university faculty and teaching resources, particularly those in the humanities.

"As part of this Campaign for Progress there is a seemingly unlimited and unreported campaign budget that is privy to no one and which operates at the whim of our administration to fund questionable new ventures such as the communications initiative about which you will hear shortly.

"Why are these funds not going to our hard working faculty and to improve our departments and our academic excellence? Do our efforts no longer matter in a world obsessed by post-graduation employment? If they indeed do not matter, or are being trivialized, then what are we as a university?

"Given all of this, about which I hear daily from our faculty, and the ignoring of our repeated requests for more transparent financial accounting for the various discrepancies I just cited, I am sorry to report to you that our distrust of this administration has now reached such a point of severity that the Faculty Senate last Thursday conducted a vote of no confidence in the present administration and has voted to conduct an independent audit of university finances."

Kravitz, having made his statement, walked haughtily back to his chair, knowing perhaps that there would be no questions.

Johnson turned to Fitz-Hugh. "Bry-yan," he asked in a neutral and unperturbed tone, "you care to com-ment?"

Fitz-Hugh smiled graciously, with understanding and patience, his expression indicating that he had been down this road now many times before with not just Kravitz but with others at his other higher education appointments.

He took the lectern and said, "Thank you, Samuel," nodding to Kravitz, "for your illuminating comments. Once we have had the opportunity to review the Senate's vote and its resolution we'll work with you and the Senate to answer all your questions and to provide whatever information necessary to clear up any present confusion.

"You know, the audit you've described is a very expensive proposition. While I'm sure you can find resources to underwrite such an undertaking, because there always seem to be individuals who would like to stir the pot, would it not be better for us to be working together as partners to have those very funds help underwrite the humanities and overall academic capability of the university rather than some seditious, divisive and unnecessary activity such as you are suggesting? I will leave you with that thought."

Johnson looked down at the agenda. "Next item, Communee-ka-tions," he twanged.

While Bryan moved seamlessly to introduce me in glowing terms and described briefly his experience and thinking in making my appointment, his careful review of my plan and its vetting with senior administration and the board of trustees, I looked around the room.

Kravitz was at his seat looking implacable and angry, but to the rest of the board members, judging by their expressions, he had already ceased to exist, the curtains had been drawn on his little drama and they had moved on to the bigger show. They were focused on Fitz-Hugh, somewhat distractedly but focused nevertheless. Fascinating.

Public speaking has often reminded me of my years playing sports, where some part of you can independently assess how you are doing even while the contest is underway. So, right away as I spoke to the first slide of the Power Point I could tell that I was on. It made sense. This was my plan; I knew it backwards and forwards, up and down. I owned it. I knew it was very good work; Fitz-Hugh knew it; Lusby knew it; Ursula; Berger; Gunderson; Fontaine; Johnson; in fact the entire board had received my Power Point summary in advance. Now even those who had not reviewed the Power Point would know it. My confidence built as I moved on from slide to slide. I could feel myself warming to the task and my delivery improving as I progressed. And their reaction? Well, there was not really a reaction. They sat there listening politely, their minds elsewhere, as if I were discussing the need to silence their cellphones.

On one hand I felt pressure to improve on what I knew was working; on the other I knew instinctively that there was no point. I had worked for months on this plan and this presentation for what I realized as I spoke was essentially a checkbox item for the Board. Bryan wanted it; he would get it. If it was good for him—that's all they needed to know. I glanced at Kravitz between slides. He was staring at me contemptuously. Lord knows how he would characterize my new communications program later. It would not be favorable, that was for certain, and it would have no bearing on the actual programming itself. It would be used to stir more trouble, more negative spin. Kravitz had made himself into essentially the anti-Sessions. What would follow?

I finished. There was polite applause. I gathered my papers and walked out, glancing at Ursula who gave me a hint of a smile. I could hear a chair moving and looked back to see Gunderson had stood, red-faced and enthused, to address his fellow board members, to compliment the report and to recommend a favorable vote. And Kravitz would have to sit there and endure it and endure the entire day of meetings. As I took the elevator down to the ramp I found myself grinning.

Back at the hotel the limousine was already waiting for me. I grabbed my things from the concierge, got into the limo and realized that my phone was still on mute. I pulled it out.

Janet had sent a text in reply to my video of the day before, which seemed like a week ago. "Don't let it go to your head!!!!" There was a text from Tommie asking me to buy Sparky a present, work emails. Halfway to the airport the phone rang. Ursula.

"We are on the morning break."

"How'd it go?"

"You were wonderful. I've read your plan and seen the slide show numerous times and still found it interesting. The board was a bit distracted but Gunderson spoke up for you, Berger said that he sits on three Fortune 500 boards and that your plan was as sophisticated as any he has seen."

"Wow, he said that?"

"Yes. And of course Bryan had given you the glowing introduction, so the plan and your appointment were passed unanimously."

"Fantastic. I take it Kravitz didn't say anything?"

"It would not have been his place to, but there is trouble with him. He has talked to Fein and Fein is putting together a plan for a press conference in which Kravitz will announce the Faculty Senate vote."

"Oh shit. How do you know this?"

"Lusby found out. I don't know how."

"What do you do about *that?*"

"We are coming up with a plan."

"Damn."

XVI
Glock

"SO, WHAT THEY GOING TO DO NOW?" Zoltan asked.

The next day, Tuesday, we were sitting by the fireplace in the club after work, Zoltan as usual trying to extract pretzel loops from the bowl in front of us, having just taken a large draw on his vodka. We had begun with him telling me about how he was setting up his new lab and I had just finished telling him about the board cocktail party and dinner and the meeting the following day, Kravitz's remarks and Ursula's call to me on the way to the airport.

The temperature outside was in the low 20s and the air was so dry that on the way to the club the new snow underfoot made crunching noises. The fireplace had been converted to gas as part of the energy efficiency movement Fitz-Hugh had initiated shortly after his appointment, but we appreciated the warmth of its flames nonetheless.

"Hell if I know," I replied. "I haven't had a chance to catch up with Ursula since I've been back. She's been in meetings the whole time. I texted her on the way over here and am going to stop by her place for few minutes on the way home."

"Could be more than a few minutes."

"I don't think so. Janet has an evening counseling session and I have to fix dinner for the kids."

"Ah, then I walk out with you, take cab to my place."

"Yeah, good idea."

We stood, pulled our winter coats, hats and scarfs from the backs of our chairs, found our gloves in our coat pockets.

After the festive Christmas décor of the last month, the club in the New Year now seemed bare, the faint smell of Lysol and dust in the cold heat pump air that circulated through it.

Outside, Zoltan walked toward the front gate of the campus where across the street he could catch a cab from the hotel there. I crunched my way to the car. The frozen driver's side door creaked loudly when I opened it and my breath immediately clouded the windshield, the cold of the steering wheel penetrating my gloves. The car started hesitantly, the heater blasting frozen air. I put it on defrost and waited interminably for the windshield to begin to clear and then drove out the university's back entrance and around side streets, crossed the parkway and parking in the alley beside Ursula's building let myself in.

Ursula opened the door to her apartment dressed in a tight fitting thick black top and tights and running shoes.

"Nice outfit. You going over to the athletic center?"

"No, dear. I'm going to go jogging."

"You're going jogging on the coldest damn day of the year? I didn't even know you jogged."

"It has been a long time," she told me, "a New Year's resolution. Stress relief and conditioning."

"You look like black ops. Or maybe like some comic book action figure, say Catwoman. In any case, you also look great."

"My dear, this is a double-lined thermal outfit."

"No one will see you."

"Ah…" she held up a red clip-on light. "It goes here." She turned and pointed to a loop at the low center of the back of her jersey, also revealing the lovely silhouette of her hindquarters. "And…" She pulled a woolen headband from the counter. It had an impressive LED light attached to it. "So," she told me, "I can see, and any *dummkopf* I certainly hope can see me."

"Terrific… So what happened after the board meeting?"

"The board was fine. They love you. Bryan met with Fein privately afterwards and told him he was aware of his work with Kravitz and that if he wanted to keep his job that work needed to stop immediately and never occur again."

"I take it that was effective?"

"Very. Fein almost shit himself."

I laughed. "Yeah, I can see that."

"Kravitz we will handle also."

"Okay, good. How?"

Ursula brushed off my question. "I must get out before it becomes even colder, plus, my dear, if we stay here much longer you may distract me."

"Likewise. And I'm expected at home. So, tomorrow?"

"Tomorrow may be complicated. We will see."

"Okay."

Ursula put on her headband and walked to a small display table on the way to the door. She reached into the drawer and pulled out a small pistol.

"Jesus Christ, you've got a gun!"

She smiled at me as if I were an idiot. "You better have one if you want to be jogging in this city. You are not familiar with firearms?"

"Hell no."

"This is a pistol, my dear, a Glock 42, the smallest handgun Glock makes. I am an excellent shot—it was my sport in college. I have a special holster for it," she reached into the drawer and pulled out a small nylon holster, put the pistol in it, "that clips on the back of my tights and fits nicely in the small of my back so that it does not interfere with jogging." She lifted the back of her jersey and put the holster in place. "You need not worry. It is registered; I have a concealed weapons permit."

"God damn, you're full of surprises."

"You do not know the half of it."

She gave me a light buss on the cheek. We walked out of

her apartment together. "*Au revoir*." She waved casually and headed for the elevator and I the back stairs.

At home, when I walked into the family room from the garage, Janet was waiting for me, standing by the couch, hands on her hips, glass of white wine on the table beside her, looking very peeved.

"Where the hell have you been?"

"What do you mean, where have I been? It's six o'clock. I had my usual wind down drink with Zoltan. You wanted me home, I'm home like I normally am, like you asked me to be."

"Well, you missed the fireworks."

"What's Tommie done this time?"

"Not Tommie. Sarah."

"Sarah?"

"Yes, Sarah. I caught her smoking dope in her room. Had her window cracked and was blowing the smoke out through it.

"Ohhh, shit."

"I really let her have it. The whole screaming Wicked Witch of the West bitch routine."

"And?"

"She giggled at me. I grounded her so hard. Took her cellphone and her computer. What the hell are we going to do?"

"You're the counselor."

"Yeah, but it's not so easy when it's your kid."

"Okay. Pretend she's not your kid. What do you normally recommend?"

"Drug test at the local clinic. It's a major embarrassment and a pain in the ass. Threaten to do it weekly. Plus you never know whether it's just marijuana. I had a mother and daughter see me last year. The daughter, Mom said, seemed listless, unmotivated, wasn't doing well in school. Against all objections, as a condition of continuing, I ordered a blood test. Lord, Thomas, it came back with traces of cocaine, PCP, Adderall, Oxycontin and alcohol. They came back and I said to the mother, 'Your daughter isn't unmotivated, she's completely and utterly blasted, stoned to the gills.'"

"And Mom's reaction?"

"Total denial. Not her wonderful child. She and daughter stomped out never to be seen again."

"Jesus."

"Yeah. Too sad."

"Where's Tommie?"

"Oh, Tommie Town. Who knows what the hell he's doing down there. Sparky's with him. They probably have a bong."

I started to laugh and Janet after a moment joined me. It was a good laugh, one that brought tears to our eyes even while we both knew her comment seemed funnier than it was. We hugged.

"Okay," I said, "not the end of the world. God, I need a drink. I take it you're not going to your counseling session?"

"No, I called it off. I hate this kind of drama."

"Get used to it. She's only 15. Long ways to go."

"Couldn't we have one child who was normal?"

"We do. This is normal."

"Shit."

"You want me to handle this, right?"

"Yeah... I tried to get to the bottom of what's going on. I already got the accusatory 'You drink; this is no different.'"

"No concept that it's illegal for her to do either?"

"Not really. It's all just a cover-up anyway, defensive."

I went upstairs and rapped on Sarah's door.

No response.

I rapped lightly again and then opened her door gingerly.

Sarah sat on her bed, her arms around her knees, looking unconvincingly defiant and convincingly sorry.

"You okay?" I asked.

"No.... Dad, I'm incarcerated in this house and with this family."

"Yeah? Tough life; tough world. What are you going to do about it?"

Silence.

"You know as well as I do that we're not going to ever accept drug use in this house, or anywhere else for that matter. That's the way it is."

"It's not fair."

"Nothing is. Our rules are our rules. While you're here you have privileges; but you have no rights. Understand?"

"No."

"Okay, Sarah. Be that way. You decide how you want things to go: continual loss of privileges, loss of trust, random drug testing or cooperation with our rules. Mom's going to take you to the clinic and get a blood test, because you've broken our trust. That's the basic proposition. Not that we don't love you. We've just seen and know of a lot of troubles caused by drug use—friends, family, our friends' kids, on and on. Plus, it's against the law. Think about it… I'll leave you alone."

I shut her door gently and went downstairs.

"How'd it go?"

I shrugged. "Oh, about what I expected. She's entering that phase. This is not going to be a lot of fun."

"You're so encouraging."

"Yeah."

We could hear the thudding of Tommie beginning to climb the basement stairs. The door to the basement burst open and Sparky bolted into the room, a toy fireman's hat on her head, held there by an elastic strap looped around her collar, a small red cape also flowing from it, held in place by a strip of packing tape. She ran around Janet and hid behind her, shaking her head to get the hat off. Janet bent to remove the hat and cape.

"Jee-sus… Tommie!!!" I said to him as he walked through the door. "What are you *doing* to this dog?"

He was dressed in his fireman's suit over his school clothes, an outfit he'd cobbled together from the generosity of the men at the fire station and rummaging at Goodwill—an oversized fireman's hat, rain slicker, black neoprene snow boots.

He came slogging toward us in his boots, the buckles jiggling, his eyes wide yet blinking, his face ticking. "Dad, there was a big five alarm fire in Tommie Town and Sparky the Fire Dog is helping me put it out!"

"You're not to do this again—torture the dog. Do you understand?"

"Dad, we're just play-ying." Tommie was looking from Janet to me and back again with odd twists of his head.

My cellphone suddenly buzzed in my pocket. I pulled it out and checked the number. Ursula, at the office.

"It's the president's office," I told Janet and took the call.

Ursula's voice was grave, shaky. "Thomas, there's been a terrible tragedy."

"What?"

"Dr. Kravitz. He has killed himself."

For several moments I could not respond, my thoughts reeling as I tried to understand and cope with the reality of this news.

"Are you there?" she asked.

I let out a long exhalation. "Yeah… I don't what to say. I'm in shock. It makes no damn sense. You're sure?"

"The police found him in the park in his car. He shot himself… Bryan wants you to come in and help craft his remarks. He is with the family now. The press and TV will be all over this; they will want a statement from him. Fein will handle setting up a brief press conference with them. We will want to say as little as possible. Our concern needs to be with his family."

"Okay, I'll get there as soon as I can."

I ended the call and turned to Janet.

"What happened?" she asked.

I did not want to tell her. I knew the information would be destructive. She had just worked her way through Compton's demise and now this.

I sighed and said as evenly and simply as I could, "The provost, Kravitz, has killed himself."

"Oh, my God, no."

"It's true. Ursula just told me. Fitz-Hugh wants me there to help with what he's going to say. I can't believe this."

"Why would he have done this?"

I shook my head. "I haven't a clue. He's such an arrogant and feisty bastard. It doesn't make any sense. Except his presentation to the board did not go well. They more or less blew him off. Plus Bryan got wind that Kravitz was about to conspire with Fein to set up a press conference on the Faculty Senate vote to do an independent audit of the university and he shut down Fein big time. So maybe that was enough to send Kravitz into a spiral. I don't know. There could be other things going on in his personal life. Who knows? But it makes no sense. Terrible. Leaves his wife, two kids in the early stages of their careers, grandchildren. Awful."

As I expected, Janet was not taking this news well. The ugly reminder of Dr. Compton's demise was all but repeating itself before her eyes.

"Look," I said, "I've got to go. Are you okay?"

Janet sighed deeply. "In a word, no. But I'll hold up."

Driving to the office, my mind kept coming back to Ursula. Her gun had spooked me. Now Kravitz's death had shaken me. That she was out jogging at the very same time when, and in the very same general area where, Kravitz took his life was probably a coincidence, but it was one that gnawed at me and caused a great wave of anxiety to well up inside. I found myself shaking my head slowly.

XVII
Aftermath

Bryan Fitz-Hugh looked like hell—puffy dark circles under blood shot eyes, a pallor, fine stubble showing on his drained face. He had just come from the Kravitz household and had called Ursula and me into his office where he was sitting behind his desk, slumped back in his chair. I had arrived about ten minutes before to find Ursula in her office in the same black thermal running outfit she had been wearing when she left her apartment.

"Bryan, are you okay?" Ursula asked as we sat in front of him.

He gazed at us, looked down at his desk. "Truthfully...I don't know... That was as awful an experience as I've ever had. Joan is beside herself. He blew his brains out and she had to go identify him at the morgue. She had to call Natalie and young Samuel. Oh, Jesus. You never know, do you, what tragedy is going to confront you on any particular day? I must tell you, I did not see this coming..." He paused, thought for a moment. "What's going on here?"

"Fein has set up a brief press conference, for you to read a statement, no questions," Ursula told him. "Thomas has written your remarks." She leaned forward and pushed a single sheet of paper that slid across his desk and stopped in front of him.

He picked it up, glanced through what I had written. "Okay, this is good. Nice work, Thomas. I need a damn drink."

Ursula and I looked at one another. She said, "After the press."

He looked at her, obstinacy flashing across his face, and then control exerting itself. "Yeah, you're right. Have you alerted Celeste about what's happened?"

"Yes. It is all over the evening news."

"Shit... Not that I will say anything tonight of course, but we need to get Don Powers in Psychology lined up as the next provost and hopefully as president of the Faculty Senate. He's a good consensus candidate and he's one of our loyalists. I think the faculty would vote him in. Get Wentz on it so we can be sure that scenario plays out as I think it can. We need this done ASAP."

"Yes."

"Thomas, I want you to call Howard—ostensibly to see how he's taking this news, but actually to see what his thoughts are about this tragedy and its impact on the faculty. He'll be a good barometer."

"Okay."

"How long until the press conference?"

"Fifteen minutes."

"Okay, leave me alone. I need some time to myself."

"Sure," I said.

We rose and left the office.

As we headed down the hall, I softly grabbed Ursula's behind, and then, as if to steady myself, reached up and felt the holster. The Glock was firmly in place.

"Thomas, this is no time for ass grabbing."

"Sorry, I couldn't resist."

"Down boy." She half smiled.

"Is Frank around?"

"Yes."

"You've got things to do. I'm going to check in on him."

"Fine. After Bryan's statement we can all go home."

"Yeah, I'll give Howard a call from the car."

Lusby was sitting in his office in the dark, chair turned to the window, looking out at the stark, ghostly landscape of snow lit by incandescent lights.

"Hey," I said lightly.

With a small, desperate exclamation he sat bolt upright and swung his chair around so hard it again almost fell over.

"Oh, Thomas... God you startled me." He shook his head slowly. "I was a thousand miles away...with a girl from high sch... Hell, never mind. Come in." He looked embarrassed at having revealed his dreaming.

"Thanks." I walked into his office and sat in a chair in front of his desk. "What do you make of all this?" I asked.

I could barely make out the deep frown that crossed his face. "Utterly tragic."

"You think it was suicide?"

"I have no clue."

"Okay."

"That being said, it's not smart to play with fire."

"Hmmmm."

"This whole situation may drive me screaming into the woods."

"Are we still getting wire transfers?"

There was a long ruminating pause. "Yeah. We've received almost $24 million now."

"Shit. Any better idea of their source?"

"Nope."

"What's going to happen with the Faculty Senate vote?"

Lusby thought for a moment and then smirked, shook his head. "Oh, it'll work out just fine. The incoming provost is a master at putting things to sleep."

"Sounds like it's a done deal."

"It ought to be. I've been working behind the scenes on it for two months. Except it was inferred that the provost was going to resign, go back to teaching."

"Wow."

"Yeah, our president thinks ahead."

"Why would the provost resign?"

"I have no clue. I don't ask questions."

"Why, if you've been working on this for two months, did the president just tell Ursula to get Wentz on it?"

Lusby shrugged. "That's the way it's been choreographed. Wentz is a heavyweight, no pun intended. He has the academic credentials and reputation of making things happen. I grease the skids; Wentz slides down 'em. The faculty knows he's the president's guy—another feather in his cap. Wentz is going to want his own presidency sooner rather than later, so Bryan is being an ally and an enabler. That and they'll be an early appropriation to the humanities from the Campaign for Progress of two million bucks. That'll sooth a lot of souls. Bryan's coming through for them in their time of need."

"Fuck."

"Yeah, fuck."

Lusby reached over, opened the bottom drawer of his desk and brought up a bottle of George Dickel Barrel Select, pulled the cork, took a long slug and handed the bottle across the desk. I did the same. The harsh taste and burning felt good and brought just a hint of relief.

I handed the bottle back to him. He corked it and placed it back in the drawer.

"Okay, time for the president's statement," I told him.

"Yeah, I'll walk down there with you."

On the way my cellphone buzzed in my pocket.

"Zoltan."

"Yes. What the hell has happened? It is terrible. All over the news."

"I can't talk now. We're about to watch the president's statement. I'm going to be tied up with calls and other crap until tomorrow."

"See you at the club then."

"Yeah, that would probably be best."

The press conference was held in the center atrium of the administration building. A folding table with a white tablecloth spread over it had been placed near the far wall. A lectern with a microphone, reading light and university seal had been placed in front of a folding chair at the center. Behind the chair stood the state flag, university flag and American flag.

We stood in the back, away from the intense television lights and the cameras and TV crews. Fitz-Hugh came in and sat down.

As he did, someone moved in on my left and stood next to me to get a better view of the proceedings—a woman reporter, cellphone in hand to record the statement.

At a technician's signal, Fitz-Hugh began, "We are stunned, saddened, shocked by this tragic turn of events. We have lost one of the pillars of our university family…"

I looked over at the reporter. She glanced over from the phone in front of her, looked at me quizzically, then went back to the task at hand.

Bryan did a nice job with my remarks then noted that, given the situation and out of respect for the family, there would be no questions.

The reporter turned to me as she stuffed her phone in her purse. "Hi," she greeted and held out her hand. I took it. Her hand was small but with long, strong fingers. I was running through my head the quickest exit excuse and the closest door. Lusby had vanished.

"Emily Sayzak," she introduced herself. "Mind if I ask you a few questions?"

My spirits sunk.

She had a somewhat disheveled look, her cheap blue slacks and white blouse rumpled from a long day of work. Her overly thick, tousled blond hair surrounded a long, too small face. She had alert eyes, a nice physique, just a hint of makeup.

"What's your role here?"

I shrugged. "Nothing really, just happened to be around."

"Okay," she said, "I was just curious. Are you an administrator, professor?"

"Professor of communications."

"Oh, that's interesting. I took a number of communications courses in college, Washington and Lee."

"Yeah, they have a terrific School of Journalism."

"Thanks. Where did you go?"

"Undergrad, UVA, for my PhD, Columbia."

"Impressive," she smiled. "Let me give you my card, just in case. Doesn't this whole thing seem...I don't know...strange?"

"Tragic is more like it."

"Yeah," she sighed, "that too... I just get the feeling there's more to this than meets the eye."

"Well, you certainly sound like a journalist. Sorry, I've got to get home."

"No problem, pleased to meet you, uh,..." she pulled out her cellphone to record my name.

"Okay," I said, "first name 'No,' second name 'Comment.' Pleased to meet you." I turned and walked away.

I walked to the car, the temperature now in the teens, the cold piercing through my clothes, overcoat, scarf, knit hat, kicking myself for being entrapped by a reporter, even if she was attractive in an off-beat kind of way.

The car barely started. While it warmed up and the windshield cleared I called Janet.

"How are you?" was my first question.

Long sigh. "Been watching the evening news. Awful. Bryan looked terrible."

"Yeah, this has hit everybody hard."

There was an awkward pause.

"Janet..."

"Yes."

"This is going to sound stupid, but it's really good to hear your voice."

"Well, that's nice to know. Thanks, honey."

"It just keeps getting crazier around here."

"I know."

"I keep asking myself what the hell I've gotten myself into."

She laughed a short, uncertain laugh. "So, do I."

"Okay. I'll be home shortly."

"Good. I need you here."

"Thanks."

I got underway and called Howard.

On one hand it was comforting to hear his foggy voice; on the other I felt a pang of guilt at my ulterior motive for calling. Under normal circumstance such a call might never have occurred to me.

"Howard, can you believe all this?"

"I am in shock. The only sense I can make of this is that Samuel was turning into a reprobate. His jealously was driving him. Perhaps he saw that he could not win and in his mind would be disgraced. In reality his cause was quixotic. Difficult to know whether there was anything to it other than his enmity. In any case, he's gone and I grieve for that and his family."

"Yeah. Bryan said that Joan is taking it very hard, had to go to the morgue."

"How gruesome; how utterly bereft."

"What will happen now to the Faculty Senate vote?"

"The Faculty Senate vote! No one cares about that. I was amazed that resolution passed, and it was only by a couple votes—Kravitz's cronies. Look, Thomas, no one wants a fight. We all just want to do our work. Yes, we're frustrated, but most of the faculty is drinking Fitz-Hugh's Kool Aid. Now that Samuel is gone so is the resistance. He was the backbone of it all."

"Yeah, I've just stayed away from the whole issue. Didn't even attend the vote."

"Well, how could you given your position?"

"Correct. Well, I'm headed home. This event has really had a negative impact on Janet."

"No doubt, Thomas. I'm sure she needs you now."

"Yeah. Thanks."

I hung up and called Ursula.

"I talked with Howard. His feeling is that the whole issue of the independent audit was being driven by Kravitz and will now more or less evaporate."

"Good to know. Thank you dear. Who was that woman you were talking to at the end of Bryan's statement?"

"Nosy reporter cornered me."

"They always want to stir up trouble."

"Yeah. I was less than thrilled. Didn't even give her my name, rank or serial number."

"If she is any good, that will not stop her. Let us know whether she contacts you again."

"Sure."

It was after ten when I got home. Janet was at her usual spot on the couch in the family room, reading. She had poured a glass of wine for me, which sat on the side table next to hers.

Sparky came running to me, wagging her tail, making noises and jumping excitedly at my arrival.

Janet stood and we hugged.

"What a day," I sighed.

"Awful."

"You got it. Plus a damn reporter tried to corner me before I could get away."

"Oh no."

"Yeah. I shunned her but it doesn't help to have that happen."

"No."

I picked up my glass of wine, took a long draught and sat down next to her.

"How's Sarah?"

"Pretty much back to normal. I've returned her computer but kept her cellphone. I need to see more contrition and groveling."

I laughed slightly in agreement. "That's the spirit."

"Tommie?"

Deep sigh. "I don't know. The same. Caught up in his fire engine world. Oblivious to everything else."

"Well, at least there's one constant in the universe. One last thing we can count on that is totally predictable."

"Today at least."

"Yeah."

XVIII
Places to Go, Things to Do

I T WASN'T UNTIL THE FOLLOWING FRIDAY THAT ZOLTAN AND I COULD FIND THE TIME TO GET TOGETHER.
Dealing with the follow-up communications challenges from Kravitz's suicide and my transition to the administration was overwhelming. Work never stopped. I simply worked until I could work no more, arriving home at around 10pm each evening, exchanging a few mumbled words with Janet and crashing into bed only to be up and out the next morning before dawn. All reports from Janet were that Sarah, on the surface at least, seemed back to normal and that Tommie was behaving in his normally abnormal manner. Nevertheless, a small warning light was flashing in my subconscious and sometimes conscious thinking that I could not keep this up without consequences, physical or familial.

Two days after Kravitz's death, when the initial chaos and tumult began to settle down, I packed up my office of twelve years in Hart Hall, throwing much of the accumulation away, said a brief, awkward goodbye to Howard and supervised campus movers carting my boxes and files and merging them with new furniture and equipment in a suite of offices on the second floor of the administration building, the university's new Communications Center. It was a good space in the corner of the building facing the outside of the campus, looking out at an open area along an access road, a parking lot on the far side and woods beyond that with a nice wide view of the sky.

Lusby poked his head in around lunchtime on my second day there, looked around approvingly and said, "Just remember one thing."

"Yeah?" I asked.

"The first to decorate is the first to depart, and it usually ain't pretty. In other words, don't get all high and mighty and full of yourself."

"Last thing on my mind."

"Good man."

During the day I had meetings with Fein, Ursula, Lusby, Ramis, Wentz and Fitz-Hugh to get fully up to date and oriented and began to scope out space in Sessions' auditorium where a broadcast studio could be installed.

It helped that it was a cavernous old building with some remarkably large areas hidden away in its basement that could be converted into usable space. Converting it would be a question of jack hammering and bringing into the building the electrical, infrastructure and technological elements for a whole new studio, a very expensive proposition.

In the interim, we would continue to produce media out of the existing outdated facility in the Student Union.

After-hours were spent writing up position descriptions for an assistant director, administrative assistant, producer, writers and various techies and then spending days dealing with the bureaucrats in HR and requisitioning additional equipment, supplies and furniture.

In all of this, with our different responsibilities, Ursula and I were more or less passing ships in the night. I saw her for meetings, or in meetings, but we had no time to ourselves, both of us working through lunch each day. To some degree this was at least on my part welcome. I had enough pressures to deal with. As well, now that I was fully part of the administration, working out of the same building, a continuing liaison with her seemed far riskier than it had before, probably because it was. It was not lost on me that this might be an opportunity, as Zoltan and I had agreed would be best, to let the whole affair fade away. And of course, this being said, a not inconsequential part of my psyche and physique wanted her.

That following Friday, mid-morning, I also got a call on my cell from Berger.

"How'er you doin'?"

"Managing, barely. Just all hell breaking loose around here. Calming down a bit day-by-day, but a mess. The campus is still in a state of shock. A memorial service has been scheduled for tomorrow. Psychological counseling has been offered to faculty, staff and students. This is very hard for people to accept. Even to those that didn't like the SOB it's a big shock."

"Yeah, I figured as much."

"Where are you?"

"Singapore."

"What the hell time is it there?"

"Umm...closing in on midnight."

"How do you deal with all the time change?"

"Sharks don't sleep, Thomas."

"Yeah, right."

"A little Ambien helps here and there."

"That sounds more like it."

"What do you think happened?"

"You mean with Kravitz? I don't know. Frankly, I'm mystified."

"So am I... Makes no sense. He wasn't that kinda guy. You know an Emily Sayzak?"

"I know who she is. Nosy reporter."

"Yeah, she's been calling."

"You haven't talked to her, right?"

"Nah. But she is asking a lot of questions through some of my people. Seems some woman jogger was seen in the vicinity of Kravitz's car. The cops are scratching their heads. It was 22 degrees out."

My stomach dropped.

"Umph..." I heard myself mumble.

"Yeah…weird."

"Yeah."

"I get the feeling from what I've been told that this Sayzak is into the university's finances, trying to figure out why the Faculty Senate voted for an independent audit."

"Shit."

"Yeah, I called Bryan about it. He was nonplussed as usual."

"Okay."

"Keep me up to date on this stuff, will you?"

"I will."

"Great. Thanks man."

We hung up and I sat at my desk for a while thinking, concluding that there was no one with whom I would share this conversation.

By the time I got out of work and walked to the club it was dark. The day had been cold and wet and I was careful, checking the walkways to be sure that despite the sand and salt spread on them that there were no patches of ice, shuffling along like an old man, my galoshes making scraping noises.

Zoltan texted that his cab coming from the medical center was being held up in traffic, so I should wait for him.

Being a Friday, the club was crowded, alumni and their families in for the next day's home Division II basketball game, faculty unwinding from a week's work and being joined by friends for dinner. The spirit was bright and festive, a striking contrast to my experience of the week.

As I sat down at one of the few empty tables in the bar area I saw that Lusby was sitting at the bar. I got up, went over and sat next to him, waving off the bartender who reflexively began reaching for the tap to pour me a beer.

Lusby saw me coming. "Thomas, good to see you," he greeted as I took a seat. "How's it going?"

"Not exactly a walk in the park," I told him. "Not that I expected it to be. A lot of bullshit attached to everything I try to do that seems to be dragging down any real progress."

Lusby nodded his head in appreciation. "Welcome to the administration."

"Yeah. It's got me concerned, expectations out of the box being what they are."

"I hear you."

"Plus I've been thinking about these funds we've discussed."

"Yeah? You know there's a reporter snooping around now?"

"Yeah, she cornered me after Bryan's statement to the press, but I shunned her. So, here's my question: If we're getting all this money coming in surreptitiously why wouldn't we just roll it into the university's general unrestricted account? Not that that's the right thing to do, but you can't just keep throwing it into the campaign, right, because eventually it will be noticed?"

Lusby looked at me as if I were stupid. "Bryan wants the Campaign for Progress to knock the socks off all the other university capital campaigns that have gone before this."

"Jesus. So, ego, huh?"

"You got it. Plus, were we to put these gifts in the university unrestricted account it would raise a whole lot more red flags than in the campaign. The university budget is tight, every dollar counts and every dollar is scrutinized. In the capital campaign, because of all the big gifts coming in, the unrestricted account doesn't stand out so much, and frankly our accountants have more or less taken our word for it on these anonymous gifts, understanding as we've communicated to them that these gifts might be withdrawn were any of the donors' identities in any way compromised. The problem is that the more of these gifts we receive the more that account does begin to stand out somewhat. So, your initial worry is correct. It could cause questions to be asked that we don't have any answers for. But I have a possible solution."

"Yeah?"

Lusby took a sip of his martini. "The campaign itself is going well. Bernie, the campaign leadership and Bryan are still calling on the top hundred prospects; Fritz and Bryan are double-teaming the board campaign. That's almost finished with one or two major solicitations to be done. One of them is Berger by the way. All the spadework is being done regionally by Bernie's minions along with some of our company's folks to recruit leadership and build momentum for the next phase, which will set goals and raise money in 12 major U.S. cities and another eight cities internationally. It's all going according to plan. So, here's my question for you.

"We have this philanthropic research screening service where if you submit the name of a prospect it kicks out a very nice report on their giving history to other organizations and to politics. Then, using real estate, stock market and other public wealth information, such as club memberships, boat and airplane ownership, it gives us an estimate of that person's philanthropic capability."

"Interesting. Not something you exactly want to broadcast."

"Very confidential. So, what do think Berger's capacity would be?"

"Oh, geez, infinite would be my guess."

"Yeah, you're not far off. Wentz was more or less joking when he talked about our getting a billion dollar gift in this campaign. The fact is Berger could do it."

"Really?"

"I'm not saying he will. But if he did, or even a portion of that, it sure would make it easier to cover up, say, about $27 million or more of anonymous unrestricted fluff, wouldn't you say?"

"Yeah… You think that more anonymous giving might come in?"

Lusby looked glum. "It keeps coming. Bryan seems to have a secretive Midas touch with someone—or several someones or somethings."

"If Berger's gift came in at that scale, you wouldn't even need that anonymous money, would you?"

"Be nice if that was the case, but any gift that big is going to be designated, probably for a host of endowed professorships or to name a new school, build buildings, things like that. No, Bryan will continue to covet these anonymous gifts because of their unrestricted, discretionary nature. They're what's powering his international ambitions."

"Got it. You're not asking me to help with Berger, are you?"

"Not if it wouldn't work."

"It wouldn't. We are friendly; we may even be friends, but money, frankly, doesn't matter, isn't a part of it. There's just no basis for the conversation. I mean, I'm not a business partner; I'm not a peer. There's a genuine connection there for whatever reason but it would be totally wrong to bring it up. Plus, I worry that it would ruin whatever relationship we have."

Lusby sighed a deep, almost mournful sigh. "Yeahhhhh, I believe you, Thomas. You're a very fortunate guy to be able to keep things real and be genuine. That's probably why Berger likes you guys. You might even have a chance to be happy. I envy you."

"Don't."

Lusby eyebrows went up. "Okay."

Out of the corner of my eye I saw that Zoltan had come in and was sitting at the table I had left a few minutes before, a vodka and snacks already set out in front of him, plus a beer at the seat across from him.

"Zoltan's here. I'm going to join him. You care to join us?"

"No, I'm on my way out," Lusby said. "Have places to go and things to do," he added in a manner that indicated he might have absolutely nowhere to go and nothing to do but also preferred not to have company. An empty Friday night, perhaps communing with brother Smirnoff.

I left Lusby at the bar and sat with Zoltan.

"How'er you doing?" I asked.

"Setting up new lab. Thomas, they give me all this space in new research complex, give me big budget for hiring people and buying equipment. I have to really think hard to know what to do first, what to do second. Lot of stress to get it right and move it along."

"Oh, Lord, do I know what you're talking about. Exactly what's going on with me. Plus I've got Bryan looking over my shoulder. He's pretty distracted at the moment but I'm guessing that won't last for long and he'll be back to his quest for total world domination soon. In the meantime, I've got to hustle."

"Yes. So, how Lusby?"

"Pretty much the same. Worried and uptight as hell."

"So, what is happening with you?"

"What isn't happening? I just seem to be getting myself deeper and deeper into this mess."

"Which one?"

"All of them, except maybe Ursula. Not seeing a whole lot of her these days."

"Yes. That good. Let it go, my friend."

"Yeah... How's Kristina?"

"Good. We just enjoying one another every day, every week. No thoughts or pressure about the future. Content to just have what we have now... So, what is this with Kravitz? He kill himself?"

"I'm not sure."

"What you mean?"

"Ursula was out jogging in the same area and at the same time he supposedly killed himself. I've just got the worst, most anxiety-ridden feeling about all this."

"Thomas, someone see woman jogger in area. Police suspicious about that. Plus he leave no note."

"Yeah. I'd never seen her have any interest in or ever jog before. Twenty-two degrees out and suddenly she has to go jogging. New Year's resolution. So, this 'coincidence' is really freaking me out."

"Hmmmm. Yes, that strange."

"Oh, and she had a Glock with her neatly tucked into a holster that fits into the small of her back."

"They found gun in the car with Kravitz fallen from his hand."

"Yeah, and she had her Glock with her when she was back in the administration building, so that would seem to more or less put her in the clear."

"Gun they found with Kravitz had serial number file off. Police wonder about that too."

"Yeah."

"Thomas, she could have two guns."

I thought for a minute, alarmed. "God damn it. I hadn't thought about that."

Zoltan and I looked at one another, ordered another round. We talked the whole situation through again, coming to no further conclusions but certain that something was not right.

About a half hour later we shuffled to my car and I dropped Zoltan off at his place. On the drive home the wind pushed the car around and sleet tapped on its body and windshield in small random hits, freezing on the wiper blades as they futilely scraped the windshield, the defroster blasting away without sufficient effect, empty tree branches being tossed by the wind moved in and out of my headlight beams.

So what had happened? Had Kravitz actually gone into deep despair over his rejection by the university's board? He certainly could have felt humiliated. What else was going on in his life that might have driven him to suicide? Or had Fitz-Hugh tried to cut a deal with Kravitz to get him to step down as provost and had he refused? And was that what was behind his death? Or was I completely and utterly wrong on both counts. I didn't know enough to have any real idea about the actual reality of what had happened. I reasoned that over time maybe I would know or find out more and the situation would become more clear. Right now all I had to go on was anxiety and suspicion, particularly about where Ursula did or did not fit into the situation.

I parked the car in our garage and stomped on the floor to rid my galoshes of sand and dirt, took them off by the door into the house and walked in through the laundry room into the family room. Janet was there with her book and glass of wine with a glass poured for me. Her expression was serious, pensive.

"Honey, come over here and have a seat."

"Uh-oh," I sighed. "This doesn't sound good." I walked over, took my glass of wine and sat beside her.

Janet said, "I know how busy you are. I didn't want to bother you with this while you were at work."

"Bother me with what?"

"Tommie hit one of his classmates today."

"Tommie hit someone?"

"Sharif, the boy with mild cerebral palsy. He hit him with one of his fire engines; held it in his hand and hit him with it. Five stitches, blood all over the place."

"Jesus."

"It gets worse. Apparently Sharif took one of Tommie's fire engines, wanted to play with it. Tommie grabbed it back. Sharif called him a retard and Tommie called Sharif a racial epithet before he hit him"

"A racial epithet?"

"Sand nigger."

"Oh shit… Where would he have learned that? I mean that's weirdly inventive. Does he even know what it means?"

"Unfortunately, yes. He must. My guess would be that he picked the term up at the fire station. Those guys spend most of their time racially insulting one another. They think its great fun. The white guys call the black guys 'rug heads,' the black guys call the white guys 'crackers,' the one Hispanic guy's a 'Spic.' So, anyone remotely Arab walks by, what are they going to say and be chuckling about? But who knows, it could be he got it off the internet."

"Jesus. Sand nigger. Terrific."

"He's been suspended. You and I have to go into the school, meet with the head and defend why Tommie should be allowed to continue to go to school there."

"Lord, Janet."

"What would we do if he couldn't go there? It would kill him to go back to public school."

"They probably wouldn't allow him anyway, given his prior track record."

"We might have to send him away."

"That would be terrible."

"And very expensive. At least you've got this new position and new income. That could save the day."

"Yeah, for now."

Janet and I looked at one another squarely.

"I don't trust the whole damn situation at Sessions." I told her. "Stuff is going on behind the scenes there that really gives me pause and makes me wonder if I haven't made a huge mistake getting involved with this administration."

"This all goes back to Kravitz, doesn't it?"

"Yeah. Can't talk about it really. Too fucked up and complicated and also very uncertain. Quicksand. Don't need to pull you into it."

We both sighed, looked at one another and, sliding close, embraced.

XIX
From the Midst of Wickedness

SATURDAY WAS A COLD, windy day, the low grey sky portending a storm front that promised to drop a couple inches of wet snow later in the afternoon. I hated this time of year, an onward march of overcast skies and bad weather that made any one day, week and even month indistinguishable from the next, an endless procession of dreariness.

The Kravitz memorial service was held at 10:30am in the university's Patterson Chapel. Constructed in the early 1900s, it is a postcard perfect Georgian building with white Ionic columns and a cross-topped steeple anchoring one end of the main quadrangle and serves as the university's architectural and spiritual centerpiece.

Knowing how crowded the service would be, Janet and I arrived early and hustled in from the parking lot, walking to the chapel from the other end of the upper quadrangle at McFarland Hall, the university's original education building, along the expanse of snow-covered lawn and bare elms surrounded by later halls built to house various departments and connected by colonnades and crosswalks. I glanced at Hart Hall and the window of my former office as we went by, feeling a small pang of nostalgia and regret.

The chapel's interior was open and bright even on an inclement day, thanks in part to well camouflaged house lights, large palladium clear and stained glass windows and a white painted interior and wood floors, natural cherry railings atop white wainscoted pews.

An elderly gentleman whom I did not recognize, who looked entirely too beatific and in love with the Lord given the occasion, undoubtedly a clueless chapel volunteer, handed us a service leaflet as we walked inside from the vestibule.

We sat toward the middle to escape notice, to better observe new arrivals and, while we did not mention it to one another, to make a fast escape. Zoltan was at our house taking care of the kids. In the past, we might have let Sarah take care of Tommie, but increasingly we were concerned about how Sarah might use such time to take care of herself.

A profusion of flowers had been placed on the altar and ran along the altar rail and around the choir stalls, the air heavy with their scent. Candles were being lit by an acolyte, a hungover, bearded graduate student trying his best to look pious.

The Patterson Chapel was renowned for the Muller organ, a 1920s contribution from a board member family, restored in the late '90s by the family's children. Its mass of resplendent golden pipes ascended rack by rack at back of the apse to the stained glass window of Jesus Christ, his open hands extended in a welcoming gesture. I didn't recognize the prelude being played and checked the program. It meant nothing to me. Undoubtedly Father Lanier would have selected the piece as appropriate for such an occasion. Feelings of discomfort, which I had been trying to tamp down all morning, welled up in me. We should not be here. This should not be happening. I felt as if we had been time warped into some parallel universe with no way out. On reflection I realized that it was not time that had transported us to today but circumstance. Unjust circumstance.

From what we could see the front left hand pews were reserved for family and friends. The Kravitz family was in the front row, already seated. I recognized Joan's short gray curls, Natalie with her husband and the Kravitz younger adult son, Samuel, sitting to her left. Every so often Joan would raise her right hand to dab at her eyes, Natalie comforting her as she did so.

The front right hand pews were reserved for department heads and key members of the administration. Fitz-Hugh was seated directly across the aisle from Joan, Celeste beside him. She turned to say something to Bryan, a not unattractive, steely brunette. Bryan listened, motionless, then turned slightly and nodded an ascent. Next to Celeste was Fritz Johnson and next to him Don Powers, whose appointment as the interim provost had been announced earlier in the week, Ursula next to him. The second, third and fourth rows were comprised of department heads. The following rows held key members of the administration, including Reve, Wentz and Lusby sitting together—see no evil, hear no evil, speak no evil.

Howard walked by us looking befuddled as he sized up the setting and seating. He did not see us, walked up the aisle and sat next to some colleagues in the third row.

Gradually the chapel filled, the organ prelude stopped and Father Lanier took the pulpit.

He paused momentarily, surveyed us, looked down at his remarks, then back at us and spoke in ministerial eloquence, his shifty lizard green eyes calculating the effect of his remarks as he made them.

"Many religions do not accept the taking of one's life, believing that always an individual must choose life, that the taking of one's life is not an acceptable solution for pain. Given this, perhaps this chapel is a more tolerant and forgiving place to memorialize Samuel's life. For we must accept his choice for whatever reasons there were for him to make such a decision, and we must also recognize that Samuel, while he has left us with a great loss, a deep hole in our lives, has also left us with a legacy that will live on with each of us in our daily lives. Each of us must revere and recognize this legacy as we go forward. Let us pray."

We recited The Lord's Prayer.

Natalie rose, pale, a resolute expression on her face, and made her way to the pulpit. She carried a single sheet of paper and was clearly trying without success to contain her distress. She read haltingly in tears, her voice alternatingly strong and quavering.

"A reading from the Book of Wisdom (4:7-15)

> *The righteous, though they die early, will be at rest. For old age is not honoured for length of time,*
> *or measured by number of years;*
> *but understanding is grey hair for anyone, and a blameless life is ripe old age.*
> *There were some who pleased God and were loved by him, and while living among sinners were taken up.*
> *They were caught up so that evil might not change their understanding or guile deceive their souls.*
> *For the fascination of wickedness obscures what is good, and roving desire perverts the innocent mind.*
> *Being perfected in a short time, they fulfilled long years;*
> *for their souls were pleasing to the Lord,*
> *therefore he took them quickly from the midst of wickedness. Yet the peoples saw and did not understand,*
> *or take such a thing to heart,*
> *that God's grace and mercy are with his elect, and that he watches over his holy ones.*

The Word of the Lord"

I found myself wondering for the first time whether the family might have some of my concerns. Emily Sayzak's name flashed through my consciousness. Would she have had the gall to talk to the family? I knew the answer and a strong anger welled up in me. The Goddamned little bitch.

Bryan Fitz-Hugh, in a dark blue suit, a brilliant white shirt that highlighted his deep tan and golden hair and the darkest violet tie, rose and took his place in the pulpit. He looked at us, seemingly at each of us, his expression one of compassion and understanding heavily tinged by the tragedy of the occasion.

"Samuel was our conscience, our compass, our protector, our friend and our ally," he began.

Janet leaned over to me and whispered, "Did you write that?"

I shook my head and whispered in return. "This is all Bryan. Notice, no notes. Extemporaneous. From the heart or whatever the hell he's got in there."

"Samuel was a man of great brilliance. His facility with languages and the deep understanding of many different cultures created a man of unique perception. His love of and service to his university, entwined as it was with his family's devotion to us, his strong principles and willingness to fight for that which he believed, his caring for others, for the humanities and for his fellow faculty, his love of his family, will forever be remembered by us all...

"Today we recognize—we revere—the remarkable life of our dear friend and his contribution to this community, recognizing even as we do the tragedy and loss of his departure. These are difficult times; yet we must endure; we must move forward to each of our individual destinies and fulfill our own lives and those of our families. That is our lot; it is what our individual faiths and our human instinct demands of us. But in doing so we must keep and cherish Samuel's example and we must keep it close. For me, personally, I will miss his ever-thoughtful counsel at our monthly cabinet meetings, where he invariably provided insights that helped move our university forward. I will recall too his love of this university, his remarkable scholarly attainments and his fierce loyalty to this faculty. The Kravitz family comprises a strong part of the fabric of this university family and we have lost a key thread. If there is but any consolation it is that Joan, Natalie and young Samuel have our continuing support, love and affection to rely on in the future. We cannot—we must not—lose or neglect Samuel's memory and his values. We must hold him dear in perpetuity and in the same spirit support his loved ones."

Fitz-Hugh descended and took his place next to Celeste as young Samuel, Samuel Kravitz II I saw from the leaflet, walked with an aggressive stride to the pulpit. He looked strikingly like a young version of his father as he took his place behind the pulpit and looked out at us. His whole posture was one of anger.

I turned to Janet and whispered, "Uh-Oh."

She glanced at me quizzically.

"I have lost," he said in a young voice that echoed his father's, "my best friend, my mentor, my father, who was the best dad anyone could have had." On this last word his voice broke. "Why?" he asked all of us loudly.

He surveyed us. "Dad was not only a great father but he was above all else a survivor. I'm sure you are unaware of our family history, but my grandparents survived as children in the Holocaust. My father's interest in the humanities and languages was due in part to his being raised by multi-cultural parents and multi-lingual grandparents who stressed the need and ability to survive through a comprehensive understanding of humanity and international relations as a touchstone value in their and our lives and in my father's life. It makes no *damn* sense that he would take his own life."

He paused to let his words sink in. In the stark silence I could hear the faint electric buzz of the lighting system and small sounds of wind buffeting and whistling on the stain glass windows. There was a single cough.

"What you also do not know is that my father was a survivor in the literal sense. The fact is that he survived prostate cancer, had a successful surgery five years ago and was elated when the results came in that the surgery was 100 percent successful. So, why would he now take his life? Leave us? We will never know, and that may be the greatest tragedy of all."

He paused again and then added declaratively, "So, does someone want to tell me what the hell actually did happen?"

I could see uncomfortable movement, the slightest squirming in the body language of those sitting up front.

The silence continued for what seemed an interminable time, finally ending with young Samuel saying, his voice echoing loudly, "This does not end here today. We will keep looking for answers. Trust me."

He left the pulpit and marched angrily to the front pew and sat down with the family. The organ burst into a recessional but the audience in the chapel sat there stunned. The acolyte appeared and began the ceremony of extinguishing candles. Finally a few random people stood and everyone else did the same and began exiting.

The tears in my eyes took me completely by surprise. I glanced over at Janet who was pulling Kleenex out of her purse and gratefully accepted her offering. I tried to think of the last time I had cried and could not remember.

Fitz-Hugh stood and went over to Joan Kravitz and the Kravitz family for what I would presumed were further words of comfort and connection. Howard walked by blinking and red-eyed. Ursula stood near the altar, tears streaming down her face, her expression one of the deepest agony, as if she had confronted the full tragedy of Kravitz's loss for the first time. I felt the need to comfort her and felt the alternative pull of self-preservation pushing me along with Janet toward the chapel's door.

Outside the weather had turned colder, greyer, a light snow beginning to fall. Janet turned to me and said, her breath steaming out into the cold, "Was that supposed to make us feel better? I'm a wreck."

"Yeah, same here."

"I felt so sorry for Joan, Natalie, Samuel. The others, Lanier and Fitz-Hugh, they were just going through the motions, weren't they?"

"Yeah."

"What do you think happened?"

I shook my head. "I honestly don't know. People these days like to stir things up at any occasion, particularly the press. I don't know whether that's it or something else occurred. There are weird circumstances, but they don't prove anything. I think the police are suspicious but don't have much to go on." I shrugged. "It's just a huge tragedy, no matter how you look at it."

Janet sighed. "Yes, it certainly is."

We drove home in silence, lost in our own thoughts as the weather turned more spiteful, and parked in the garage.

When we entered the family room, Zoltan and Sarah were watching a National Geographic special on lions.

"Where's Tommie?" I asked.

They both looked at me as if I was stupid.

"Where you think?" Zoltan asked. "How was service?"

"Awful," I told him. "Kravitz's son took the pulpit and asked everyone what really happened."

"You serious?"

"Oh yeah."

"My God, that send big ripple through the university."

"Yeah."

Zoltan waited a beat as we all thought about possible under-currents going forward, then said, "To change subject, Thomas, Janet...I have been talking with Sarah about this situation with Tommie. I want to go with you to meeting at school."

Janet looked shocked and said firmly, "That's not a great idea Zoltan. The school's head, Ms. Olin, is a psychologist. I think she'll resonate with me as a fellow professional and with Thomas as an educator. I think you would intimidate her."

"Yes. That what I thinking. Nicely of course. I reason with her."

Janet thought for a moment more about the prospect of Zoltan joining our meeting. "No," she said with finality. "It wouldn't help. It might hurt. It's too many people for one thing; it would get confusing."

"But I uncle. I am educator. I am professor. I smart guy. I can help."

"No, this is a matter for just our nuclear family."

"What nuclear have to do with this? I help nonproliferation. Keep Tommie here."

Janet smiled indulgently. "Do me a favor, okay? Let us handle this."

Zoltan stared us down for a moment and then gave a huge shrug of resignation. "Well, I be available if you change your mind."

Sarah broke in, "But you can't let them expel him. You can't let him be sent away. He's my *brother!*"

"Yeah, honey. That's our thought too. Dad and I will do our best."

"What this Ms. Olin like?" Zoltan asked.

"Nice enough, certainly caring," Janet told him, "but a bit of a stick-in-the-mud rule follower, inflexible. Plus she's relatively new to the job, so once she makes a decision she's probably not inclined to back down from it or change her mind. Fortunately she seems to be a bit on the fence about this situation, so there's room for some discussion."

"We see how all this work out. You keep me in loop. I want to help."

"Okay," I said to help end the conversation.

There was a thumping on the basement stairs. The door to the basement flew open and Sparky ran out into the family room. Despite our daily instructions and scolding that Tommie was not to dress the dog up in fire station costumes, she again had a fireman's hat tied around her neck that had fallen off her head and was bouncing off her front legs, a red cape knotted to her collar trailing behind her. She ran to Janet and hid behind her as Tommie trailed into the room. He was dressed in full fireman's regalia—hat, slicker, boots, plastic hatchet hanging loosely from a rope tied around his waist.

"Sparky's being a bad fire dog!" he said much too loudly, almost a wail. "She doesn't want to help me anymore!"

"That's because you're torturing her!" I heard my voice rising to meet the volume of his, a rush of emotion coming up in me at the thought of how many more times would I have to endure this kind of behavior, which only seemed to get more and more dysfunctional and problematical. It seemed that no matter what one said to Tommie it just went in one ear and out the other as his compulsiveness ruled his personality and life. I was flooded by feelings of both anger and hopelessness.

"Thomas, you don't need to use that tone of voice," Janet said disapprovingly.

Tommie looked at us, stricken, his upper lip quivering.

Zoltan, in all his height and girth, stood and calmly walked over to Tommie, went down on one knee, took Tommie's hand and looked him straight in the eye.

"Tommie," he said, "you like your life here?"

Janet and I looked at one another, acknowledging with one glance that we were on the wrong track and very definitely did not have a clue about how to proceed, and that we should let Zoltan continue, however risky that might be. He seemed to have some sense of Tommie that we did not, and seemed to know what he was doing.

"Yeah…sure," Tommie responded tentatively.

"You love your parents? You like Tommie Town? You love Sarah and Sparky?"

Sniveling, "Yeah…"

"You want to be a good boy, I know."

"Uh-huh…"

"So, what happen with this Sharif?"

"He took my fire engine! He called me," Tommie screwed up his face, "a…re-tard!"

"Okay… I see. Look, Tommie, I'm going to say something. I want you to repeat it. Okay?"

"…Yeah…"

"'What they say doesn't matter.' Repeat that."

Tommie said hesitantly, "What they say doesn't matter."

"Whenever anyone call you name or say something bad, that is what I want you to say to yourself. Do you think you can do that?"

"…I guess."

"No, Tommie, this very important. You can never let what happen with this Sharif boy happen again. You must believe that when anyone calls you a name it does not matter and must say this to yourself. You know why, Tommie?"

"…No."

"If you ever let what you do to this boy ever happen again, Tommie, your school will not let you come back and you will have to go to special school in another part of the country. You must never do anything like this again. No name-calling; no hitting. What is important is for you to stay here, be with your family, Sparky, Tommie Town. That's why whatever anyone say or do to attack you, you must tell yourself, it doesn't matter."

"But he called me a re-tard!" Tommie was crying now.

"It just a stupid name, Tommie. Names do not matter. It what in here," Zoltan struck the center of his chest, and then reached out and lightly touched the center of Tommie's chest, "that matters. What you think they call me at school?"

Tommie looked at Zoltan. It was obviously a revelation to him that anyone had ever dared call Zoltan a name.

"They call me a giant retard. How you think that make me feel?" He reached out and tickled Tommie, who started to giggle even as he was crying.

XX
You Will Be Fine

O<small>N THE SECOND</small> T<small>HURSDAY IN</small> F<small>EBRUARY AT</small> 10:30 <small>AM</small> <small>THE ADMINISTRATIVE TEAM ASSEMBLED IN THE PRES-</small> <small>IDENT'S OFFICE FOR THE FIRST PRESIDENT'S CABINET</small> <small>MEETING SINCE</small> K<small>RAVITZ'S DEMISE</small>. We sat in awkward, sub-dued silence. As always at random moments the forced air heat came on with a rush and its scents of outgassing and dried dust washing over us.

Wentz, Depew and Fitz-Hugh were absent, leaving us to wonder whether they were caucusing separately before our meeting or were simply randomly late.

I was spending most of my time now with new hires, re-viewing plans for the new studio, commissioning and manag-ing the president's upcoming first interactive webcast town hall meeting with alumni and friends, trying my best to let the tasks at hand distract me from any reflection, passing Ursula in the hallway as we acknowledged one another with distant, respectful pleasantries, sitting well apart from one another in meetings while I tried with a total lack of success to ignore her scent, her sensuality and her every motion. Work was the easiest part of my employment; everything else threatened to overwhelm me.

We had all taken our same seats—except of course for the seat Kravitz had occupied previously. In his place was the ho-mogenized niceness of the new interim provost, Don Powers. Powers was an attractive, pleasant fellow, tall with blow-dried coal black hair, a small mouth, eyes spaced far apart, long fine-boned fingers and an ever-present smile. At the moment he was smiling self-assuredly, his underlying anxiety and nervousness at this new situation palpable. Lusby was looking ever more reddened and despondent. Ursula was distracted by her iPad, examining different screens with a whisk of a finger. Reve was staring off at something across the room, contemplating per-haps his travel schedule and different scenarios for his interac-tions with top prospects. Ramis sat ramrod straight in his white clinician togs, light glinting off his titanium framed glasses, an impenetrable expression on his face. Fein was pensively and unconsciously chewing his fingernails, alternating between one hand and the other. I was distracted by the fact that at 4:00 pm that afternoon Janet and I were to meet with the head of Tom-mie's school. I kept rehearsing the case for Tommie to stay at the school, playing out different scenarios, what the head was likely to say and how Janet and I would respond.

There was a click of the door lock and Fitz-Hugh, Wentz and Depew entered. Mystery solved—they had been meeting.

Fitz-Hugh went to his desk to drop off some materials and pick up a legal pad. Wentz sat in his usual chair, glanced around the table, nodded to us. He was in serious mode today. Depew deposited his odd little body in his chair. He looked around at us through his yellow-lensed aviator glasses, his insouciant face surveying us as if we were an arrangement of furniture. Fitz-Hugh joined us. He cleared his throat.

"I've been meeting with our colleagues this morning," he nodded at Depew and Wentz, "to discuss the financial feasibil-ity of moving forward with our next international center, a very exciting prospect. It appears that we've garnered enough unrestricted funding through contributions to the Campaign for Progress to organize and launch plans, which will be coor-dinated under the experienced guidance of Dr. Wentz in con-sultation of course with Dr. Powers for our next center in…" he paused for effect… "Brussels."

Wentz made an almost imperceptible nod. Powers' smile intensified and grew a bit more rigid. The rest of us tried our best to put on expressions of surprise and approval.

Fitz-Hugh continued, "We have at present a sphere of influence in Asia; we will now begin efforts to create a sphere of influence in Europe. At points in the future, should funding become available, we will in due course look at the potential for centers in Latin America and the Middle East.

"Regarding Brussels, Dr. Wentz is presently talking with several universities there about establishing our program in their on campus facilities. I believe from what he's telling me that they fully understand, and are eager for, such a partnership. The program would begin as a cooperative student abroad exchange initiative but rapidly morph over 24 to 36 months into an interactive international center. There would be undergraduate and graduate programs at Sessions for their students and vice-versa, on-site academic admissions and administration personnel in Brussels to assist student recruitment and exchange programs and shared curriculum development. So, give me your thoughts on this new venture."

None of us spoke. I looked around and realized we were all holding back. What was there to say? This was a done deal.

Powers finally broke the silence just as Fitz-Hugh was beginning to get an irritated look on his face. It made sense for him to speak first; he had the most to lose or gain. "If I may be so bold, this forms a natural bridge between Sessions and Europe. For instance, our program in urban planning would now be open to interchange with students and faculty engaged in problem solving in European cities and vice-versa. As you go down each discipline—English, History, Political Science, the sciences—there are very interesting connections to be made with our European counterparts. The possibilities and synergies are endless, open only to our own inventiveness and imagination."

"Not to mention to what sells," Wentz observed with a slight smile. "Once up and running, it's got to be a self-sustaining enterprise. There will need to be a big federal and foreign government grant writing effort on its behalf, not to mention a strong fundraising effort among individuals, corporations and foundations interested in forwarding international relations."

"Yes, good thinking," Powers observed.

I thought about how Kravitz would have reacted to this new initiative. He would have noted that Brussels would have been his choice for Sessions' first international center and would have lectured us about the inherent risks of Beijing. He also would have been completely up in arms about the financial feasibility of the Brussels Center, asking where the money was coming from to run not one but two international ventures. I could almost hear him. And regarding this last thought, I wanted to ask Lusby the same question.

Ramis commented, "The opportunity to link arms with our fellow researchers in Europe through symposia, peer review and clinical trials would be most interesting and productive. They are onto things that have yet to be approved in the U.S. for instance. Knowing how those trials or research discoveries are faring and the next steps they are taking would be very helpful. Of course, it most likely would be the same for them. This is a very good development, Bryan."

"From a PR and communications standpoint," I added, "it adds heft to the concept of Sessions as a global university that we can make a part of all our materials. As well, we can develop branding of this new center as linked to our global image but with a separate and distinct identity. The potential for collateral programs from alumni trips to webcast programs focusing on issues relating to the European Union and its issues and challenges and how they affect the U.S. is huge."

"Good," Fitz-Hugh beamed. "I was sure you would all get it." He looked at Wentz. "Let's move forward."

Wentz nodded.

Fitz-Hugh turned back to us. "We'll be reporting back to you in more detail as time goes on and will use the cabinet as a sounding board. Your input will be greatly appreciated and very useful. I'd like to get this in front of the board of trustees this spring as a complete package for their approval with the cabinet's endorsement."

Wentz and the rest of us nodded in agreement.

"Other business?" Fitz-Hugh asked.

Silence again, then Fein timorously raised his hand, as if he was back in grade school. "What'll I do about these Kravitz inquiries? We have this woman reporter asking for the minutes of the last Faculty Senate meeting and she and the police keep interviewing people, even the family, asking questions."

"We have no comment," Fitz-Hugh said sharply and rather caustically. "Refer them to the family's attorney. That's what he's being paid for, by us I might add. That was the least I could do to help Joan."

"Thank you," Fein said meekly.

"Other questions, issues?"

We went on for another fifteen minutes on other issues— disputes between departments about assigned parking, another movement emerging to change the name of the university because Joshua Sessions at one point had owned a cotton brokerage business in Norfolk, Virginia, a planned student demonstration over transgender discrimination, a conservative faculty member posting an out of line blog featuring his considered opinion about local and national politics. All this was treated as business as usual by those of us in the room.

As I was walking down the hall back to my office, Ursula came up beside me and said softly, "Do you have some interest in joining me for lunch?"

I stopped dead in my tracks, turned and looked into her eyes. Her whole expression spoke to me of need.

"Okay...see you in a half hour or so."

Back in my office, I answered a few emails, answered some questions from staff, returned a phone call and then casually, as if I was going to pay a call on my old department in Hart

Hall, walked across the lower quadrangle, climbed the stairs to the upper quadrangle and then retraced my previous route to Ursula's apartment, déjà vu. Everything felt the same. The weather was the same, cold, damp and grey. The route was now the same. What had changed? Everything.

I let myself into her building through the alley door as before and climbed up the back stairs to her apartment, thinking about my last visit, about her black thermal tights, her Glock in its holster, her *au revoir* at the elevator. I felt anxious almost to the point of nausea, yet here I was. Insanity.

Ursula was on me before I could close her door, slamming me against it.

If intercourse can be an assault, over the next five minutes we were both guilty of it, releasing the pent up emotions and lust of weeks of denial. We went deep. Thinking faded away completely as we descended into the act, animals, hammering away in a void, feeling only the need for ecstasy and working as hard and fast as we could to find it, knowing it was there, wanting it. And finally it arrived, with supernatural intensity. I realized we were both screaming.

It was a long time before either of us could speak, her apartment silent. I listened to our labored breathing gradually subside, feeling that I might never move again, drifting in space, my mind still blank. After a time, the faintest street sounds began to nibble at the silence.

"Fu-uck," I heard myself declare suddenly.

We both began to giggle.

"Yes," she said. "Epic."

"Academy award winner."

We uncoupled and she snuggled up and threw a leg over me. "Yes."

We lay there for a time, lost in drifting thoughts until the reality of where we were and what we were doing slowly dawned on me.

"What the hell do we do about this?" I asked Ursula.

There was a long silence. I could feel Ursula pulling into herself even as we lay entwined.

She moved her leg and we now faced one another. "I am going to be leaving the university."

"What?"

"This whole episode with Kravitz is driving me crazy. I cannot get my job done. It is a total distraction. I've talked to my parents about the situation; I've even talked to my birth parents. They have all urged me to get away from this place and this situation. I have to go."

"Where?"

"I do not know yet. I am working on it."

"Does Bryan know?"

"He senses what is going on. He is giving me my space to work things out, I can tell. In his heart, he knows it would be better for me to leave. So, my dear, this is *au revoir* to our relationship. It is better for you anyway, for your family. But I must thank you many times over for your affection and companionship. They have meant a great deal."

"Thanks, I think… I'm…"

I was grappling with a cascade of emotions, relief being one of them, pain, disappointment, a huge sense of loss and regret all out of proportion to what I would have expected—not far from devastation.

"You will be fine, my dear. Just let this all play out. It is for the best."

I sighed. "I guess."

I walked back to the office in a daze, went through the motions of working until 3:00, then briskly took my leave, nodding at my staff on my way out the door, having informed them of the school meeting earlier in the morning, and drove out to our place to pick up Janet.

On the way, I alternately played out my romance with Ursula, our lunchtime together and our ending interspersed with thoughts about what to say to the head of Tommie's school. I was a basket case, totally frazzled and trying to keep myself together and fake normalcy.

Janet came out of the house when I pulled up, got into the car, looked at me and asked, "What's wrong?"

"Work is driving me crazy. Plus this little meeting has made me a bit anxious."

"Me too."

"How's Tommie?"

"Oblivious. Not a clue of why he's been home from school this week, despite Zoltan's talk with him and all the warnings. Just more of an opportunity to go back down to Tommie Town and be in his own little world. I told him he couldn't have Sparky down there and Sarah promised to keep her in the family room." She thought for a moment. "Actually, let me correct that. He has a clue; he simply chooses to ignore everything, prefers his own world to ours."

"Yeah," I shook my head. "That's the truth. You sure we're okay leaving Sarah to take care of him?"

"What choice do we have? We should only be gone a little more than an hour."

Schossler Academy, Tommie's school, was in an ancient mansion house left by a former board member and located at the top of a narrow twisting road up a steep hill. Thanks to incessant fundraising campaigns and heavy debt financing the school now had a gym off to the left, an auditorium off to the right and small playing field carved out of the woods.

Its spooky antediluvian, dark brick and verdant ivy exterior was offset by an interior that had been redesigned and redecorated to be warm and accepting with contemporary furniture of natural wood and soft primary colored cushions, wide open spaces, bright indirect lighting and substantial noise canceling ceilings and drapes. It was a place filled with children who seemed to have some purpose to everything they were doing and what they were doing at the moment at the end of the school day was what was called "work detail" where for 45 minutes the students were charged with sweeping the building, emptying the trash and otherwise cleaning up the facility before sports.

It felt very strange sitting in Ms. Olin's outer office reception area, a too-small room surrounded by glass with shatterproof embedded wiring with an empty reception desk, unkempt but healthy potted plants scattered around, the smell of stale milk in the air and vestigial, meant-for-children chairs whose design and color fit the décor perfectly but were hell on my back and hindquarters.

I could see through the glass in Ms. Olin's office door. She was turned from us, working at her computer monitor. We had met in passing at parent events. A not unattractive woman, her brown hair pulled back into a bun, black glasses, too serious an expression that could melt with humor and pleasantry when the moment called for it. Could not be easy being a head of a school for special needs children, I reflected. No easier than being a special needs parent perhaps.

She glanced at her watch, looked out at us, saved whatever she was working on and came out to offer her greetings.

"Thank you for coming by. Good to see again. I'm so glad we could have this conversation," she said as we walked into her office and sat thankfully in more comfortable, adult chairs.

I took a quick glance around. The usual diplomas, some generic prints, framed pictures of different graduating classes, a picture on her desk of her husband in a rustic setting in plaid shirt, jeans and hiking boots.

Ms. Olin looked at us a moment, from one to the other, sizing us up, deciding how to proceed. I could follow her thought process. We might appear to be a bit anxious, but she could see she was dealing with rational, not angry people. Janet was a fellow psychologist; I was a professor at Sessions, a fellow educator. She decided to play it straight.

"I must tell you," she said, bringing her hands together, "that I am a bit perplexed."

Janet and I glanced at one another, puzzled.

"How so?" I asked.

"Well, initially I was prepared to recommend Tommie's dismissal." She held up a hand signaling that we were not to respond. "Don't worry, that's not how we are going to proceed."

Janet and I both gave an audible sigh of relief and all of us smiled in reaction to how loud it was.

Ms. Olin continued, "We simply cannot tolerate violence and/or abuse of one child to another. The children we have in this school in particular must have as tranquil and structured environment as possible if we are to have a chance of success with them."

She paused to make sure we were following her line of thinking and to see whether we had any thoughts or questions.

We had not a clue what to say.

"Then I was prepared to recommend Sharif's dismissal."

We looked at her with surprise.

She acknowledged it, expected it.

"Not because of Sharif, but because of his parents. I have never in all my days met as obnoxious and hectoring set of parents as Sharif's. They called me numerous times every single day to repeat the same denunciation of Tommie and demand that he be separated from the school. There is such a thing as due process and I wanted to be sure I could speak with you to fully understand Tommie's background and history and to hear your side of this story and answer any questions you might have.

"Then this Tuesday, I received a call from Sharif's parents in which they told me they had been considering the matter with Tommie over the weekend and that they realized that they may have rushed to judgment, that these kind of flare-ups can occur among children and that they wished to withdraw their request to see Tommie separated from the school; in fact, they wanted to apologize for their being so upset and would like to encourage us to keep Tommie enrolled."

She began to smile. "And they did not stop there. They went

on to say that they did not understand until this weekend that Sharif had taken Tommie's fire engine away from him as a first act of aggression and that he had called Tommie a very unfortunate name. I'm not sure where they got this information. Did you talk with them?"

We both shook our heads. An inkling of suspicion crept into my consciousness.

"Well, they would be very happy to put this incident behind them. I have given this news and their revelation a good deal of thought and I now understand that Tommie did not initiate this incident and that Sharif not only took a prized possession from him but then called him, well, it's perhaps the worst thing any child here could call another. So, I have decided that we should let Tommie continue here at Schossler, but I must tell you that we cannot tolerate any future actions like this on Tommie's part again. Physical injury to another child is quite simply grounds for expulsion. In this one case, given the parents' turnabout and given the evidence that Sharif was indeed the instigator, I will let this go. But you need to make sure this doesn't happen again. I'd start with following our rule against bringing toys of any kind to school."

"Yes," we both said simultaneously, nodding vigorously, not wanting to tell her that such a rule had been in place in our household for years, that Tommie was as sneaky with hiding his toys as an alcoholic hiding miniatures.

We parted with Ms. Olin very amiably and as Janet and I walked out of the school toward the car, she turned to me and said, "That was really strange. What do think happened with Sharif's family to make them change their minds?"

"I'm not sure," I said, but I had an idea.

We got in the car and as we wound down the twisting hill driveway my cellphone rang.

Zoltan.

"So, how meeting go at Tommie's school?" he asked.

"Really, really well. They're not expelling him, but he's on a short leash from here on out. Hey, I am very sure I never told you when this meeting was. How did you know to call just now?"

"Oh, sometime I just know things." Zoltan began to chuckle.

"You bastard. What did you do?"

There was a moment of silence on the line and then Zoltan could not control his desire to tell us.

"Well, I deeply worried about our boy, Tommie, so I talk over with Kristina what to do and we agree on a plan."

"God damn it, Zoltan. You interfered. You could have ruined Tommie's future with the school. Sharif's parents could have brought charges or sued. What the hell do you think you're doing?"

"Just trying to help, Thomas, protect Tommie. I did good, yes? Look at result."

I found myself shaking my head. I glanced at Janet whose mouth was a firm line.

"Okay, what the hell did you do? Wait a minute. Let me put you on speaker phone." I reached the end of the drive, pushed the speaker phone symbol and set the phone in a cup holder between us before turning onto the county road to drive home.

Zoltan began to talk. "On Saturday I call Sharif's parents and talk with father, tell them I child's uncle and Godfather, medical professor at university, and often caretaker of Tommie and that we very sorry for what happened and that I want to explain, could they see me? At first he very bitter and wife in the background hurling insults and complaints until I say very directly that I want to make it up to them. After I repeat that several times, using my great charm, they stop and think and they agreed to see me.

"Je-sus."

"You had *no* right to do that, Zoltan," Janet added, furious.

"Yes, I agree but I did it to help you, help Tommie.

"So, I go see them and at first they really scared because of how I look, aren't even going to open the door but after I beg and plead and am super nice, they come outside and we talk and then after a while they invite me inside and then we have nice talk and they begin to understand and begin to see things my way."

"Why would they want to see things your way?"

"I pay Sharif tuition for next year."

"Oh, shit. You *bribed* them!"

"No, not at all, we just reach a good understanding of how make the situation better. Sharif agree he will be nice to Tommie from now on. Parents happy. You happy. Head of school may be happy sometime, who knows?"

For once I was speechless. I looked over at Janet and she shrugged and shook her head as if to say, "What can you do?"

"Okay, Zoltan. Look, understand something. You got the right result; for that we're grateful. But otherwise we're fairly pissed."

"Yes. You should be pissed. But understand too, I love you guys."

There was a pause in the conversation. Janet and I looked at one another again. I was beginning to feel like we had no more control over Zoltan than Tommie. "Okay," I said. "We get it. We'll talk to you when we're in a better frame of mind."

"Yes, Thomas. Good day."

I drove home, Janet and I in something of a state of suspended animation, each of us trying to process the meeting at the school and the conversation with Zoltan. Nothing ever seemed to turn out like we thought it would.

I parked the car next to our dusty box-covered Bimmer and as we walked in from the garage found myself wishing Janet would take an interest in it again.

Sarah was in the family room, munching on popcorn, watching her cool kids show, Sparky sitting at her feet, looking up intently at the bowl of popcorn, clearly hoping for some additional dropped pieces. Sarah picked up the remote and muted the TV.

"Hey parents. How'd the meeting go?"

There was the faintest trace smell in the air. I breathed it in, thought about it. Marijuana?

"God damn it, Sarah, have you been smoking dope again?"

"*Au contraire, mon pere*. You're probably smelling the couple of kernels of burnt popcorn."

"…Maybe…"

"But how did the meeting go, Dad, Mom?" she asked again, urgently.

Janet seemed oblivious to the smell. "The head of the school is going to let Tommie stay."

"Oh, yea! That's fabulous!"

"Another incident like this and he's gone," she added.

"That's not so good."

"No. Sarah, they don't want him bringing toys to school anymore. We've tried to stop him, but he's sneaky. Could you talk to him? He seems to listen better and understand better sometimes when you're the one explaining things to him, like Zoltan. And could you keep a lookout for him hiding toys to take to school. I'm very concerned. He just doesn't comprehend the trouble he can get into. We'll probably ask Zoltan to talk with him too."

"Sure, Mom. That's the least I could do."

Janet breathed a small sigh of relief. "Thanks."

Suddenly I caught another whiff of the smell, much stronger this time, acrid, burning plastic and wood.

"FIRE!" I shouted. Simultaneously, we heard a jet like whooshing sound from the basement. The sound of a fire extinguisher. Sparky stood and began barking in alarm.

I rushed to the basement door as Tommie's wail began to sound through the house. The basement stairway was filled with smoke.

"SHIT, GOD DAMN IT!" I heard myself exclaim in horror as I bounded through the smoke and thumped down the basement stairs.

Tommie Town was on fire, flames taking out one of his hotels and feeding off the plywood below, as in real life getting ready to spread to adjacent structures—a pharmacy, a dry goods store. The smoke wasn't as bad at this lower level but I was coughing from inhaling it on my way down. Tommie lay on the floor. The large fire extinguisher we had placed under Tommie Town—in the hopes we would never have to use it—was on top of him. I saw immediately what had happened. He had tried to put out the fire but the extinguisher was too heavy for him to hold in place and when he pulled the trigger it had caused him to fall over backwards. He lay there helpless in his confusion and grief, wailing.

I ran to him, grabbed the extinguisher and in a moment, with some judicious but heavy applications, had sprayed the fire out of existence.

I turned to Tommie, furious, coughing out, "You are going to god damned *kill* us all! What the *hell* have you done?"

Tommie lay on the floor wailing inconsolably. Janet came thumping down the stairs, ran to him, knelt and took him in her arms. Sarah and Sparky were close behind and joined Janet as they soothed our distraught child, Sparky jumping around them, licking at them, confused. The air was already clearing as the smoke trailed up the stairs into the house.

I surveyed the damage. A significant portion of Tommie Town was a mess, would have to be rebuilt. We'd have to scrub down the walls of the basement, repaint the place. I exhaled a large sigh of relief. Then I saw the magnifying glass covered with fire repellent lying in front of the hotel in a shaft of sunlight coming through one of the four basement casement windows. It was an ornate antiquity, originally my grandmother's, one of the few heirlooms we had, and normally resided on my desk where I used it as a paperweight.

Obviously, Tommie had taken it and used it, as every child does, as I had done as a child with this very same magnifying glass, to focus the sun in an intense beam, to create a fire, only in this case the small fire in Tommie Town which he intended to heroically put out, saving the citizens and the town had morphed into a mini-conflagration before he could stop it.

Janet looked up at me and said levelly in a voice full of reproach. "It doesn't do any good to yell at him like that."

"Yes it does," I said angrily, feeling less and less under control as a tsunami of emotions from Ursula's goodbye, my new job, the Kravitz situation and Tommie's destructive tendencies crashed across my consciousness. I was losing it. Better keep my mouth shut.

Janet looked at me with reproach.

I stood there and stared back at her, hostile.

"Maybe you should just quit your job, go back to teaching communications. It doesn't help to have you be so stressed out, half the time distant in some other world. We're going to need you here, now more than ever."

"Yeah, I could do that," I said cynically. "Fitz-Hugh would probably have me murdered or something."

"Thomas!"

"Just kidding. On a more serious note, maybe it's time to raze Tommie Town and do away with all our enabling. Maybe bring Tommie back into the real world."

Janet, holding Tommie curled up in a fetal position, and Sarah beside her both looked up at me as if I had lost my mind. Clearly a Tommie Town urban renewal project was in our future.

XXI
A Three Letter Word

WITHIN A FEW WEEKS, as February accelerated toward March, life at Sessions seemed to move more or less back to business as usual, at least on the surface.

Below the surface, in the hearts and minds of those of us in the central administration, things had changed irrevocably. Any *esprit de corps* was gone, replaced by careful, guarded behavior. The smell of suspicion was everywhere. The whole atmosphere only served to strengthen my sense that a great injustice had been committed and that Samuel Kravitz had lived for naught.

Winter continued on with a gray sameness to all the days, however there were also small signals of spring approaching. Basketball season was winding down. Lacrosse practice would soon begin indoors, as well as in the ice and mud. The baseball team was planning to decamp to Florida. Courses wound their inevitable way through their syllabuses with exams as the final endgame. I could sense among the students I saw around campus a palpable restlessness as spring break approached.

The president's first interactive webcast town hall meeting was to occur next week, the first week of March. The pressure was really on—this was the first event under my management in a new position, a total national and international exposure with a blizzard of details, uncertainties and decisions.

By Wednesday afternoon, after a series of meetings where problems kept surfacing like Whack-A-Moles, the thought of ice-cold beer crossed my mind. Not only did I need a drink but I needed to get out of the administration building, away from meetings, and breathe some fresh, moist air.

Normally I would have waited until 5:00pm. However, Janet and I had made a pact that instead of my going to the club after work I would come home directly so that I could be even more attentive to both Tommie and Sarah, Tommie because he needed it whether he wanted it or not and Sarah because we had capitulated to her desire to apply to programs for underage gifted and talented youth at different universities, and she wanted—and needed—our help with the applications process.

So, if I wanted an after work drink now, I had to sneak out an hour early, which I had not done until today. Too busy, too risky.

But today I walked out of my office and down the hall as if going to the restroom, then took the back stair out of the building an hour early.

The walk to the club was damp and cold, the wind blustering out of the northeast. As I reached the flagstone stair to the club's deeply varnished front door, I noticed a few crocuses, some lavender, some orange, peeking out from the half melted snow by the stairway's wrought iron railing. They brought a momentary smile to my face.

At this early hour the club was empty. As I entered the bar area, my attention was drawn immediately to a distant wall where I saw Frank Lusby sitting at a small table near the drapes trying his best to drink a martini while fading into the scenery. I went over to his table and sat across from him as a waiter saw me and drew a beer at the tap.

Lusby looked terrible, his face reddened and drawn at the same time, pulled down by a deep frown almost as if he were in some acceleration chamber.

"Frank, you look awful," I told him as I sat down.

Lusby picked up his martini, took a slug and looked at me. "I am awful."

"What's the problem?" I asked as the waiter set my beer in front of me.

He put down his martini, reached out and stirred it with the toothpick that had held four olives. "More money."

"Anonymous?"

"Yeah... $4.7 million in six different wire transfers from abroad, different countries, arrived over the last few days."

"Jesus."

Long sigh. "Yeahhh... I feel like a grenade has been lobbed into my office every time one of these gift notices pops up on my screen. But this is why Bryan's all hot to trot on this new center in Brussels."

"I was wondering about that."

"Wonder no more."

I paused, thinking for a time, then asked, "So, Frank, something I'm not sure I understand. Why are these international centers so important? I mean I get the whole global university theme and I understand Bryan's Washington ambitions and I see how it increases Sessions' importance in the world, burnishes its reputation, helps international relations overall, but I get the feeling there's something else going on. I mean what's going on with these wire transfers, Bryan's aggressiveness with the implementation of the centers, the involvement of characters like Wentz and Depew? You know what I mean?"

Lusby stared at me, appraising me and the situation before he said, "Well, Thomas, you're a bright guy. You've got good instincts. Answer your own question."

"I'm not sure I want to."

"Good man. You don't. Ignorance is bliss, truly." He paused, reached down, took a final long draw on his martini, placed the empty glass back carefully on the table, raised his hand and made a circular motion to the waiter signaling another round, then looked me squarely in the eye. "I can give it to you in one three letter word, beginning with S, ending in Y, with a P in the middle."

For several moments, as I ran what Lusby had said through my consciousness several times, I was speechless. "Shit…" I looked him over to be 1,000 percent sure this wasn't some badly timed put on. "You're kidding me."

"Wish I was."

"Well, the suspicion had crossed my mind on a couple occasions. But is this for real? You're sure of this? It seems just… surreal."

"Yeah, it's real all right. Can't get into it, but I've been there on a couple of occasions where Bryan let things slip. I just acted as if I hadn't even noticed or heard anything. It's not that the whole premise and program isn't legit for these centers. They truly are what we say they are and operate for all the excellent, cooperative reasons for being that our president so glibly espouses. But I get the really strong feeling that they also have a few integrated, embedded personnel and operations whose purpose is entirely different from that expressed in the program and course catalog."

"Jesus. It all makes sense. Yeah, sphere of influence all right. But why? What's the motivation?"

Lusby shrugged. "My guess is that Bryan and Greta Hauser, Madam Secretary, are in this together, maybe not directly. Folks like this always have go-betweens representing them. He's serving her and our country's interests in return for future rewards. Not like his next move would be into another university presidency. He has far greater ambitions."

"Damn, Frank, who knows this other than you?"

"I would guess besides our president and Depew, maybe Wentz, you, me and I would guess shortly, Zoltan."

"Zoltan can be trusted."

"I'm sure you are right."

"Ursula?"

"Who do you think is running the show? It ain't Wentz."

"Jesus Christ," I heard myself mutter. In my heart and soul I knew it was true. I knew he was right. I suddenly felt a great sense of loss and regret. "Why haven't you told any-one this?"

Lusby shrugged unhappily. "Got no one to talk to. Who would I tell? Bryan? My colleagues at Blakum? Hell, they'd treat me like a leper. Emily Sayzak? The Kravitz family? Hell, I could always call the secretary of state. Besides, what proof do I have? You're the only one who is more or less in the same boat—who I can talk to, who I trust. Just like you're the only one Ursula can talk to."

I felt my face turn crimson.

"Except I'm sure that in your various conversations this par-ticular subject has never come up, right?"

"Right."

"Don't worry. You and Ursula is just another guess on my part, a thought I have shared with no one else."

"Thank you." I drained my beer and stood to leave. I felt a sudden strong urge to go home.

"Don't mention it."

I walked out of the club and across campus toward the park-ing lot, the sun long gone, the overcast gray of the sky fading into darkness, the walkway lights blinking on, the wind bluster-ing harder, preoccupied with rehashing my conversation with Lusby. As I skirted the botanical garden, I became aware of someone walking up from behind me, a woman from the sound of her heels on the asphalt.

I picked up my pace and turned slightly.

Emily Sayzak.

Shit.

"Hey, Dr. Simpson. Could I have a word?" she said as she hus-tled up beside me. She wore a tight fitting, belted, lined trench coat that accentuated her small waist. I picked up my pace, but she matched it. 'Nice set of legs,' I thought and then shook my head to rid it of that and any other observations in that direction.

"Or should I call you Dr. No Comment?"

"Uh, how 'bout we call me Gone."

"Actually I thought the Dr. No Comment was kind of cute...
So, now I know you are Dr. Thomas Simpson, the new director
of university and campaign communications. You don't seem
pleased to see me."

"I'm not."

"What was behind the Faculty Senate vote for an independent audit of university finances?"

I stopped. She stopped with me and we faced each other. She
was too close. Light gray eyes, long lashes. "Look," I said, "I
don't have anything to say, plus I'm in a hurry. Good to see
you."

Emily Sayzak looked at me closely, considering me. "You
have pretty eyes."

"Oh, Jesus. Cut the crap. I have nothing to say, because I
know nothing. Okay?"

"Did you know that a woman dressed in a jogging suit was
seen in the vicinity of Provost Kravitz's car?"

"I've heard that but what difference does it make? Women jog
all the time in the park."

"In 22 degree weather?"

"People are crazy. Doesn't surprise me."

"Don't you think it's kind of suspicious that the gun Kravitz
used to kill himself had its serial number filed off so that it
could not be traced."

I felt my stomach drop. "That is strange," I admitted.

What was it about reporters? They dressed badly, in cheap,
ill-fitting clothes, always rumpled like they had slept in them,
always trying to fashion random facts into a plot of some kind,
always looking for 'the story,' sniffing for it like a mouse sniffs
for cheese. The good ones had some sort of sixth sense and
were scary. Right now I felt like a large piece of Roquefort.

"I have nothing to say," I told her.

She reached into her bag, pulled out a card and handed it to me.

"Let me give this to you again. My work, cell and home phone
are on there in case you'd ever care to say something or just get

together for a drink or whatever," she said in a friendly and familiar manner that both scared me and attracted me.

"Okay. Thanks." I took the card, turned and hustled away, leaving her standing there.

As I drove out of the university parking lot, I placed a call to Ursula at her office.

She answered immediately, "Yes, Thomas?"

"Emily Sayzak just ambushed me on the way from the club, wanted to know what was behind the Faculty Senate vote for an independent audit of the university finances, why there was a woman in a black jogging outfit in the vicinity of Kravitz's car and why the gun he used had its serial number filed off."

"What did you tell her?"

"Nothing. I walked away."

"Good. Thank you. We will handle it."

"I hope not."

"What do you mean, Thomas?"

"Not like you handled Kravitz."

"No, no, no. You are talking silly. No connection, my dear."

"Okay. Whatever you say."

I hung up and stared long and hard at the road ahead, my mind racing in a thousand directions when my cellphone rang.

Berger. Fuck.

I thought momentarily about not taking the call, then picked up the phone.

"How's it goin'?" he asked.

"Business as usual on the surface; very uneasy below."

"Hmmm... Yeah, that figures... Say, I got a question. I'm looking at the campaign balance sheet and the university budget and yah know what?"

"What?"

"I'm beginning to have the same questions the former provost had. In fact, I gave these reports to my man, Ziggy, and he had similar concerns. The word he used, preceded by a string of expletives, was 'cover-up.' Can you shed any light on this?"

There was a long pause as I tried to stifle an immense panic overtaking me and think of what to say. Classic that the board and even Berger had never really focused on the budget and campaign numbers comparatively until now. Their trust and confidence in Bryan had lulled them into total head nodding complacency.

Berger said, "I take your silence to mean you know something."

"Yeah. Where are you?"

"Bah-ston."

"Got time for a quick trip down here?"

"Yeah, maybe."

"Call Lusby. Have him meet you for a very private drink at the Intercontinental."

"You're not wasting my time, Thomas. Right?"

"Nope. It's better if you hear things from him. He's closer to knowing what's going on than I am."

"Okay, man. Never had this conversation, did we?"

"Sure didn't. Thanks."

"I may owe you some thanks."

"We'll see."

I hung up and speed dialed Zoltan.

"Yes, Thomas," he answered.

"We need to talk, man."

"At club?"

"No, I'm already on my way home. Part of the new regimen."

"You not want to talk on phone?"

"Yep."

"I come over to your place after dinner, bring Kristina. She here with me. You and I take walk around neighborhood."

"That'll work. Say 7:30?"

"Yes."

When I came in from the garage, Sarah was in her usual seat watching her usual cool kids show. I was pleasantly surprised to also see Tommie there, laying on the rug, a sheet of paper beside him, copying spelling words into a small bound notebook.

One of our objectives was to keep Tommie out of the basement and Tommie Town by making him do his homework first. We had talked with his teacher who pointed out to us that she posted daily homework assignments on the class's webpage, a fact we had somehow missed. Without this knowledge Tommie would have normally told us that he had done the work in school or did not have any homework, but now we could check daily to see what he had skipped over, blown off, ignored or where he simply had not understood the instructions.

As well, we had given him some daily responsibilities with Sparky, like taking her for a walk and picking up after her. Of course, one of us, usually a somewhat resentful Sarah, accompanied him.

So, I made no comment, nodded to Sarah, who gave me a passing wave of her hand, and walked into the kitchen where Janet was rustling up a more or less instant dinner. The glasses of white wine she had poured for us were on the counter.

"What's with Tommie?"

"He's doing his homework."

"Wow, what a concept. How'd you pull that off?"

"Bribery."

"That figures."

"Yes. I promised him you would take him to the fire station this Saturday if he got with the new program."

"Hmmm… You really went all out on the self-sacrifice there, didn't you?"

She laughed, stirring instant scalloped potatoes into a stainless pan of boiling water. "Brilliant, I thought."

"Oh yeah. Not that I had any plans or anything."

"I know what your plans are or were. Get up, eat a pensive breakfast and then sneak off to the office."

"Hmmmm… Yeah…it's this town hall meeting…"

"Honey, it's always going to be something."

"Yeah… say, look, after dinner Zoltan and Kristina are coming over."

"Really? That'll be nice. What's the occasion?"

"I need Zoltan's sounding board advice about stuff going on at Sessions."

"Ummm, serious?"

"Yeah... can't discuss it."

"Okay, you guys can take Sparky for a walk. Kristina and I can see the kids off to bed. I'll call her and see whether she wants to read Tommie a story."

"Okay," I said, hearing myself exhale a sigh of relief that Janet had not asked any further questions. Picking up my glass of wine, I reflected that a normal child would have long ago outgrown the need to have a bedtime story.

DINNER WAS THE USUAL, a series of muted and truncated conversations at the kitchen table in which the adults tried to pry information from the kids and the kids did their best to resist through monosyllabic responses, although they were a bit more keyed up than usual at Zoltan and Kristina's impending visit.

As we were clearing plates, the doorbell rang and Sparky began barking excitedly

When I opened the door, the kids and Sparky beside and around me, a light snowfall was drifting around outside, the smell of it fresh and pleasant.

Zoltan stood there, his presence blocking the view.

I caught a small glimpse of Kristina, blond hair and tan knit cap behind him.

He stomped on the mat on the front step to shed any snow or grit off his boots and came into the hall.

Kristina followed, bringing in a cellophane covered plate of sugar cookies and under it a children's book of stories.

"These are Belarusian stories," she told us, handing the plates of cookies to Janet. "Frankly, a bit odd, more parables than stories, but Tommie may find them interesting."

Sarah said, "Cool. I'd like to listen in. Could you read some of it in your language?

"Of course."

Zoltan knelt down next to Tommie and said, "Tommie, you being a man of the house and doing your homework like you supposed to?"

"Yeah."

"Well my young man, for that you get a medal."

He reached into his coat pocket and pulled out a small plastic ziplock bag with a cerulean blue military medal in it, fluted iron cross, Russian looking.

"Wowwwww," said Tommie as he carefully took the medal. "Coolllll. Thank you!"

"Where'd you get that?" I asked.

"Same theater person who lend us Thanksgiving dress up."

"Ah…"

"Now, Tommie, you must keep this in a safe place. And what else, Tommie?"

Tommie looked at him, puzzled.

"Where can this medal absolutely not go?"

"Oh yeah…school."

"That is right."

Tommie had taken his medal out of the plastic and was examining it closely. "I can put it on my fire station jacket, like for bravery."

"Yes."

"Okay, Tommie," Janet said. "Time for bed. You go to your room and get in your pajamas and brush your teeth. We'll be up in a minute for Kristina to read you a story. We'll put the cookies away for tomorrow."

"Ohhh-kay," Tommie said unwillingly, still gazing at and fingering his medal.

I opened the hall closet, pulled Sparky's leash from a hook, called her and clipped on the leash and Zoltan and I walked out the front door into the cold, clear air and the light snow.

Our neighborhood consists of wide streets with paved cut-through walkways throughout to help keep our families and their children off the roads. At this time of night they were deserted.

Zoltan pulled a pint bottle of Stolichnaya from an inner pocket of his overcoat.

"Here," he said after taking a voluminous slug, "clear head."

"Hah. Right." I took my own slug.

We made our way along the walkways, our breaths blowing out before us as from two stable animals, Sparky finding fascination in every dog pee marking on either side while I explained the latest developments to Zoltan, both of us taking pulls on the bottle.

When I had finished, he said, "So, what you telling me is that Ursula some kind of secret agent running spy ring out of president's office that extend into new international centers?"

"That about sums it up."

"That unbelievable."

"Plus, Ursula told me she's leaving, so she/they must be feeling the heat from all the suspicion surrounding Kravitz's death. Maybe this situation will resolve itself."

Zoltan shrugged. "You pie in the sky. You also too close to risky situation. I think you need to have health issue immediately. Maybe we fake mild heart attack. Let Berger figure things out. He in a much better place to do something."

"Jesus. What a big fucking help you are. For starters, I've got the president's first town hall coming up next week."

"After that perhaps. In any case, you lay low, get sick, disappear, break leg, hurt back, something to get you out of that building."

We walked for a time while Zoltan ruminated seriously.

Finally, he said, "I think about this. Will not share this discussion."

I shook my head. "Let's just see what happens."

We walked back to the house lost in our own thoughts.

By the time we returned, Janet and Kristina had finished putting Tommie to bed and were in the family room, bottle of wine open, glasses for us on the table. Sarah apparently had enough Belarusian immersion and decided to leave us alone.

"So, what is this all about?" Janet asked out of curiosity once we were all seated.

"I had this reporter after me today, asking a lot of questions about Kravitz, plus now Bryan wants to start a new international center in Brussels. Just a lot to absorb and react to. I wanted Zoltan's thinking on some of it."

Kristina cocked her head when I mentioned the Brussels center. "Fritz Johnson was in Washington last week," she told us. "We only know because someone at State called our dean wanting more information on him than his Wikipedia biography. You know, 'what is he like,' 'who does he know' kind of things."

"What was he there for?"

"I do not know. We were left with the clear impression that this was not a social visit."

"Well," I told them, "I'm just going to lay low, do my job and we'll see what happens.

XXII
Birth Parents

NOTHING HAPPENED. At least that's what it seemed. Perhaps I was too busy preparing for the town hall meeting, focusing on getting the details right, to pick up on any subtleties.

It wasn't that difficult a project technologically, but it had a lot of different moving parts that had to be coordinated and, as with any public broadcast, while we wanted it to seem like an open forum, it had to be rigorously controlled.

Basically it was set up as a webcast in our existing university studio, which had been upgraded for the occasion with rental and new equipment we could move to the new studio once completed. Dr. Don Powers was serving as a friendly moderator and master of ceremonies, a very clever move on Fitz-Hugh's part. Powers would get literally worldwide exposure as the incoming provost and academic partner to the president's administration. Plus, he had exactly the right broadcast persona; he was attractive, bland, friendly and intelligent, with enough experience and acumen at this sort of public discourse to manage his scripting for the conversation adroitly.

Alumni and friends worldwide could register online, which allowed us to know who was out there, and they could submit questions via email so that we could screen and chose among their questions for those few with the best or most interesting content, as well as cut out all those that were seditious, axe grinding or reflecting mental illness.

In our key cities, nationally and internationally, as a benefit for our supporters and our older alumni, particularly those of wealth, some of whom were not technologically savvy or even computer owners, we held regional meetings at various conference centers where we served refreshments. Their questions had been solicited beforehand so that we could cherry pick one or two from the most wealthy or that actually had significant merit. All of this boiled down to a dozen questions that Fitz-Hugh had in advance and would have well-rehearsed responses to.

As moderator, Powers helped referee the proceedings by introducing the president and leading off with some softball questions about recent news and developments, particularly in athletics, then moving into some background questions regarding Bryan's goals for the university, his educational philosophy, key initiatives he had undertaken at Sessions and how these were moving the institution forward. Bryan would hit these out of the park with grace, power, inspiration and articulate brevity, making eye contact with every viewer, doing his best to bring them into a trance like state of adulation before the alumni and supporters' questions began. I had no doubt that he would succeed in wowing his audiences; he was that good. My main objective was not to let technology or some other glitch foul things up.

Choreography was as important as technology in an endeavor like this. And naturally the press had to be involved, locally and in each region where they had their own pressroom, so as not to intermingle or interfere with our alumni and supporters.

So it began, Powers just right in his respectful, inquisitive obeisance, Fitz-Hugh in a blue suit, TV blue shirt and Sessions University rep tie at his most charming, sincere, brilliant self. I thought to myself, 'God damn he's good.'

As I was sitting near the engineer in the control room watching both Powers and Fitz-Hugh in the studio through its surrounding glass, the broadcast on the monitor above, Emily Sayzak sat down beside me.

I jumped.

"You need to leave," I whispered to her. "Now."

I glanced back at Bryan and found him answering a question from an alumna about dormitory facilities for women, articulating the perfect response with a flicker of a side-glance at me and Sayzak.

"Get out of here, please. You are about to cost me my job."

She had noticed Bryan's reaction. "Okay, but I have another question or two. Could we meet somewhere?"

"Hell no. Get out of here or I'll have you removed."

"Okay." She smiled at me, placed a hand on my leg, let it linger for a moment, stood, turned and walked out.

I turned back toward the studio and found that I had broken into a hot sweat, soaking my shirt under the armpits.

Bryan had just finished his response and seemed refocused and composed as he listened to the next question from an alum who was now a faculty member at another university, asking how he might best acquaint his administration with the green initiatives at Sessions.

The rest of the program went well, an hour and fifteen minutes of exchange with Powers concluding the session smoothly. It had gone brilliantly, I could tell. All those out in Sessions land should be quite happy to be led by a man of Fitz-Hugh's stature, vision and acumen.

Fitz-Hugh shook hands with Powers, made his way out of the studio and poked his head into the engineering room.

"Finish up here and come to my office," he commanded flatly.

I reconnoitered with my staff. Everyone was fist pumping, shaking hands and back slapping, a few hugs here and there, celebrating. I faked my own congratulations and enthusiasm. Then I walked across campus dreading my upcoming meeting and on the way passed by Ursula's office.

She looked at me in sympathy and said, "He's furious."

"But I didn't do anything."

"It's that reporter."

"I didn't even know she was here. How the hell did she even get in the studio?"

Ursula shrugged slightly. "She found her way in one way or another. That hardly matters now. Just do not defend yourself in there. Everything is 'Yes, Bryan.'"

"Okay."

At Fitz-Hugh's office, Ms. Bemis looked through me and said, "You may enter."

Fitz-Hugh sat behind his desk, red-faced.

Before I could sit down he pointed at me and said angrily, "Haven't I done well by you, Thomas? Promoted you? Supported you at every turn?"

"Sure," I said as I sat before him, "and I'm totally appreciative, doing my best to help you and Sessions."

"What the *hell* is it with you hanging out with this reporter?"

"I'm *not* hanging around with her. She's *stalking* me. I've given her no encouragement and have completely shut her down. But she keeps turning up. I have no idea how she got into the studio."

Fitz-Hugh was having none of my explanation. He pointed a threatening finger at me. "If I ever see you with that woman again, or even hear about your being near her," he punched his finger at me, "you *will* hand in your resignation. Is that clear?"

"Yes sir."

Fitz-Hugh closed his hand, lowered his arm, half turned toward the window behind us and gathered himself. I watched the transformation, fascinated, as he morphed into his normal charming persona.

He turned back to me. His eyes met mine. "Now, there's something else. We're having lunch in the private dining room at the club with Mark Berger on Friday to ask him to be vice chair of the board, our strategy for securing a very significant gift from him. As you know, the vice chair serves more or less as an understudy for the chair and is expected to be his successor. I want you to be there; Berger likes you, and your presence provides some reassurance that the publicity surrounding his appointment will be handled adroitly."

"You mean the lack of publicity."

"Exactly." Fitz-Hugh smiled at me in appreciation of my understanding. He was now my best friend and colleague again. "It'll be you, me, Berger, Fritz Johnson and Reve. High noon at the OK Corral."

"I'll be there." I stood to leave, suppressing my feet's desire to scamper the hell out Fitz-Hugh's office, and walked under control to the door, turned and gave him a small wave, which he returned, and stumbled out into the hallway.

Ursula was in her office staring at her monitor when I walked in, closed the door and sat down.

"Do you think maybe he has one of those multiple personality disorders?"

She turned and looked at me. "Bryan?"

"Yeah. He just had me into his office to threaten that I'm to resign if he ever saw, or caught wind of, my being around Emily Sayzak again, and then promptly turned around and invited me to a luncheon on Friday where he and Fritz, with Bernie and me in tow, plan to ask Berger to be vice chair of the board."

Ursula looked at me some more and then said carefully, "Bryan does not have a lot of time. Sometimes that means you see two sides of him in the same meeting. It has happened to me."

"I should just accept this?"

"Yes. I will do what I can to calm him down. I do have some influence."

"You do. I'm not sure I understand it, but do your best."

Ursula gave me a look I had never seen before, full of pathos and angst, from a woman whom I thought until this moment had none. "Bryan," she said, and her voice caught before she could continue, "is my birth father."

I found myself looking at her as I might have looked at the stump of my leg had my foot just been blown off.

"What?"

"Yes. He and Greta Hauser are my birth parents. They had me out of wedlock and put me up for adoption those many years ago. So, yes, I am able to talk to Bryan like no one else."

I sat there stunned for a time. Finally, I told her, "This is all beginning to make way too much sense."

"Yes. Now you know. No one else does."

"Why are you telling me this now?"

"You will understand soon."

"Okay."

I stood to leave. She came out from behind her desk and caught me by surprise before I could turn to open the door, embraced me and gave me a long, passionate kiss.

"Remember me, Thomas."

"How the hell could I ever forget…?" I mumbled, confused, shaking my head.

I wandered down the hall in a daze.

Back in my office I sat in my chair, pivoted around to look outside. Buds were beginning to show on the trees, a few sprigs of green were in the woods beyond the parking lot, the lawns still brown and muddy.

My cellphone buzzed in my pocket.

Berger. Je-sus. Why did he always call at some crisis moment, I thought, then reflected that lately there had not been any moments when there wasn't a crisis.

"Hey, how you doin'?"

I heard myself give a long sigh. "Not so great. This reporter who's been stalking me came into the studio during the town hall, sat next to me before I could shoo her away. Bryan saw her, called me into his office after the meeting and said if he ever saw us in proximity again, or heard of it, he wanted my resignation. Ursula says she'll talk to him and try to straighten him out."

"He's feeling a lot of pressure, I guess. Great broadcast though. You ought to be able to generate a ton of good publicity from it."

"Yeah… You talk to Lusby?"

"Yeah, I did… Been a long time since I've seen a grown man cry."

"Really?"

"Yeah, bawlin' like a baby. I put an arm around his shoulders. He told me the whole story. He's a good soldier. Caught in a damn impossible situation."

"Sure is."

"I told him to keep a low profile, keep his mouth shut, cut down on the drinking and palsy-walsy shit with Wentz and others to assist that goal. Don't think you'll be seeing him at the club much. At least I hope not. If you do, let me know."

"Don't know that I'm going to be at the club after work much myself. What are you going to do?"

"Can't say."

"Ah…okay."

"Speaking of the club, I understand we're having lunch on Friday."

"Yeah, so I just learned."

"I think you'll find it most interesting. In the meantime, just keep layin' low."

"Zoltan suggested that I should have a mild heart attack just to get out of the middle of this mess."

Berger snorted in appreciation of the humor. "Nah, don't do nothin', my friend. Lay low. Act normal."

"Sure thing."

ON FRIDAY WE WERE TO MEET IN THE PRESIDENT'S OFFICE FOR A BRIEF REHEARSAL PRIOR TO WALKING TO THE CLUB FOR OUR LUNCH WITH BERGER.

For once, Fitz-Hugh was there before we arrived. In fact, Ms. Bemis instructed Reve and me to wait outside for an interminable ten minutes or so. It occurred to me that Fritz Johnson was probably in there with Fitz-Hugh conducting other university business. I spent the time glancing furtively at her as she turned her attention to her monitor while Reve fidgeted and glanced at his watch every thirty seconds of so.

Today she was dressed in a magenta outfit with large lapels over a high neck magenta silk blouse and a long magenta skirt of full pleats. Massive spangled earrings resembling small wind chimes pulled at her earlobes. How the hell could she use a keyboard with those sword-like—also magenta—nails? I watched in wonder as she tapped a few keys. What was she paying attention to on her screen: University business, Costco sales, unimaginable porn? Eventually she turned slightly toward us and commanded, as if speaking to a spectral presence, "You may enter." How the hell did she know, I wondered, that now it was acceptable for us to open Fitz-Hugh's door whereas a moment before it had not been?

I had guessed right. Fitz-Hugh and Johnson were sitting at his office conference table smiling at something Johnson had just said, something lewd by the look of them.

"Well, boys," he said as Reve and I took seats, "let's see whether we can make our day by baggin' this little Jewish sucker."

We all laughed uncomfortably.

"Ah say that with great affection," Johnson clarified. "Bernie, what you got for us, son?"

Bernie shifted from the pensive and nervous-as-a-cat person outside the office to the charming raconteur we all loved to be with.

"Gentlemen," he said, placing his fingertips before him, and then expanding both hands outward as he spoke, "we have a remarkable opportunity before us... Mark Berger is a fan of Bryan's. He's become very involved in helping steer our endowment investments. He's been on the board over two years, so he's fully knowledgeable of Sessions, its goals and plans for the future. He's very careful in his commitments; hard to pin down; difficult to gauge his philanthropic interests, so the strategy here is to give him ownership of our university and its future. We need to forget about the numbers; that is, put out of your mind that this is a man conservatively worth over seven billion dollars and focus on our personal relationship. This isn't solicitation; it's a recruitment. We're all friends. Small talk beforehand.

"We get to the meat of our conversation toward the end of the meal. Bryan, you should lead. Fritz, I want you to follow and slam dunk the ask. You need to tell him how proud you'd be to have a man of his stature follow you as board chair. Thomas, you're there as a good friend. No need to do any more than be that. I'm just there to help get things on track should they go off track, which is not gonna happen with Bryan and Fritz. They're veterans," he began to laugh, "hardened criminals."

We all began to chuckle, a bit nervously, but I could see Bernie was working his charm and we were beginning to relax.

"Now let's go," Bernie said, standing.

We stood to leave and Fritz said to Bernie, "So, I hear through the grapevine that our buddy, Berger, is settin' up a big financial services business in Puer-to Ri-co. That right?"

We walked to the elevator and out of the building listening in as Bernie said, "Absolutely, Fritz. First, Puerto Rico is part of the U.S., so no regulatory hoops to jump through, easy access, don't need a passport, no customs, a lot of flights in and out, just a couple hours away. Second, like the U.S., there's good infrastructure, medical care and all the amenities of real civilization. Third, and here's the clincher, extremely low tax rate, both personal and business—so, all the advantages, none of the penalties. Very shrewd."

"Yeah," Fritz, agreed. "I've actually put it in my mind that some of our boom and bust boys in Texas might do well to park some of their play money with Berger in the good times, so they have somethin' to fall back on when they go belly up like they do once a decade."

"Makes sense," Bernie observed.

I noticed that Bryan was unusually quiet. Normally he would be adding something no else knew about the situation, either about the regulations in Puerto Rico or something of interest or import about Berger.

The weather was reasonably mild, a heavy wind rushing past us, tossing the just budding trees, penetrating our coats and suits.

I had now taken to scouting my surroundings, hoping fervently that I would not spot Emily Sayzak anywhere, looking for her around doorways and corners and even wondering whether I should be checking out trees and bushes. Definite paranoia.

When we entered the club Berger was standing in the hallway, dressed in a blue pinstripe suit, white shirt, Sessions tie. Clearly he knew the importance of the meeting.

I walked up and shook his hand, said, "You going to court?"

"Hah!" he laughed. "Maybe! I'm not really sure."

We sat in a small, private room off the main hallway.

Once our drink and menu choices were taken, Bryan talked in his glib and charming way about the new Brussels Center; how it was coming together; how he hoped the board could be brought into the conversation; that he hoped Fritz and Berger might assist him in leading the way, all of which Fritz and Berger nodded to amiably. Bernie gave a quick and very positive update for the Campaign for Progress. There were compliments from Fritz and Bryan for me about how well received the town hall forum had been. I was pleased with how the lunch was proceeding, establishing a proper level of comfort and exchange before the real task at hand.

Then, as our lunch plates were cleared, Fitz-Hugh said to Berger, "You know, Mark, in the context of things to come like this new center, let me take a moment to convey my great personal thanks to you. While you've been generous to us with your contributions, your investment advice has contributed many times more than your philanthropy. That, and your level-headed and wise perspective on so many things, is valued by the board and by me personally."

"Ah can certainly attest to that," Johnson added. "Fact is, ah don't know what we'd do without ya. So, it's occurred to Bryan and me that we'd like to more or less lock you in for a while." He held up his hands, palms out to prevent Berger from responding, which he was about to do.

"Mark, my friend, indulge me for jus' one moment and let me tell you how our former president, the wise and resourceful Gordon Milton, recruited me to be vice chair of our board. I'd always wondered at his success in getting so many good people to serve, but I'm a busy guy—maybe not as busy as you, but ah can only afford so much time to help our fine university. At least that's what ah thought in those days. So, Gordon, knowin' or sensin' that I might be inclined to put him off, calls my missus, outta the blue, and says, 'My dear, I wanted you to be the first to know, your wonderful husband is about to be accorded a great honor by his university...' Well, what the hell could I say after that?"

We all chuckled along with Fritz.

"Well, Mark," he continued, "you got no missus, least that ah know of," he laughed, "so ah got to put this to you directly." He paused for effect. "Ah would be mighty proud to have a man of your stature follow me as board chair. You're the right man for the job. You've got the right temperament, the right smarts and, Mark, you can lead us. So, Mark Berger, on behalf of our board and our president, ah'd like to ask you to consider serving your alma mater, Sessions University, as vice chair of our board, workin' with me and with Bryan to complete his vision for our university. It would be a great honor, sir, for you to join with us in this endeavor... So what do you say?"

All of us had turned our entire attention on Berger.

Berger looked around the table at us, a considered expression on his face, musing for a moment. It was difficult to determine exactly what he was thinking, and then he said, "Well, that would a great honah, Fritz, and I deeply appreciate that you, Bryan and others would think so highly of my capabilities and service. And the fact is that I'd be happy to consider your invitation, but with one condition."

"What might that be?" Fritz Johnson twanged.

"A team of my auditors is on the front step of the administration building tomorrow morning when the doors open. I wanna go over all your books."

There was a long moment of shocked silence.

I watched Bryan. His demeanor was calm, unfazed, but a fine line of perspiration appeared on his upper lip. Quickly he picked up his napkin and wiped his mouth.

Reve's round eyes told me that he had at least some notion of the problems Berger's audit team might discover. Of course, I thought, he monitored the progress of the campaign daily, tracking progress across the board and the different details of donor crediting and allocation of their funds. He couldn't help but notice a glaring overage in the campaign's unrestricted account and its anonymous nature. That he had never to my knowledge asked Lusby about it was fascinating. Sometimes your sense of self-preservation tells you that there are certain things you do not want to know, lest someone ever ask you about them. But clearly he knew that now trouble was brewing.

"Isn't that a bit irregular?" Fitz-Hugh queried Berger mildly.

"Nah...normal course of business for my due diligence with any organization, profit or non-profit, where I'm asked to consider playing a leadership role, investing my time and my money. Don't take it personal."

"I see," Fitz-Hugh said with a hint of unhappiness.

"Well, do we have a deal?" Berger asked, looking directly at Fritz Johnson as if he were a used car salesman going for sale.

"Well certainly!" Johnson boomed. "We're jus' so pleased yawl wanta join tha *team!*"

Suddenly a certainty washed over me as if I had just plunged into a warm water pool that Johnson and Berger were working together and I felt myself smile. Just the slightest crestfallen look ran across Bryan Fitz-Hugh's face before our waiter came in with a bottle of champagne on ice, popped the cork, filled glasses that we passed around to each other. Fritz raised his glass. "To our new vice chairman of the Sessions University board of trustees!" Bernie Reve raised his glass, now one with us.

Our mood was sufficiently ebullient that we ordered another bottle of champagne and after downing that and listening to various war stories we headed off toward the administration building with Berger accompanying us for some follow-up conversations with Bryan and Fritz.

Our walk took us by the reflecting pond in front of Stewart House and along the grounds of the Farr Botanical Garden. Just as the path wound down to the university's main drive, Emily Sayzak came walking around the corner curve of boxwoods.

Seeing us she jumped slightly, had the sense to pick up her pace and walk by us, but as she passed she looked at me directly, gave a small wave with her hand and winked at me.

I felt as if I would just melt right there and flow rapidly into the nearest culvert.

"You know her?" Reve asked.

"Not really. She's been stalking me," I told him and looked over at Fitz-Hugh. His expression was baleful.

XXIII
He Will See You Now

S O I DID WHAT ANY INTELLIGENT BEING WOULD DO UNDER THE CIRCUMSTANCES. I took a week off. If Bryan Fitz-Hugh was pissed at me, then he could stew for all I cared. Perhaps Ursula could calm him down. In any case, proximity was not a good idea. With auditors now ensconced on the fourth floor, who knew what kind of mood Fitz-Hugh might be in. Plus, on campus there was the possibility of running into Emily Sayzak again. Lord knows for all I knew she was ballsy enough to show up asking after me at my department. Finally, truth be told, I needed to get away from the place, its dry heat and urethane air, its byzantine and clandestine politics, all the insincerity and manipulation that accompanies ambition.

My task for the week was to, as best I could, rebuild Tommie Town as a father/son project. Of course, Tommie's obsessiveness, routine distraction, imaginary pantomiming of work and poor motor skills when he actually tried to do something made the job twice as difficult as it needed to be, but he seemed to revel in his imaginary and our actual daily progress and accomplishments. While he was at school, I went to the hardware and hobby stores and purchased all that we'd need for that evening's work, after his homework was completed of course. We had already bought online, or at the hobby store, all the requisite new buildings and had been assembling them. Janet and I had cleaned up after the fire as best we could, throwing out burnt plywood, model structures and charred shrubbery and trees and melted humans and cars. The most difficult task had been deodorizing—the scent of the deodorizer being perhaps worse than that of the acrid smell of burnt plastic, model glue and plywood. Finally, we had reached more or less of a stalemate where the basement contained trace smells of French bordello and funeral pyre. We kept two of the casement windows across from one another open to try to air the place out with a small, fireproof space heater on to keep the space habitable.

I found this rebuilding project, especially during the day, to be therapeutic. While on any particular task, I could let my mind drift among my life's and work's complications or simply shut them out and concentrate. Often I found myself wishing I was back in my office in Hart Hall preparing the next day's lesson plan.

Janet and I had had a long, frank to a point conversation about Sessions. I brought her up to speed with Berger's appointment as vice chair, the audit, the Sayzak stalking and Bryan's look when she walked by. We were both concerned but had no idea what to do, other than have me hang out at home, out of harm's way. Perhaps all the good reviews about the town hall forum would also work in my favor during my absence.

So, I was mildly hopeful about my situation until Thursday when around eleven my cellphone rang. The president's office. Ms. Bemis: "Your presence in the president's office is requested for 2pm this afternoon," she communicated coldly.

"What's this about?" I asked, hearing my voice rise defensively.

"Shall I communicate that you will be present?"

"Um…sure."

"Thank you." The click at the other end of the line seemed deafening, the chop of a guillotine.

Oh, fuck, I thought, he's going to can me.

I called Ursula. She was neither at her office, nor was she answering her cell.

I called Janet, asked her assistant to put me through despite that fact she was in the middle of a session.

"Yes," she answered, mildly irritated, distracted but very professional.

"I've been called into the president's office at two."

"Oh dear…"

"Yeah… Well, I just wanted you to know. I'm not sure whether I'll be back before the kids get home from school."

"Okay. Thanks for letting me know. I'll cancel my last appointment and come home."

"Good. Thanks."

"And I'll keep my fingers crossed."

"Thanks." My mouth had become dry.

Distractedly, I finished the installation of a firehouse, fixed myself lunch and then went upstairs, showered and shaved, felt the need to put on my most expensive suit and drove to campus, numb with apprehension. It was another grey day, a bit more temperate but with the same blustering wind that had plagued us for weeks. I parked in the lower lot and trudged to the administration building, took the elevator to the third floor.

Ursula's office was empty, devoid of any personal presence as always.

Ms. Bemiss looked past me. "He will see you now."

I walked into Bryan Fitz-Hugh's office steeling myself, preparing to say something collegial, genial, to put him at ease, then stopped in my tracks and gaped.

Sitting with his hands behind his head in Fitz-Hugh's leather office chair, behind Fitz-Hugh's ornate desk, feet in worn deck shoes propped on it, was Mark Berger, grinning.

"Hey, I could get used to this," he said and swung his feet to the floor, stood and put out his hand. "Good to see yah."

"What the *fuck* are *you* doing here?" I asked, delighted and relieved as I took a few fast steps and shook his hand.

"Jus' warmin' the seat for a few minutes. Seemed like someone should."

"What *in the hell's* going on?"

Berger shrugged, sat down, propped up his feet again, put

his hands back behind his head. "Ah, just a bunch of good news. Don't yah think the world's a wonderful place? I mean a regulah *It's a Wonderful Life* kinda place?"

"Not exactly."

"Well, yeah, but we can pretend, right?"

"Pretend what? Where's Bryan?"

"Ah..." Berger raised his eyebrows. "Have a seat...."

I sat down.

"You mean the newly appointed undersecretary of state for the European Union?"

"Bryan?"

"Yeah, announcement is imminent. He's already 'transitioning.' Be a pretty smooth transition. Bryan gets a nice severance package courtesy of the capital campaign. He and Celeste are in DC right now looking at houses. Her law firm has offices there. Kids can finish out school here and have the summer in their new digs while Bryan works his way outta here with the interim president, a certain Dr. Wentz. The board launches a search for a new president next week. We'll need a lot of help from you to design the communications roll out of all this news."

"You fucking pulled this off, didn't you?"

"I had a lotta help. Fritz Johnson came through big, negotiated most of this behind the scenes with Madam Secretary's folks. I think everyone down there is very appreciative of the adroit delicacy with which this situation has been handled. Fritz is now owed big time. Don't be surprised if he's not off to Washington for a cabinet appointment somewhere in the next year or so. Don't be surprised if Hauser recommends Bryan to be the next secretary of state when she steps down, presuming the president is reelected."

"So, if Fritz gets an appointment, he'll have to resign as chair of the Sessions board and then you'll be board chair?"

"Yeah, looks that way."

"That would be fantastic."

"We'll see."

"What about all this clandestine money?"

"Ah, yeah." Berger took his feet off the desk and sat up, facing me. "My guys are doing forensic accounting, will work with Depew to clean up and reconcile the last three years of books. It'll be a bitch but it can be done. Depew, by the way, is now a consultant to the university having been relieved of his comptroller duties. My guys will handle all that shit for the time being."

"Damn you work fast. But what about the money?"

"You mean the wire transfers?"

"Yeah."

"All being returned to the sources, via wire transfer, of course. Bet there'll be some raised eyebrows in certain quarters internationally."

"You're zeroing it out?"

Berger smiled indulgently. "Nah, it looks like the university has found some dumb schmuck billionaire to make it up. You know any dumb schmuck billionaires who could make this sudden transfer loss disappear?"

"No...I don't," I said emphatically, smiling.

Berger laughed. "I'll cover it. I believe the term our friend, Bernie Reve, would like to apply to this new, anonymous gift is that it is an 'Organizational Enhancement' grant. It will make the anonymous donor look farsighted and visionary when the fact is he's always been nearsighted and delusional."

I laughed. "Yeah, and a wise ass."

"That would be me... But the fact is, our international centers and all their good programming will proceed as planned, minus any embedded spooks of course. Bottom line: Bryan did a great job here and that's the way we'll play it. The party line is that no one could expect him to turn down such an incredible government appointment. These things happen. Our job on the board is to manage a smooth and successful transition."

"What happens with the campaign? What about Lusby?"

"Ahhh, Lusby. I've talked with his company. He's been placed on leave, going to detox for a month or three, has his appointment here to come back to when he's done. We'll continue to pay their tab as well as for the detox, which is being done by a private clinic we've used successfully for a couple of my employees."

"That's damn generous."

Berger raised his eyebrows. "Yeah, it is. Frank's a good guy. It also buys his silence."

"Yeah."

"As for the campaign, Fritz and I with Bernie's help and probably some help from Wentz get in planes, trains and limos and visit all the major donors to date to reassure them that Sessions continues to move forward, that Bryan's new position is a feather in our cap and helps Sessions in all sorts of ways with Washington and that we'll all survive. It's not like Bryan won't continue to be our ally. All this reassuring will be a bit arduous but no big deal. We've already started making calls."

I hesitated for a moment, but then shrugged my shoulders and asked, "Where's Ursula in all this?"

"Ah, now there's the surprise. You're not gonna believe this... She's on *Calypso Too* with Jean Claude. Right now they're sailing down the Bahama chain, going to hang out in Tortola for a while and then head over to the Med. As I understand it, she's applied for a position in the German Embassy. Dual citizenship has its advantages. I have to admit, I did not see that one coming."

"Yeah..." I wanted to add, 'You're not the only one.' I was shocked and felt simultaneously loss, regret but also relief with some added emotions of anger and disappointment at being deceived, almost as an afterthought. However, as I assessed my overall reaction it dawned on me that our romance, if you could call it that, more or less emotionally and situationally had ended in a tie, no loss, no gain. I was free. The thought made me smile stupidly.

"You find all this funny?"

"More like funny as in bizarre," I said, shaking my head. "So, yeah, I do, except for Kravitz. Why the hell was that necessary?"

"Desperation, loyalty, fear I guess. The really disturbing thing: they got away with it. That is, if in fact, he didn't kill himself. Guess we'll never know."

"Yeah."

We looked at each other for a long moment.

Mark Berger stood. "Okay…now I need you to get outta here. I gotta a lot of work to do before Wentz's fat ass gets in here toward the middle of next week. Take the rest of the week off, like you planned. See you Monday."

"Sure."

We shook hands and I turned and headed out the door as the heat came on and began blowing dry urethane and dust-scented air.

I exited the administration building and began walking toward the parking lot. The wind was still gusting, blowing a few of last year's brown leaves and some plastic bags around. I looked at the lawns, wet, muddy but beginning to green and at the stark black branches of the trees with sprigs of green waving around against the grey sky. Then I became aware that Emily Sayzak had walked up beside me.

"Hi, Dr. Simpson. You're looking like a happy camper today."

I kept walking but asked her, "Isn't there a point, like some kind of statute of limitations, where you just drop all this inquiry and go on to the next story? This assignment is a dry hole, don't you think?"

"You're beginning to sound like my editor."

"I don't know whether that's good or bad, but I do know one thing. There's bound to be more news in the next days or weeks that will push this inquiry of yours to beyond the back page."

"You may be right. In any case, I'd still like to get to know you better."

I stopped for a moment and faced her. We looked at one another openly. "Not going to happen. Look, sorry, I've got to go home. My presence is required, if you know what I mean."

"I don't."

"That's okay," I said, suddenly impatient to walk through the door to the family room and see Sarah on the couch watching her cool kids show, and Tommie doing his homework or off in his imaginary world obsessing about Tommie Town, having Sparky come happily to greet me and see Janet in the kitchen in good spirits doing her best to throw a meal together.

I turned and felt my phone vibrating in my pocket.

Zoltan.